"ALLOW ME, MISS GREY."

He dropped to the ground, looped his reins over his arm, and came to assist her. Once again, Letitia lay her hands on Lord Brerely's magnificent shoulders, but this time, as he assisted her down, he held her closely. A strange, but pleasant, *frisson* of excitement tingled through her veins. Almost shyly, she looked up at him.

"Shall we walk the horses, my lord?"

"Yes. Shall we enter the woods . . . or turn back?"

"I would like to stroll through the woods, but we'd best return home. My father will soon arrive at the stables and find that I've gone out without a groom. He won't be pleased about that."

"No, you shouldn't go out unaccompanied." He grinned. "But then, *I* am with you."

And who will save me from you? she wondered.

Letitia

CATHLEEN CLARE

AVON BOOKS NEW YORK

LETITIA is an original publication of Avon Books. This work has never before appeared in book form. This work is a novel. Any similarity
to actual persons or events is purely coincidental.

AVON BOOKS
A division of
The Hearst Corporation
1350 Avenue of the Americas
New York, New York 10019

Copyright © 1994 by Catherine Toothman
Published by arrangement with the author
Library of Congress Catalog Card Number: 93-91014
ISBN: 0-380-77667-7

First Avon Books Printing: July 1994

AVON TRADEMARK REG. U.S. PAT. OFF. AND IN OTHER COUNTRIES, MARCA
REGISTRADA, HECHO EN U.S.A.

Printed in the U.S.A.

RA   10   9   8   7   6   5   4   3   2   1

*For my niece,
Anna Jane,
and in memory of
the real Racky*

Letitia

1

"Never in my life have I heard of anything so appalling, so absolutely disgusting!" Lady Grey stared at her husband with outright rage blazing in her eyes, her lips so tightly pinched together that a thin band of white encircled her mouth.

"What's wrong with it, m'dear?" he asked mildly, rather taken aback that she was failing to fall in line with his brilliant idea.

"The scheme is so obvious! Why, everyone will know what we are about! People will laugh and laugh!" Wildly, she fluttered her fan, her head snapping from side to side in disagreement. "Letitia and Julianne must have a Season, just like any normal girls of our class and our means!"

Viscount Grey shook his head. "I can't afford it."

"Oh—yes—you—can," she said in measured tones of accusation. "You are not a poor man."

"That new stallion I bought cost me dear. I'll need time to recover, for I won't touch my capital."

"You've more capital than you could ever crave!" cried his wife. "Your daughters need husbands! Letitia is nineteen; Julianne is seventeen. There is no time for experimentation with such a ridiculous venture as this! It won't be long before they are on the shelf!"

"Balderdash!" He chuckled and winked at the two young ladies sitting quietly in the window seat. "Not my gels! They'll be snatched up quick as you please."

"They won't be snatched up if they are buried in the country! Alfred, you must reconsider!"

"No!" he said vehemently. "We'll do this my way! My plan is a good one."

"Your plan reeks of blatant manipulation! Whoever heard of a house party to which only eligible bachelors are invited? Everyone will know that you are desperately attempting to marry off your daughters."

His snicker increased to a full-blown laugh. "If we go to town, everyone will know it, too. Isn't matrimony the prime goal of the London Season?"

"No, it is not," Lady Grey retorted. "It is a time of sociability, of seeing old friends and making new ones. The girls must be introduced to all of Society, not just to young men. They should be presented at Court and meet the patronesses of Almack's. They must learn something of the world! It is their birthright."

"Then let their husbands do it," he stubbornly declared. "I don't like London. It is too expensive, and it is not a good environment for my horses."

"A pox on your horses! That is all you ever think about. Those damned horses!"

"Goodness, my dear, what a thing to say! And such language! It boggles the mind." With feigned shock, he mopped his brow. "Whew!"

"My speech is well-suited to the occasion. Horses! Why must everything revolve around those featherbrained beasts?"

"There are far worse things for a man to pursue." His blue eyes twinkled with the pure joy of nettling his wife. "Things such as gambling and womanizing."

"Alfred!" she gasped. "You must not talk of such practices in front of the girls!"

Lord Grey cast a doleful glance at his daughters. What beauties they were! With their rich brown hair, their expressive green eyes, and their sweet faces, they would catch the eye of any young man worth his salt. His wife was wrong. They'd snag husbands with ease once they set their minds to the task. He smiled kindly.

"A thousand pardons, m'dears, for my plain speaking, but it is the truth, you know, and you should be aware of it. Too many members of my sex engage in disgraceful pastimes. One never knows what evils lurk behind a handsome facade, ha-ha! That is why I have carefully screened my guest list. Only the most honorable, upright young bucks will attend my gathering. Thus, my plan is far superior to your mama's."

His wife groaned, rolling her eyes toward the ceiling.

"In London," he continued, "a young lady may fall victim to countless dishonorable lures, despite the constant vigilance of her parents. My house party offers a controlled atmosphere. Tell me, Letitia," he asked his eldest daughter, "wouldn't you rather make your debut in the country?"

"There is no *debut* to it!" Lady Grey harshly interrupted. "They will not be introduced to Society. They will meet a handful of gentlemen who will take to their heels as soon as they realize that you are hosting a Marriage Mart instead of a house party."

"Tish?" he pressed. "Favor us with your opinion."

At that moment, there was a scratch on the door, and a footman entered with a tray of refreshments. Grateful for small miracles, Letitia breathed a sigh of relief. There was no way in which she could answer her father's query without offending one of her parents—most likely, her mother. That was the reason her sire had directly put the question to her. He assumed she would be on his side.

Strangely enough, her mind was divided on the issue. One small part of her had been fascinated by the prospect of a London Season. It would be exciting to dress in lovely clothes, to dance at the glittering balls, to attend the opera. It was a world she had never experienced. That unknown existence might be a bit frightening, but it was undoubtedly enticing.

On the other hand, there was great comfort in the familiar. She loved the country, her horses, her dogs and cats. She would probably be homesick in London. Hers was not an outgoing personality like that of her sister. She would probably appear to greater advantage here at Greywood Manor, especially to the sporting gentlemen that her father was likely to invite.

Julianne rose to pour the tea. Letitia watched her, knowing from the dejected set of her shoulders that her sister was distressed by this turn of events. Julianne had been cheerfully anticipating the Season. With her bubbly good nature, she would sparkle in a London ballroom. Gentlemen would flock to her side and offer her all manner of inflated flattery. It would be a shame for her to miss it.

Letitia smiled encouragingly as her sister presented her with a cup of tea. Perhaps her father might agree to foot the bill for just one of them to have a Season. She would be happy to relinquish her opportunity to Julianne.

"Letitia?" Lord Grey prompted, as soon as all had been served. "Let us have the benefit of your opinion."

She pensively gazed at each of them. "I thought, perhaps, that it might be possible for just one of us to go," she suggested, "and Julianne would be the perfect choice."

"Impossible!" Lady Grey condemned, almost before the words were out of her daughter's mouth. "Letitia, you are the elder. Your sister cannot come out before you do. It isn't done."

"I truly don't mind."

"Absurd! Do you wish to be an old maid?" the lady demanded.

"No, ma'am," she answered softly, a blurry vision of a handsome husband floating through her head. "But I do feel that Julianne is more suited to the requirements of a Season. I prefer quieter surroundings."

"Everyone is wasting words!" Lord Grey denounced. "We will not go to London. My party is a far better idea. For one thing, there will be no competition for our girls to deal with."

"I am not afraid of competition," Julianne murmured, returning to her seat beside Letitia.

"What's that?" Her father humorously cupped his ear.

"I said . . ." She cleared her throat. "I said that I am not afraid of competition."

"Excellent! Then you can attempt to challenge your sister on horseback."

"On horseback?" Julianne cried.

"Indeed. Our guests will be sportsmen. They'll be impressed by a female who rides well. With my fine horses, of course," he said proudly, "you'll be mounted superbly."

"Papa!" she wailed. "You know I am not adept at riding!"

"You shall be adequate. I'll mount you on a seasoned animal. You need but sit there! After all, you will not try to be more proficient than our guests." He raised an eyebrow, favoring Letitia with a glance of warning. "It wouldn't do to outshine the young men."

"Mama!" Julianne appealed. "I am afraid of horses! I cannot do it!"

"This is ridiculous!" yelped Lady Grey. "It is absolutely mortifying! Gracious, Alfred, what other nonsense do you have up your sleeve? Is this a house party or a *horse* party?"

"Bit of both, I'd say." He grinned good-naturedly.

"No one will attend!"

"Oh, yes, they will," Lord Grey said confidently. "My stables are famous throughout the land. No true lover of horseflesh will turn down my invitation. Naturally, my foremost criterion is that the gentlemen be excellent horsemen, so there will be a great deal of equine entertainment."

Letitia found her interest piqued. It sounded like fun! She pitied poor Julianne, whose equestrian ability was atrocious, but she was excited for herself. Riding was a sport in which she excelled. In fact, she secretly considered herself to be just as accomplished as most men.

"What are your other criteria?" Lady Grey asked dreadfully.

"Wealth, of course," he readily replied. "I don't wish my future son-in-law to spend all of his blunt on horses and have none left for his wife."

"Isn't that what you do?" his own wife scoffed.

"No, madam, it is not. Isn't that a new dress you are wearing? When have you ever lacked for whatever baubles and bibelots you desired?"

She ignored his challenge. "The simple truth is that you do not wish to stir yourself to go to London, isn't it? Go on with your other prerequisites."

"The man must not be a dedicated gamester. A reasonable amount of wagering is sporting, but he must not do it to excess, hazarding only that amount which he can afford to lose. Nor must he overindulge in drinking or wenching."

"Alfred!" she admonished.

He smiled sheepishly. "We must be rational, my dear. You may trust me. My eligibles are well-rounded gentlemen. All of them are considered prize catches, the cream of English bachelorhood!"

Lady Grey gently rubbed her temples in dizzy disbelief. "No one will attend," she repeated. "This affair is just too obvious for words. I shall not agree to it."

"You haven't much choice," her husband replied exuberantly. "I've already sent out the invitations!"

There was an awful silence. Letitia glanced back and forth between her parents, waiting for the storm to break. Lord Grey's thin face remained alight with merriment, but there was a glint of challenge in his blue eyes, such as that which he possessed when laying down a massive bet on one of his racehorses. Lady Grey bore a stony countenance obscuring any inward turmoil, except for the tiny twitch at the corners of her mouth.

"Well," said the viscountess, coldly. "So this matter is irreversible."

"Indeed it is, madam."

"Then I have a great many preparations to make," she proclaimed, "among which shall be a trip to London to purchase new wardrobes for the girls. If they are to be merchandise on display at this preposterous Marriage Mart, they shall be well-attired. Also, I shall obtain a variety of fine wines and epicurean delicacies which are not readily available in the country. Furthermore," she added, coolly smiling her counter-challenge to her husband, "there are any number of desperately needed household articles of comfort and decoration if we are to host such august gentlemen-about-town. We entertain so infrequently that I have allowed the house to become rather shabby."

Lord Grey recognized defeat when he looked it in the eye, but knew he had won the major conflict. "Very well, m'dear," he agreeably granted. "Just so long as I do not have to accompany you! Hate the city, you know. I hate it!"

"And you claim to be short of money," muttered his wife. "Fustian!"

The fragrant scent of flowers floated through the garden window of the library at Brerely House in Park Lane. Summer had arrived, bringing with it the end of the Season. Soon, the fashionable members of the *ton* would depart to the country, or to one of the popular spas, to escape the city's searing heat. Christopher, Lord Brerely, and his younger brother, William, sat before the empty fireplace, sorting through a collection of house-party invitations. The stack had been growing for the past week, and it was time they made their replies.

"First, we'd best go home and visit Mama and Papa," William stated. "They'll never forgive us if we don't."

"Of course," the earl agreed.

"Later, I'd like to go to Freddy's parents' gathering. Were you invited to that one?"

He was, but he wasn't enthusiastic about attending. Freddy Scott-Havens was William's age, and his parents were rather elderly. The guest list would reflect that fact.

"You go, Willie," he said. "I think I'll go to Brandon's."

"Oh! Is the duke having a party at the same time? I'd like to go there."

Chris sighed. Since William had left Cambridge and come to town, the young man seemed to think he should sit in his elder brother's pocket. Up to a point, that was all well and good, for it eliminated the possibility of Willie falling in with the wrong crowd, but it was becoming rather stifling for the earl.

There were times when he wished to be alone with his friends, without his ever-present sibling. It was not that the fivesome did anything to be ashamed of. The Duke of Rackthall, the Marquess of Singleton, and the Earl of Abingdon were happily married men, no longer given to wild pursuits. He and Aubrey Standish remained the only bachelors, and they had long since outgrown their unrestrained ways. It was just that Willie, at the age of twenty-two, didn't quite fit in with the older men. There seemed to be a vast chasm between the early twenties and the early thirties. Chris wondered if his friends weren't tiring of his brother, too.

Willie was a nuisance on other occasions, as well. Whenever Chris played cards at his club, his brother hovered behind him, gaping into his hand and making him and the other gamesters a bit nervous. It was impossible to concentrate under such single-minded scrutiny.

One of the worst episodes, however, occurred on the evening William tagged along when Chris went to visit his mistress. Chris had tried to explain the circumstances to his brother, and the young man seemed to understand and to agree to go on elsewhere. But when they arrived at Felina's house, Willie had decided to accompany him inside. To avoid a brangle on the sidewalk out in front, Chris had permitted it and was forced to turn the anticipated pleasurable interlude into a social call. Felina had been angry and had demanded a vastly expensive diamond necklace as reparation for her disappointment.

It was time to wean his brother from his coattails. He didn't want to hurt him, but he had to have some freedom. Chris took a deep breath.

"The duke isn't having an actual house party. It's merely an informal gathering of the five of us, and the wives," he said gently.

"I see. I am not invited," Willie murmured painfully.

"No, it isn't really *that*. My friends would always welcome you. It's just that I would like to get off on my own now and then. Do you understand?"

"I enjoy your company, Chris."

"And I enjoy yours! We've grown closer this year than ever before. That's the way brothers should be. But we ought to have friends of our own, as well." He smiled encouragingly. "You've made some good friends in London. Wouldn't you rather be off on your own with them sometimes?"

"No," said Willie.

"You went to that cockfight with Scott-Havens. Didn't you have a better time without me?" Chris urged.

"Not particularly."

The earl choked back his frustration. "Willie, you'll just have to understand that I need some time to myself," he said flatly.

His brother chewed his lower lip, worriedly knitting his brows. "Do you want me to move out?"

"Good God, no! We can still do lots of things together. I just need an hour or two once in a while . . ."

Willie brightened. "All right, Chris." Blithely dismissing the subject, he picked up another invitation. "Look at this. It's from Lord Grey, the *horsy* viscount. We're both invited to his estate. Damme! I wonder if he'd consent to sell some of his thoroughbreds?"

The earl shrugged. "Grey sells nothing but his culls. On the few occasions that someone has talked him out of a good horse, the price has been gigantic. This is strange, however. He is a rather reclusive sort of man when it comes to entertaining. I can't ever remember hearing of his hosting a house party."

"Well, here it is." Willie tossed the paper across his brother's desk. "I've never met the man. How well do you know him?"

"Scarcely at all." Chris thoughtfully examined the contents of the message. "I've a nodding acquaintance with him, but that's all. I'd never expect to be invited for a visit."

"Well, now you are! He's included me, too. Let's accept, Chris! Maybe he's in dun territory and has to sell off some of his stock. By Jove, I'd like to get my hands on one of Grey's thoroughbreds!"

"Lord Grey is one of the wealthiest men in England. If he'd lost his fortune, we'd know of it." The earl ran a hand through his dark hair. "This is most intriguing. It's just not like the man."

"Wouldn't you like to see his breeding farm?" Willie prodded.

"Of course," he answered readily. "It's said to be a model facility."

"Then let us accept!"

"Not so fast, Willie. It might be well to ask around a bit first. Let's see who else is invited."

His brother gave a grunt of impatience. "Gad, one would think you were afraid of Lord Grey!"

"Don't be ridiculous." Chris laid the invitation on the pile of those to be accepted, when answered by his secretary. "All right, we'll go, but it still seems highly unusual."

Over supper at the club with his friends that night, he brought up the subject of Lord Grey's

invitation. "Did any of you receive an invitation
to Lord Grey's house party?"

The other four exchanged grins.

"So you're one of the chosen few." Lord Standish smirked. "Even though all London is laughing,
it is a sort of honor, I suppose."

Chris eyed him suspiciously. "What is that supposed to mean?"

"Curious, isn't it?" Aubrey returned, prolonging
the suspense. "The five of us are known to have a
great interest in horseflesh, yet only you and I were
invited."

"I was," William added.

"Sorry, Willie. Forgot about you! How old are
you? Twenty-two, isn't it?" Lord Standish laughed.
"You're probably too young to be in peril. No, your
brother's the target here! Grey probably invited
you for politeness's sake."

"I have money," Willie said defensively. "I can
afford to buy horses."

"Horses? You're off the mark, m'boy! We're talking of two-legged fillies here."

Chris frowned. "You'd best explain."

Aubrey guffawed, leaning forward. "Lord Grey
has marriageable daughters. This isn't a house party. It's a husband-catching trap! From what I hear,
only eligible bachelors have been invited. I wouldn't
go within ten miles of the place!"

The earl cast his brother a look of disparagement.

"How was I to know?" Willie mumbled. He
bowed his head and took a sudden interest in
polishing off his beefsteak.

Brandon Lacey, Duke of Rackthall, glanced at
Chris, a devilish glint of amusement in his blue
eyes. "Have you sent your acceptances?"

The complete silence provided all the answer
necessary.

"He has!" the Marquess of Singleton jibed. "Before the summer's out, he'll be caught in parson's mousetrap!"

"See here, Harry," Chris said firmly, "just because I will attend doesn't mean that I'll be caught. No one will trap me in such a shabby fashion!"

"So *he* thinks," Brandon taunted. "Best lock your door at night, my friend, else you may find yourself standing stud to a 'grey mare'!"

His interest in his meal fading, the earl laid down his knife and fork. "A man can't be ensnared if he doesn't want to be. I'll stay for a few days, have a view of Grey's equine facilities, and be on my way. It's just as simple as that!"

"Shall we make wagers?" Harry Singleton goaded.

"Of course," the duke agreed.

"Actually," Brougham, Lord Abingdon, mused, entering the conversation, "if a man were seeking a wife, one of those girls might be an excellent prospect. Grey's as rich as Croesus, and his stable is top-of-the-trees."

"That may be," Chris amiably replied, "but I am not interested in marriage at present."

"Have to be wed sometime," Brandon asserted, and the other two married men nodded their agreement.

Chris knew that the duke was right. In fact, his father had recently been hinting at the very same thing. But he just wasn't ready for that formidable step. Brandon, Harry, and Brough were lucky in their choice of wives. There just couldn't be many more women like Allesandra, Ellen, and Clarissa. Once he had made up his mind to seek a mate, it would probably take him a very long time to find the right lady.

He took a sip of port. "I'm not prepared to take on that responsibility, and when I am, *I'll* do the catching. I'll go to Lord Grey's to examine his stables, not his daughters. He won't trap me on his Marriage Mart! Why don't you change your mind and come along too, Aubrey?"

Lord Standish violently shook his head. "I have to exercise enough of my wits running from Tina."

The friends laughed. The pursuit of Aubrey by Ellen Singleton's best friend, the vastly attractive Lady Christina, was a well-known fact. Large wagers rode on the outcome.

"You might miss buying a horse," Chris pointed out.

"Not me! I wouldn't want one of Lord Grey's culls," Aubrey said derisively, "and *that*, my friends, includes his daughters!"

Letitia gave the newborn foal a final stroke and rose, brushing the straw from her skirt. "He's perfect, isn't he?" she said smilingly to the groom.

"That he is, miss," the servant boasted proudly, as if the colt were his own.

"When Papa returns from the squire's, he'll be disappointed that he missed being among the first to view him."

"I can't see why," came a voice from outside the stall. "One colt looks much the same as any other."

"Julianne!" Letitia cried. "What are you doing here?"

"Looking for you," her sister replied, leaning cautiously over the polished oak half-door.

"Come in and see the baby," Letitia invited.

Julianne shook her head and quickly stepped back when the mare lifted her nose to sniff at her sleeve.

Letitia sighed. "I'll be right along." She glanced one more time at the newborn animal. "Take good care of him, Donald. With his looks and breeding, he should be a winner."

"Yes, miss. I'm hopin' so!"

She let herself out of the box and joined Julianne for the walk back to the house.

"Letitia!" the other girl bubbled as soon as they had left the foaling barn. "I've been trying to catch you alone all day. What do you think of Papa's awful scheme?"

"Just that. It's awful." Letitia adjusted her stride to her sister's shorter pace. "But it does have some merit. I really wasn't desirous of spending such a long time in London."

"Mother and I were."

"I know, and because of that, I'm sorry. Still, I can't help being relieved."

"None of those gentlemen will ask for either of us," Julianne predicted sorrowfully, "not on the basis of one encounter."

"It does seem rather farfetched," Letitia acknowledged.

"If they do, it will be due to reasons of business, and not because of love. Can you accept that? Wouldn't you rather fall in love?"

"Certainly, but I think we should be practical. I've been thinking about the whole thing. For me, at least, Papa's plan might be suitable. I love animals, horses in particular. These men will be the best bachelor horsemen in England. I'd probably be well-matched with one of them."

"How can you think of it so coldly?" Julianne wailed.

"I don't think I'm being indifferent," she protested. "Favoring the same things is the first step in friendship. I'd like to be friends with the man I marry."

"Well, I'd like to be in love with him," her sister said tartly.

"That would come."

"Not necessarily."

"I know you're unhappy about this," Letitia said consolingly, "but look on the bright side. We'll be meeting eligible men. One of them might be exactly what you want."

"I doubt it. Papa's stratagem is too audacious. None of the good prospects will come." Julianne kicked angrily at a piece of gravel. "I wanted to go to balls, and parties, and the opera. I wanted to take drives in the park. I wanted to go to Vauxhall Gardens! Having a Season seemed so dazzling, but what do I get? Nothing! Around here, it's nothing but horses, horses, horses!"

"I'm sorry," was all that Letitia could think to say.

The young ladies walked the rest of the way in brooding silence.

2

The soft-cushioned, well-sprung carriage bullied its way through the busy London streets and drew up in front of the magnificent edifice of Grillon's Hotel. Within, Lady Grey chattered indefatigably to her two daughters about the vast number of purchases they had made that morning and how much they had accomplished overall, given the short amount of time they had in London. Unfortunately, she lamented, this was their last day in the capital city, but truly, one more expedition to the shops should be sufficient.

Only half-listening, Letitia surreptitiously worked at slipping her aching feet back into slippers that suddenly seemed too small. Her mother and sister might regret leaving town, but she did not. She was weary of being poked, pinned, and prodded by the fashionable modiste and her assistants, of being measured and fitted by boot and glove makers, and of being hustled around to a variety of other shops in search of the perfect accessories. It was terribly enjoyable to possess a marvelous new wardrobe, but it had taken pure, hard, boring work to achieve it.

Their life in the hotel was rather dull, too. For such a disappointingly brief stay in the city, Lady Grey had chosen to lodge herself and her two daughters at Grillon's instead of opening the town house.

Though the establishment had more than lived up to its reputation for excellence, it was rather confining for one who was used to roaming at will. Letitia longed for the open space of Greywood Manor.

"Get out of here!"

Intrigued, she leaned forward to peer out. Now this was diversion from the dull routine! What could have caused the disdainful doorman such dismay?

"Get out of here!" he shouted once more at the two ragged waifs who stood in awe before him. "Take yourselves off from these premises! We'll have no solicitation from the likes of you!"

His strident voice continued to distract Letitia from her mother's prattle as she, Julianne, and Lady Grey disembarked from the coach. She paused curiously, while her parent and sister, followed by two footmen bearing the enormous load of purchases, marched into the hotel.

"Our clientele don't want anything like that!" the doorman railed. "Strange beasts! Sneaky-looking! Don't belong in England!"

Letitia drew closer, her attention centered on the wooden box beside which the two children were standing. Strange beasts? This she had to see!

"Get them out of here!"

"Just a moment," she intervened. "What have you there?"

"Nothing a lady'd be interested in," the doorman sniffed.

"I shall be the judge of that," she said severely, peering into the box.

Two sets of dark, beady eyes adorned with little black masks stared back at her. Goodness! She'd never seen animals like this before! The beasts were very small and furry, their thick coats a mixture of shades of gray. They had pointed snouts, tiny hand-like paws, and rings around their tails. They were the oddest, most adorable creatures that she had ever seen.

"What are they?" she asked.

"They're baby raccoons," the older child announced.

"Raccoons." She rolled the unfamiliar word on her tongue. "What, pray tell, is a raccoon?"

"They're from America, miss," he told her. "M'dad's a sailor. 'E brung back their mammy for a pet. Didn't know she was gonna 'ave babies."

"They're darling!" Letitia said admiringly.

"Lots o' fun, too, miss. But we can't keep 'em all, so Pap said we 'ad to sell these."

"May I pick one up?"

The boy nodded.

Letitia reached into the crate and lifted out one of the beasts, cuddling it to her shoulder. The raccoon, however, was not content to lie still. It began to explore her as thoroughly as she was examining it, poking its nose under her jaw and grasping the collar of her spencer with its leathery little hands. Letitia giggled as both animals set up a loud chittering trill.

"Are you sure that they are old enough to leave their mother?" she asked. "Can they eat?"

"Yes, miss. They eat all sorts o' things."

"Garbage, most likely!" hooted the doorman.

The scene had drawn several interested onlookers. A well-dressed lady and a little girl hesitated on their way into the hotel. After watching Letitia for a few moments, the child fearlessly reached into the box and picked up the other animal.

"Mama, please! May I have him?" she begged, gently stroking the fluffy fur.

"I'm interested, too. Let me hold one," someone else said.

Letitia quickly made up her mind. "How much are you asking?" she inquired, before anyone else could claim the darling little fellow that she held.

"Well . . . ah . . ." The older child stammered.

With her free hand, she reached into her reticule and pulled out a guinea. "Will this do?"

"Oh, yes, miss!" the boy replied. The children glanced at each other, eyes ablaze with excitement. "Thankee!"

"Please, Mama!" cried the little girl. "May I?"

"Rather extravagant, but very well." Laughing, the young woman dipped into her purse and paid the children for the other.

"Is there anything we should know about the care of these animals?" Letitia asked.

"Just treat 'em like a cat or dog!" the elder youngster said, and the two dashed off down the street.

"Grillon's won't allow you to take such beasts inside," the doorman warned superciliously.

Letitia's spirits fell. She hadn't thought of that.

"Oh, yes, they will," the mother of the little girl replied, "for I am a relative of the owner. There shall be no problem whatsoever. Come, Flora. Let us see if we can obtain a saucer of milk for the little creature." With that, she swept through the doors, Letitia hard on her heels.

What wonderful luck, Letitia thought as she climbed the stairs to their rooms. Alone, she would probably have had a difficult time with that haughty doorman. Now she need only face her mother. Hopefully, Lady Grey would be so enthusiastic about her shopping adventure that she would take small notice of one tiny raccoon from America. Taking a deep breath, she opened the door and went in.

"Where have you been, Letitia? What is that?" gasped her mother.

"It's a raccoon," she explained, and swiftly related the story of her purchase.

"He is so adorable!" Julianne rushed over to pet

the soft bundle. "Mama, just think of the attention he shall garner! He is much better than a lady's lapdog! May I hold him sometimes, Letitia? When gentlemen are present?"

"Of course," she agreed magnanimously.

"Well . . ." Lady Grey frowned thoughtfully. "I am in the habit of disliking indoor pets, but you may be right. A young lady with a little dog or cat presents the sort of gentle picture that a man appreciates, and this beast is so unusual that it will definitely attract attention. Just see that it does not dirty the carpet, girls!"

"We'll take care!" Julianne laughed. "What shall you name him, Letitia?"

"I don't know," she confessed, and sat down, allowing the animal freedom to crawl up onto her shoulder and from there, to the back of the chair.

"Let's call him Racky," the younger girl suggested. "It's short for 'raccoon,' and it will be easy to remember."

"All right. That's a good name."

"Let me see the thing." Lady Grey plucked the raccoon off its perch and held it up. Racky immediately reached out and pinched her nose.

"Heavens! You're a mischievous little tyke!" Quickly she returned the animal to his roost, but she laughed.

Chattering gaily, the creature climbed down head-first and romped across the room, shinnying up the draperies.

"Obviously, trees are of great importance to these animals in their natural state," Lady Grey remarked dryly. "You must watch him closely, Letitia. I will not have my house destroyed by this beast."

"I shan't allow that to happen," she promised. "When he becomes accustomed to us and to his surroundings, I imagine that he will settle."

The raccoon reached the valance, crept expertly

across it, and skimmed down the panel on the other side. He cavorted across the room and stopped in front of Lady Grey. Emitting a little warble, he tugged at her hem.

"He likes you, Mama!" Letitia declared with relief.

"Well, he certainly isn't shy." The viscountess smiled.

"No, it is evident that he has had kind treatment. Come here, Racky." Letitia scooped him up into her arms. "Let us ring for something for you to eat. And perhaps the hotel has a box that you can live in, when we cannot watch you."

The animal gibbered and poked his nose into Letitia's ear.

She giggled. "I cannot wait for Papa to see you! What on earth will he think of our trip to London?"

"Yes, what will he think?" mused Lady Grey, eyeing with satisfaction the heap of parcels she had purchased that day. "This ridiculous house party will save him scant money. A Season in London would have cost little more and would have produced the desired results. I hope he learns a lesson from his absurdity!"

"Mama?" Julianne said wistfully. "Is there any chance whatsoever that he will relent and allow us the Season?"

"Of course there is. When none of those gentlemen ask for either of your hands, he will be forced to listen to me! We can only hope that this sad business has not affected too greatly our chances of success."

"Why should it?"

"People talk. I am certain that the scandalous news of Lord Grey's Marriage Mart is being bandied about this very moment. Our reputations will not emerge unscathed from this piece of work. Oh, no, you may be sure of that! You girls might not be able to look so high for husbands. You may have to settle for less than ideal."

"But if we find gentlemen who love us, they will not care!" Julianne protested, walking to the window and staring down at the street below.

Woefully shaking her head, Lady Grey took a seat. "I'm sorry, dear, but you must understand that if we are the butt of gossip, there is only a limited number of men who will desire to pursue an acquaintance. You and your sister are very pretty girls, but comeliness will not overcome notoriety. An upstanding lord of fine family will not afford you a second glance."

"Surely it cannot be that serious," Letitia joined in, seeing her sister's shoulders begin to tremble.

"It can, and it will," the viscountess predicted direly. "Your father should have consulted with me before he embarked upon this misguided scheme. Not that he would have heeded me, though! He can be such a *stubborn* man."

Julianne sniffled. "Why should he do such a thing to us?"

"Because he does not wish to leave his damned horses for any appreciable time!" her parent snapped. "He is besotted with the beasts! He only enjoys leaving home when he is going to a racetrack or an auction. Fustian! I cannot comprehend why I married him!"

"You told us that yours was a love match, Mama," Letitia reminded her.

"Yes, it was." She smiled fleetingly before resuming an expression of irritation. "Therein lies a lesson for you! Marry with your head and not your heart!"

"Don't you still love Papa?" Julianne asked, turning, her inquisitiveness overcoming her distress.

"Of course I do. It's just that he *frustrates* me so!" She threw up her hands in surrender. "Do you know where we went on our honeymoon? To Newmarket! I sat in the inn while he attended the races!"

"Why didn't you go with him?" Letitia inquired.

"A racecourse is not the most salubrious place for a lady to go," she said deprecatingly.

"I'd love to see a horse race."

"Goodness, Letitia!" her mother scoffed. "It is a most uncomfortable experience. There are all sorts of disagreeable men, some of them in their cups, sporting and frolicking like a batch of children. The odor is breathtaking, and the flies . . . Gad! A race-track is not a proper facility for a lady."

"I would still like to go," Letitia said reflectively. "Perhaps Papa will take me someday."

"He will not. I absolutely forbid it! No daughter of mine will set her pretty foot on any racecourse!"

Letitia's eyes twinkled. "Then perhaps I shall be lucky enough to wed one of Papa's chosen bride-grooms, and he may take me to Newmarket on *our* honeymoon."

"Humph!" Lady Grey pursed her lips. "I hope you are jesting, child. Any gentleman who lowers himself to attend this ridiculous house party will be searching for a brood mare, not a companion. Most likely he would take you to his estate, get you in an interesting condition, and depart."

Julianne winced. "I will not be treated like that! The man I wed will love me and want to be with me!"

"Then he won't be one of your father's horsy heroes!"

"We shall see," Letitia said saucily, setting the raccoon on the floor. "There, Racky, what do *you* think of the matter?"

The creature trilled, scampered once around her, then attempted to climb her skirt.

Her mother shook her head. "There is one thing

certain. Your husband, Letitia, must be a devoted lover of animals!"

A breeze, bearing on it the scent of new-mown grass, drifted through the library windows, ruffling the curtains and shifting several papers on the big walnut desk. It was a beautiful day in the country, not too hot and not too cool, just right for any outdoor activity. Chris wished that he could take a ride across the estate, but that would have to wait until this conference with his father was concluded. It probably wouldn't take long. The man was direct and succinct. Whatever matter was concerning him would quickly be brought to a head and settled.

The older gentleman poured them each a glass of port, then took several slow swallows, as if he were deliberately delaying the opening of the interview. That was most unusual. Where was his customary forthright approach?

Thoughtfully knitting his brows, Chris sipped the sweet, full-bodied spirits. Whatever was bothering his father was bound to have a direct effect on him, else the man would not have requested this conversation so formally. Could it be money? The very idea seemed outrageous. The family possessed a vast amount of wealth in cash, investments, and lands. The gentleman's health? Doubtful! His father appeared as robust and hardy as ever. Something *he* had done? Impossible! Chris's intemperate days of youth had long been left behind. Now he was a suave, sophisticated man-about-town. Thrusting aside all further attempts at speculation, Chris settled back in his chair and waited.

"Well, Christopher," the Marquess of Trinarton finally intoned, setting aside his wine, folding his hands, and gazing at his son across the richly polished expanse of his desk, "I requested this private meeting to discuss a subject which of late has caused me great concern."

Chris nodded, relieved that the discourse had begun. "Whatever it is, I shall be glad to be of service," he assured his sire.

The marquess smiled faintly. "Maybe you will, maybe you won't," he enigmatically commented. "This isn't easy, son."

"Please explain."

His father chuckled. "Going too slowly, am I?"

Chris grinned. "This isn't quite in your usual manner."

"No, but this isn't an average topic." Lord Trinarton exhaled audibly. "It concerns your future, and that of the family."

"I see." Chris sobered. "Have I displeased you?"

"No, no, you've never truly displeased me, even when you were sowing your wild oats! I can only hope that you will not do so now. As you may have guessed from my letters, Christopher, I am troubled about our line of succession. You have no heirs."

Chris opened his mouth to begin a protest, but the marquess lifted a silencing hand.

"I had hoped, when three of your friends wed, that you would take the hint. Yet I see no indication of this. Have you any young lady in mind whom you might wish to marry?"

Chris sighed. "No, sir."

So that was it! Never before this summer had his father reproached him about doing his duty, but he was not surprised that the topic had finally arisen. Time was speeding by, and though there were two Brerely sons, the marquess would naturally wish to see the advent of a third generation.

Chris himself held no distaste for the marital state. Hadn't he witnessed the perfect happiness of his friends? He simply hadn't found the right lady. However, he wondered with a small measure of guilt, had he sincerely looked for her? He *was* rather content with his bachelorhood. Perhaps he had grown a bit complacent. He should visualize the traits he wished in his future wife, and begin to search for her.

His parent's next statement brought him resoundingly to attention.

"Do you wish your mother and me to assist you in finding a mate?" the marquess asked nonchalantly.

Good God! An arranged marriage? Not for him!

"Marriages of convenience are rather sensible," Lord Trinarton continued. "I believe that your friend the duke was wed in such a fashion."

"Bran was lucky," he said in a rush.

"Luck may play only a small part. Good sense and adept estimation of character on the part of neutral individuals is far superior to emotional entanglement. If I'd wed the girl I thought I loved, I'd really have been in the suds! Today, that woman is the biggest shrew in England! Fortunately, I listened to my parents and married the girl of their choice, your mother. There could be no happier marriage, Christopher, and it was one of convenience."

"I know that," Chris admitted, but he slowly shook his head. "I also know of many arranged marriages that are very *un*happy. Give me a chance, Father. I haven't really tried."

"You've had a number of years and a number of Seasons to look about," his sire reminded him. "By your own admission, you've found no young lady to whom you are attracted."

"But I haven't really *tried!*" he repeated desperately.

"I cannot understand that claim. Don't you dance and converse with eligible ladies?"

"Occasionally. Father, I . . ."

"Perhaps you are too wrapped up in that mistress of yours. Dispose of her, Christopher, and seek a legitimate union."

"I'm not ready to get rid of her," he protested. "At your age, you may have forgotten that a younger man has certain . . . uh . . . urges."

Lord Trinarton bristled. "That, young man, is a patent falsehood! *My age* has not diminished my capacity for fleshly pleasure! I enjoy . . ." He stopped, flushing deeply. "Dammit! I won't discuss my personal activities with you!"

Chris took a quick drink of port to hide his grin.

"I cannot believe my ears! My own son, questioning my manhood! Such impertinence!"

"I'm sorry, Father. It was a poor choice of words. I didn't really intend to question your . . . capabilities. I only thought to remind you of . . ."

"Enough!" The marquess tossed down his remaining wine and refilled his glass. "You won't succeed at diverting me from the original subject, Christopher. I believe we were discussing your future nuptials?"

Chris's smile faded. "I give you my word that I shall seriously consider the matter."

"I don't want serious consideration," Lord Trinarton grumbled. "I want a daughter-in-law. And grandsons."

"I understand."

"I realize that I cannot control you by threatening to cut off your allowance. I'm well aware that you've made a comfortable number of shrewd investments, and are quite well-to-do without my contributions. You're a grown man. I can only beg you to do your duty, and, if your mother and I happen to introduce you to several suitable young ladies, I do ask you to regard them without prejudice."

"Very well," he agreed, relieved that the exchange seemed to be drawing to a close.

"Your mother has planned a house party, which we expect you to attend."

Chris stiffened. "Father, I will not be forced into marriage."

"No one's forcing you. Good God! I wouldn't set a trap for my own son! I'm only requesting your presence."

He groaned.

"Now, m'boy, it won't hurt you!" the marquess said jovially. "Your mama seldom plans such entertainment. You wouldn't want to hurt her feelings."

"No, sir. Remember, however, that I have accepted several other invitations."

"This won't interfere." He meditatively tapped a forefinger on the desk. "You mentioned Lord Grey's house party. That old tight-fist would never part with a decent stallion, but he might be overrun with mares. I'm willing to go partners with you, if you come up with anything. Hmm . . . Grey has some daughters, too, if I recall."

"Does he?" Chris asked innocently.

"I am almost certain of it!" Lord Trinarton laughed. "You may come home with a different sort of filly!"

"I doubt it," he answered flatly.

Must everyone tease him about the invitation? Lord Grey and his alleged Marriage Mart were fast becoming the greatest joke of the year. By association, he was included in the jesting. He could strangle Willie for talking him into accepting!

"You'll keep an open mind, however?" his father cajoled. "Grey may be a bit eccentric, but the family is good *ton*."

"I hope that I shall never be guilty of judging anyone in advance, sir, but don't expect a match to come from that quarter. Anything Lord Grey breeds must have pointed ears, a long muzzle, and a flighty disposition." He chuckled. "No, Father. Much as I love horses, I don't have the least desire to go to bed with one!"

Lord Trinarton raised an eyebrow. "Lord Grey is a well-enough looking man, and Lady Grey is a handsome woman, if I recall. You just might be surprised."

"No," said Chris, stubbornly. "If Lord Grey's purpose is to trap me, I'll bolt at the first opportunity! No one will force me to wed. Least of all him."

3

Letitia walked the rangy thoroughbred down the drive to the stable, her tension beginning to rise as every stride brought her nearer to home and the pressures of Lady Grey. It had been three weeks since she, her mother, and sister had returned from London, three weeks of bustling, planning, and strain as everyone at Greywood Manor made furious preparation for the impending house party. The housekeeper and servants had been frantic, cleaning every inch of the house and taking especial care that the guest chambers were comfortable and well-appointed. The butler and his minions had feverishly polished all the china and the plate, and made certain that the wine cellars were admirably stocked with the finest spirits. The cook and kitchen staff had been designing the menus, cooking and baking many delectable items in advance, and filling the larders with the delicacies that the viscountess had purchased in London. The harassed Lady Grey had overseen it all, enlisting the help of her daughters and all the while haranguing them on the proper behavior to display before the gentlemen. Though Julianne seemed well-versed and happily anticipating the event, Letitia could remember less than half of what her mother had to say, and spent her days in growing dread of the ordeal to come. Only Lord Grey remained unaffected by the chaos. His stables were always in perfect order to receive even the most discriminating of visitors.

Today, everything was coming to a head. The guests should begin to arrive that very afternoon, and the party would begin. A frisson of nerves fluttered in Letitia's stomach. Suddenly she felt ignorant of what to wear, what to say, or what to do. Perhaps a London Season would have been better after all. She could have eased into it more gradually. The enormity of it wouldn't have descended upon her all at once, as this event was doing.

Unable to prolong her absence any longer, she rode the horse up to the entrance to the stable courtyard and dismounted onto the mounting block beside the archway. Stepping down, she drew the reins over the gelding's head and stroked the soft tip of his muzzle. She'd had a good ride today, cantering over the moorland, popping over several walls, and estimating the potential of the young hunter. She wondered when she'd have the opportunity to enjoy such a relaxing morning again. No doubt the gentlemen guests would be silently evaluating her equestrian skills every time she set foot in a stirrup.

Unfortunately, most ladies were not considered to be above average in riding ability. Indeed, they were often considered to be much less. Many women rode for the sole purpose of showing off their stylish riding habits, or for displaying a charming helplessness that was certain to garner sympathetic assistance from a gentleman. Letitia deplored this attitude. She was a talented, proficient horsewoman, adept at controlling the highbred, mettlesome animals she rode, putting them through their paces, and training them, too. Her father had taught her well and was proud of her.

But what would the guests think? Would they appreciate her expertise? Surely men looked for something more than equestrian prowess when choosing a wife.

Momentarily suffering her hand on his nose, the handsome chestnut tossed his head and blew.

"All right." Letitia laughed. "You don't like being petted like a baby! Very well." She gently smacked his shoulder and turned to the groom, who had ridden behind her. "See that he's sponged and cooled more thoroughly, Lyle."

It was an unnecessary request. Anyone who was employed by Lord Grey knew perfectly well how to care properly for a horse. The slightest deviation resulted in prompt dismissal.

"There you are, m'dear!" The viscount himself emerged from the stable enclosure. "Your mama has been searching for you."

"I told her I was going for a ride." Handing the horse's reins to the groom and tucking her crop under her arm, she stripped off her gloves. "I suppose I should have stayed at home. She is rather frantic about the guests' arrival."

"Pah!" Her father shrugged off any anxiety. "All will be well. She's a fine hostess."

"She is worried. She hasn't had much practice entertaining. Neither have I." She swallowed.

His eyes twinkled. "Criticizing my isolation, Tish?"

"No, not at all," she loyally murmured.

"I meet my fellows on sporting occasions. Were I to open my home to visitors, as some are in the habit of doing, I'd play host too much of the time. I'd not have a moment to accomplish anything. And I wouldn't have the enjoyment of surprising everyone with new and better horses."

"I just thought . . ." she began.

"Yes?"

"Well . . . Though Mama delights in Society, she seldom participates in it."

"Very true, but she may go to London anytime she pleases!" Satisfied, he looked speculatively after the gelding as the groom led him away. "How did he go today?"

"Very promising. I'd like to hunt him myself this fall, at times when we are assured of a small field."

He nodded vigorously, but added, "If you aren't off with a husband by then!"

Letitia twisted the gloves in her hands and returned to the topic she had introduced. "I'm rather anxious, too . . . about the guests."

"Nonsense!" He briefly clasped her about the shoulders. "You'll be fine!"

"I wish I could be as confident as you are."

"You've nothing to worry about! Our guests will be impressed. Mark my words, you'll have a husband from this! You can ride better than any gel I've ever seen."

She eyed him doubtfully. "Don't gentlemen want something more in . . . in a wife?"

Chuckling, he attempted to return to the stable.

"Papa!" She caught his arm. "Mama was not a great horsewoman, yet you, of all people, chose her!"

"This is different."

"How?" she pressed.

"You'll see. Now be a good girl and go help your mother."

This time he made good his escape. Unhappily, she watched him enter the stable yard and turn out of sight. It was the first time in her life that she had been disappointed in her father. He had deliberately avoided her question.

Frowning slightly, she started toward the house. *This is different*, he'd said. Perhaps she should simply trust his judgment. Indeed, that was what she must do. There was no time for her to develop drawing-room polish, or to improve her sewing of fancywork or her performance on the pianoforte. She must rely on her horsemanship, and on her own wits.

"Letitia!" her mother called through the open door of the drawing room as she entered the hall. "Where *have* you been? We've been searching all over for you!"

She paused, laying her gloves and crop on the hall table. "I was riding, Mama. Don't you remember? I did tell you."

"Goodness me, so you did! Now I recall it!" Lady Grey lifted a hand to her forehead. "I am all to pieces."

"All will be well," Letitia assured her, echoing her father's certainty. "The house looks so pretty, and I know you've conceived the most delightful menus. You've accomplished all this in such a short period of time! Mama, you truly are marvelous!"

"Thank you, my dear. I hope that the gentlemen will enjoy themselves, and above all, that they'll be comfortable. Never forget . . ." She cast her glance toward Julianne, who was seated by the window. "Gentlemen set a high value on their comfort. You must never overlook it, even to the denial of your own ease. If a man is comfortable, he will forgive any number of deficiencies."

"Yes, ma'am." Letitia stepped into the room. "You were looking for me," she reminded Lady Grey. "Is there something you wished me to do for you?"

"La, I can't recollect." Her mother placed another rose into the big, showy floral arrangement she was creating. "How does this look?"

"Beautiful, of course. You have such talent!"

"Fustian! It's nothing anyone couldn't do." She picked up a flower with a sadly bent stem. "Oh, yes. I *do* remember now! Letitia, you must control that raccoon. Do you know why I am arranging this bouquet at such a late hour? Because Racky took it all apart!"

Letitia sighed. When she was not present to supervise her pet, she kept him confined to her room. Lately, however, he had been escaping and getting into mischief such as this. She had not been able to determine his method of departure. Though the servants claimed they had kept the door firmly shut, she couldn't help but believe that they had been lackadaisical about it. Perhaps they had merely pulled the door to, without securing the latch. After all, how else could the little adventurer get out?

"You must watch him closely," her mother admonished, "else he will disturb our guests. Remember what I said about male comfort? That Racky can destroy the peace in seconds!"

"I'll be very careful," Letitia promised.

Julianne giggled. "Remember when he got up on the breakfast buffet? His little hands were covered with jam and . . ."

"I do not find it amusing!" Lady Grey snapped.

Julianne's smile faded. "Yes, ma'am."

"And I will warrant that none of the gentlemen would be pleased either. Really, Julianne, I cannot believe that you would laugh at such a disgusting sight!"

"But he looked so cute," she whispered.

"I shall see that he does not cause further mischief," Letitia interjected. "You need not be concerned, Mama, about his naughtiness."

"I had better not be! If there are further transgressions, he shall be sent to the stable!" she severely warned her elder daughter, suddenly fixing her with a wide-eyed gaze. "What are you doing in that riding attire?"

"I was riding, Mama. Remember?" She bit back a smile.

"You must bathe and dress at once! The guests are expected at any moment!" she cried in horror.

"But you said earlier that they wouldn't arrive until afternoon," Letitia protested.

"We must be prepared for any eventuality. It is impossible for a traveler to predict his exact time of arrival." She made frenzied shooing motions with her hands. "Hurry, Letitia! Make ready at once!"

"Yes, ma'am." With a speaking wink at Julianne, Letitia hurried from the drawing room and trotted upstairs to her chamber.

"A fine-looking establishment," William observed to his brother as they jogged up the drive to Lord Grey's estate, followed by Chris's curricle and the large traveling coach bearing their valets and baggage.

Chris nodded, his gaze sliding from the large eighteenth-century brick home with its neat box-wood landscaping to the interesting quadrangle beyond.

"That large complex of buildings must be the stable area," he commented.

"Undoubtedly," his younger brother agreed.

From their position on a slight rise, they had an excellent perspective on the layout of the viscount's equine enterprise. The main stable consisted of a quartet of brick slate-roofed buildings wrapped around a central courtyard. Nearby were several structures of identical architecture, which no doubt bore witness to periods of expansion. Surrounding this hub of activity were numerous hedged paddocks, beyond which stretched vast acreages of enclosed pasture.

"I'd like to have a place like this," Chris said admiringly.

Willie chuckled. "Marry one of the girls. Maybe it isn't entailed."

The earl laughed without mirth. "I do believe I could afford to build a comparable facility, with far less risk to my equilibrium."

"But you wouldn't have the horses to stock it with."

"Cut line, little brother! I have horses."

"Not like Lord Grey's," he teased.

"You overrate his animals," Chris said tightly.

"Not I! The man's won all the most important races in the kingdom. When his horses don't win, they're not very far off the pace. C'mon, Chris, admit it! You'd give your right arm to have your choice of Grey's thoroughbreds, and don't try to tell me differently!"

Chris vehemently shook his head. "Not my right arm, and definitely not my name!"

"Why are you so set against marriage?" Willie demanded.

"I am *not* set against marriage. I am set against being trapped and forced into it. And if it turns out to be true that Lord Grey's sole purpose in hosting this party is to snare husbands for his daughters, I shall leave at once."

"What a coward."

"Think what you will. I won't play stallion to Grey's mares."

"You're overreacting, Chris," his brother calmly proclaimed.

"No, I'm not! You should have heard my conversation with Father. Even *he* is trying to push me!"

William favored his brother with a cross glance. "Then hide in your room. I intend to have a good time, and to learn as much as I can about Lord

Grey's methods of training and breeding. The man's a genius, whether you want to believe it or not! I just don't understand you. You've been in a sour mood all summer long."

"You'll comprehend when you have escaped as many matrimonial traps and stratagems as I have."

William groaned. "Keep it to yourself. I don't want to hear any war stories. I'm going to concentrate on horses!"

"Just watch your step," Chris warned. "You're fair game, too."

Ahead of them, the road forked: a hedge-enclosed lane led off to the barn complex and the main avenue skirted the front lawn to the house. William drew in.

"Do you suppose we could approach the stable first?"

"No," Chris reluctantly replied, "it wouldn't be appropriate, even for a 'horse' party. We'll have to greet our host and hostess and receive our welcome first."

"I suppose you're right."

"Don't forget to dodge the young ladies that will be thrown at your head," he added cynically.

"Oh, *Chris!*"

Followed by their retinue, Christopher and William rode up in front of the house and drew to a halt. Immaculately liveried footmen materialized immediately and took the reins of their horses as they dismounted. On their heels appeared an elegant lady, a young woman at her side.

"She's beautiful!" Willie breathed, unable to keep from staring at the girl.

"Be cautious!" Chris quietly reminded him, and walked up the short flight of steps to the portico to bow over his hostess's hand. "Lady Grey, I am Christopher Brerely. And this is my brother, William."

"How do you do? So kind of you to come!" The viscountess's fingers trembled slightly. "This is my younger daughter, Julianne."

Chris greeted the young lady, but her gaze was not for him. She was eyeing his brother with unabashed adoration. Good God, he thought. She'd already set her sights on Willie! He wished he could leap on his horse and dash away, dragging the young man behind him.

"You must be weary and hungry from your journey, my lords," Lady Grey said merrily. "Do come in. We shall hold back luncheon while you refresh yourselves."

"Please do not go to special pains," Chris murmured, offering her his arm. "William and I can make do."

"It is no trouble at all!" she assured him. "My husband has only just returned from the stable, so our meal shall be late in any event! Please accept his apologies for not being among the first to welcome you. And those of my elder daughter, too."

"Of course."

They entered the house and paused in a large paneled hall.

"Formby," Lady Grey instructed the obeisant butler, "please show the gentlemen to their rooms and see that they are made comfortable."

"Yes, my lady."

Chris bowed again to the viscountess and followed the dignified servant up the stairs.

"Be careful," he warned his brother once more as they parted at his chamber door.

"She's beautiful," Willie marveled dreamily. Eyes slightly unfocused, he wandered down the hall behind the stiff-backed old retainer.

Irritably, the earl entered his bedroom. His brother had certainly lost all thoughts of horses. His mind was full of Grey's younger daughter, and she, the little vixen, was encouraging him. What the hell would happen now?

Guests had arrived!

Her heart in her throat, Letitia turned away from the window and rushed to her dressing room to finish her toilette. Gentlemen had arrived, and her mother was going to be furious with her for not being at hand to greet them. But goodness! How was she to know? After all, Lady Grey had first told her to expect them in the afternoon. The only thing she could do now was to dress as quickly as possible.

"Guests are here, Maudie!" she gasped to her maid. "We must hurry!"

"Yes, miss." The abigail picked up the lavender, sprigged muslin gown that had been laid out for her young mistress, and slipped it over her head, deftly fastening the tapes.

"Oh, dear," Letitia fretted, sitting down at the dressing table. "I am so unprepared that I am sure I will make a poor impression."

"Now, miss, don't you worry. I'll have you looking pretty in minutes!"

"It's not that," she quavered. "I know that you can work miracles, Maudie. It's just that I feel so deficient! All facets of charming behavior seem to have fled from my mind. I shall be tongue-tied and gauche."

"You're just overset," the maid soothed, gathering Letitia's hair into a shining knot at the nape of her neck. "As soon as you enter the drawing room, you'll be fine!"

"I hope so." She pressed her hands against her stomach. "I am full of butterflies. This isn't like me at all!"

Maudie opened her mouth to comment, but was arrested by a loud shout of masculine dismay that penetrated the very walls.

"What is that?" Letitia wailed.

The bellow resounded again.

A sense of horror gripped Letitia's spine. "Maudie, where is Racky?" she cried, suddenly realizing that the little animal was not playing with her brushes and combs as he usually did while she dressed.

"He was here just a bit ago, miss . . ." Maudie stared with alarm into her mistress's eyes.

"Oh, dear God!" Letitia sprang up and sped into her chamber. It was as she had feared. The door was slightly ajar, and there was no sign of the raccoon. Hurrying into the hall, she ran to the opened door of the nearest guest room.

"Dammit!" The cry reverberated from within.

Taking a deep breath, she pushed in the doorway, quickly surveying the awful scene. Standing with his back to her was a tall, trim, dark-haired gentleman, who was looking upward to the top of the window. High above on the drapery valance was Racky, chattering blithely and grinning down at the guest.

"What the hell are you?" the man blared. "Some sort of rodent?"

"He's a . . . r-raccoon," Letitia stammered.

The gentleman swung around, favoring her with a hard, questioning glare.

Letitia clung to the doorjamb, her knees slowly seeming to dissolve. In all of England, there could not be a male so handsome. Nor could there be one so angry.

"I . . . I am Letitia Grey," she managed, "and R-Racky is my . . . my p-pet."

Heart fluttering, she dropped into an ungainly, trembling curtsy.

4

The gentleman surveyed Letitia quickly with his expressive dark-brown eyes. With seeming disinterest, he turned back around to stare at the strange intruder once more. He shook his head.

"What in God's name is a raccoon?" he asked, his voice losing a measure of its heated anger.

"A raccoon is a woodland creature native to America." She stepped forward, praying that the necessity to function would overcome her quaking embarrassment. "Racky, come down from there!"

Her pet trilled and rolled a small item back and forth in his little hands. With a smirk of pleasure, he popped it into his mouth and licked his palm. Letitia saw with dismay that it was one of the cream mints from the dish Lady Grey had placed on the guest's bedside table.

"Sir, I do assure you that my pet is harmless. He's only a baby," she explained, hoping to distract the man from the realization that Racky had plundered his confections.

"Where did you get him?"

"In London, from a sailor's children. I thought he would make the most marvelous pet."

The gentleman raised a sardonic eyebrow. "And has he?"

"Oh, yes, though he . . . he is rather naughty at

times." She stretched out her arms. "Racky, *do* come down!"

Content to remain on his perch, the animal ignored her command.

"*Racky!*"

"He's well-trained, I see," the gentleman dryly observed.

"Letitia!" cried Lady Grey from the doorway. "What are you doing in Lord Brerely's chamber?"

"Mama!" She whirled around to see the viscountess, flanked by two footmen, frowning at her with disapproval.

"Whatever will Lord Brerely think of you?" her mother scolded. "Sir, I must apologize for this intrusion."

Letitia's heart sank to her toes. Lord Brerely was the earl, their ranking guest, the elder son of a marquess! She remembered his name from her father's list, and recalled the fact that her mother had been exceedingly surprised when he had accepted the invitation. Oh, dear Lord, why had Racky chosen Lord Brerely's room for his mischievous invasion? The gentleman would probably leave immediately and proceed to tell his tale all over England!

"Mama, I . . ."

"Go to your room at once," Lady Grey severely told her. "I cannot think why you would invade Lord Brerely's privacy!"

Cheeks burning with anguish, Letitia motioned wordlessly toward the drapery valance.

"Racky!" the viscountess gasped. "Letitia, I warned you to contain that animal! How can you have set him loose on the household? Get him down from there!"

"I am trying, ma'am," she whispered helplessly.

"Indeed," Lord Brerely agreed with a cynical chuckle.

"What is all the commotion?" Lord Grey appeared behind the group in the doorway. "I heard shouting."

"I fear that I was the one who disturbed your peace, sir," the earl explained, casting a pointed gaze upward. "In a sense," he added, pursing his lips.

"Oh, you've met Racky," Letitia's father remarked mildly, and strode past his wife and servants to shake the hand of the new arrival. "Welcome to Greywood Manor, Brerely. I trust you had a pleasant journey." He peered upward at the drapery valance. "Little rascal! Best fetch him down, Tish. Lord Brerely might not appreciate sharing his chamber with a raccoon."

"Certainly not!" snapped his wife frantically, turning to one of the footmen. "Bring a feather duster. We shall dash him to the floor!"

"No, Mama!" Letitia shrieked. "It would hurt him!"

"I doubt we need to resort to such an extreme," Lord Grey stated firmly. "Call him, daughter."

Anxiously, she complied, but the raccoon merely chattered and licked his lips.

"Perhaps we can coax him." Lord Brerely crossed the room to the dish of confections. "He seems to like mints."

"What?" screeched Lady Grey. "He has . . . He has . . ."

"Helped himself to refreshment?" His lordship smiled enigmatically.

"Just like the buffet." Julianne tittered, joining the company and realizing instantly what was causing the turmoil. "You should have seen him when he assailed the breakfast buffet, my lord. He looked so cute, sitting there with one hand in the bacon and the other in the jam. Just like a naughty little boy!"

"Julianne!" her mother moaned. "Can you not keep such appalling anecdotes to yourself?"

"But it was funny," she protested.

Once again lifting an eloquent eyebrow, Lord Brerely extended a mint toward the raccoon, but the creature merely sniffed, cocking his head from side to side.

"He's interested!" Lord Grey exclaimed. Hurriedly, he dragged a chair to the window. "Get up on this, Brerely. You're taller than the rest of us. Perhaps you can reach him!"

"What's the to-do?" inquired a pleasant, curious voice from the hall.

Letitia glanced toward the newcomer. From the striking facial resemblance, it was plain to see that the gentleman was his lordship's brother. There, however, the similarities ended. His open and amiable countenance was far less complex than that of the earl, and his eyes twinkled with unguarded interest. The younger man would be much easier to know.

He ambled into the room. "What have you there, Chris?"

"A raccoon," said his older brother.

"What's that?"

Julianne promptly drew him aside and began a giggling explanation.

Letitia returned her attention to the problem at hand as the earl removed his coat and climbed up onto the chair.

"Do be careful," she begged. "Perhaps we should send for a ladder instead."

"Let us try this first," he insisted. "Will he allow me to pick him up?"

"I . . . I don't know." She dragged her gaze from the breathtaking sight of the earl's beautifully sculptured thighs in his form-fitting buckskin breeches, only to be arrested by the well-formed muscles of his shoulders and back that were so artlessly displayed by the fine, thin fabric of his shirt.

"Miss Grey." Lord Brerely flushed slightly as he turned, catching her in the act of inspecting his masculine attributes. "I'm asking you if he'll bite me."

"I . . . I don't know," she repeated inanely, quickly looking away. "He has never attempted to bite anyone. Oh, Racky, *do* come down!"

"Grab him by the tail!" called Lady Grey. "Fling him to the floor!"

"My dear," said her husband, shocked by her outburst. "I have never known you to exhibit such cruelty toward animals."

"He has devastated my house party!"

"Nonsense! He has only provided entertainment."

"Our luncheon will be ruined!"

"The servants will keep it warm. It will be an unforgettable day. We're enjoying this interlude immensely, aren't we, Brerely?" he asked jovially.

His lordship's answer was a tight, obviously forced grin. He held the mint to the raccoon's nose, moving it tantalizingly to and fro. As the animal leaned toward it, he drew it slowly downward.

"Come on, sirrah," he crooned. "Down you go."

But Racky was too fast for him. With lightning speed, he snatched the sweet from Lord Brerely's fingers and popped it into his mouth. With a throaty purr, he eyed his audience with self-satisfaction.

"All right for you!" The earl took a deep breath and plucked him from his roost, the animal's sharp little claws pulling threads in Lady Grey's elegant new draperies.

Once captured, Racky didn't seem to mind. He loudly crunched his mint in Lord Brerely's ear and wrapped one arm around his neck. Swallowing, he planted a sticky kiss on his lordship's cheek.

"Oh, dear," Letitia murmured, reaching for her pet as the earl stepped down. "I am so sorry."

"Take him and pen him up," her mother commanded. "Letitia, *take him.*"

"I'm trying, Mama," she wailed, attempting to pry the clinging Racky from Lord Brerely's neck.

Contented to be in the arms of one who had given him a sweet, the raccoon had taken a great interest in the earl's exquisite neckcloth. Warbling happily, he tugged and rearranged it to his own rumpled design. Periodically, he poked his nose into Lord Brerely's face.

"This is awful!" Letitia cried, blinking back tears and jerking as hard as she dared.

"He likes you, Chris!" the earl's brother said with a guffaw, then was so overwhelmed by laughter that he was forced to seek a chair.

"Hold onto him," Lord Brerely snarled. "Let me see if I can loosen his hands ... er ... paws ... whatever the hell they are!"

Grimly, Letitia grasped the furry body while the earl worked to free himself from the raccoon's busy fingers.

"Let me help," Lord Grey volunteered.

With the viscount's assistance, Lord Brerely managed to wrest away one hand, while his host detached the other. Unceremoniously, the earl leaped backward to freedom.

"Hell and damnation, Brerely!" Letitia's father laughed. "I doubt you can say that you've ever received a more singular greeting!"

Clasping her pet securely to her breast, Letitia stared unhappily at the gentleman's disarray. " My lord, I do so regret what has ..."

Racky cackled and thrust his hand down the bodice of her dress.

Letitia gasped. Bursting into tears of embarrassment, she turned on her heel and ran from the room.

"Mama, I can't go down to lunch!" Letitia sobbed into her pillow. "How can I ever face him again? I shall remain in my room until the house party is over. I have never been so mortified in all my life!"

"You have brought this upon yourself," Lady Grey said severely, sitting down on the edge of the bed. "I told you to keep that creature under control!"

"But I did! I don't know how he got loose! I am certain that I shut the door securely!"

"Obviously, you did not. And you *will* come down to luncheon, Letitia. I shall not permit otherwise."

"Mama, please let me hide," she moaned. "I know it will delight Lord Brerely. He most certainly must have formed an active aversion to me!"

"Fiddlesticks! The whole incident has probably piqued the gentleman's curiosity."

Letitia lifted her head, rolled over, and sat up. Staring at her mother in frank disbelief, she accepted the dry handkerchief that Lady Grey offered. How could the viscountess believe such fustian? Piqued his *curiosity*? The whole incident had piqued his *temper*! She wiped her eyes and then mightily blew her nose.

"Mama, he wasn't amused. He was angry."

"Nonsense! His interest was aroused."

"Oh, yes," Letitia said sarcastically. "In a negative fashion."

"Then it shall be up to you to change it into a positive one."

"That would be impossible! He has received the most unfavorable first impression of me. Moreover, he is too far above me in looks, rank, and polish!"

"He is a handsome devil, isn't he?" her mother observed. "But above you? I think not. Never forget that you are descended from one of the oldest and most respected families in England."

"And so is he," Letitia groaned. "Furthermore, he shall be a marquess one day."

"Marquesses are men, just like any others."

"Oh, no, they are not! How can you say that? They are grand, top-lofty . . ."

"Be that as it may," Lady Grey cut in, weary of argument. "I shall not allow you to hide in your room. You will take your place at the table like a well-bred, mannerly daughter of this house is expected to do. And that's not all! I expect you to assist in entertaining our guests and to make yourself pleasing to them."

"*Mama!*"

"I mean it, Letitia," Lady Grey warned severely.

"But surely you must understand how I feel!" Letitia cried. "You, too, were perfectly mortified by that scene!"

"Maybe I was." The viscountess fluttered her hand as if to cool her perspiring brow. "I, however, intend to rise above it. And so must you."

"*I can't!*" Letitia shrilled, her eyes filling once more with tears.

Lady Grey rose majestically. "I shall hear no more. Young lady, you will obey me in this. Now, get yourself together, freshen your face and hair, and come immediately to the drawing room. We shall await luncheon for you."

"*Please!*"

"If you do not quickly appear downstairs, I shall come for you myself and drag you down like a naughty little girl. *Then* we shall see how embarrassed you are!"

Letitia shook her head. "I cannot believe that you could be so cruel."

"I have two unmarried daughters. I am a desperate woman!" Purposefully she strode to the door, then turned. "See that you close the door firmly. I'll not have that wild beast preceding us into the dining room!"

Letitia flinched as the door slammed shut loudly. She had no choice but to submit to her mother's commands. Lady Grey was overset enough to do just as she threatened. How mortifying that would be! She sighed.

A leathery little hand tugged at her sleeve. Racky crawled into her lap and gazed innocently up at her.

"Oh, Racky." She picked him up and held him to her shoulder, nuzzling his head with her cheek. "However am I to get through this? Lord Brerely must think me the worst of antidotes. Please, please, you must be good. From now on!"

Chris accepted a fresh neckcloth from his valet, glancing at the door as William, still chuckling, entered the room.

"If you've come to make fun of me, little brother, you can turn right around and go the opposite direction," he growled. "I am in no mood for jesting."

"Be a sport, Chris. You've had a unique experience." He draped himself across a chair, then began idly swinging his leg. "I know of no one else who's been kissed by an American raccoon!"

He snorted. "That silly female probably has."

"Miss Grey? I don't think she's silly. I found her rather refreshing. No artifice, no wiles, and vastly attractive."

"She is nothing but trouble." Chris returned his attention to the mirror, concentrating carefully as he put his personal twist to his cravat. "Dammit! I got it wrong."

"Your judgment of the lady?" Willie asked.

"No! This neckcloth!" He whipped it off and exchanged it for another. "If anything, my assessment of Miss Grey was milder than she deserves!"

"Don't be such a prig, brother. So the lady has an unusual pet! What's wrong with that? You like animals."

"I don't like them invading my room. I don't like them kissing me."

Willie snickered. "Come now, Chris. It's not Miss Grey's fault. You can't blame her for what the little imp did."

"Oh, yes, I can! She failed to control him." He completed a satisfactory knot in the cloth and stepped back from the mirror as the valet helped him into his perfectly tailored coat of blue superfine. "Her so-called pet is a menace. And I have the distinct impression that she is, too!"

"Balderdash!" Willie stood. "Are you ready?"

"Almost." He sat down and motioned Nickerson to apply the final touches to his artfully disarrayed hair.

"Hurry up," his younger brother said. "We shouldn't make them wait any longer than necessary."

"I don't give a damn. It isn't *my* fault," he murmured querulously. "If it hadn't been for that raccoon, we would be lunching right now."

"Well, I'm starving."

"I don't care, Willie! It was your idea to come here!"

"Poor Chris!" William mocked in a whining, high-pitched voice. "He's so put-upon."

The earl set his jaw and glared at his reflection. Over his shoulder he saw his valet trying fruitlessly to hide a grin. He sprang to his feet.

"That does it! I'm leaving here this afternoon!" He snapped.

"You can't!" Willie cried, sobering. "I want to examine Lord Grey's stables, and . . . and to make further acquaintance of Miss Julianne!"

"You don't have to leave."

"I can't stay if you don't! I need your support!"

Chris curled his lip. "Support? Defense would be a better word. This place is a mantrap! That girl trotted right into my room. Bold as brass!"

"There was a reason for it," his brother protested. "You're being entirely unreasonable. I've never known you to be like this!"

"I have a lot on my mind, Willie."

"Because of Father pressuring you to marry?"

"That, and this situation!" The earl threw up his arms. "I am sick and tired of everyone *wanting* something from me! Why can't people just leave me alone?"

"Chris." Willie drew him across the room to a sofa in front of an empty hearth. "No one is going to force you to do anything you dislike, and that includes the Greys. They seem like decent, honorable people. They are not going to try to set up a trap for you."

"You don't know to what lengths people will go in order to snare husbands for their daughters."

"I doubt they'll go to such extremes," his brother said patiently. "Remember all the times you've escaped in the past? You're experienced at avoiding the marital noose!"

Chris shrugged. "I suppose I am."

"Think of poor Miss Grey. She was so horribly embarrassed! In truth, I imagine that she suffered a great deal more damage than you did. If you take your leave, she'll blame herself. You're a gentleman. You don't want that!"

The earl felt a niggling stab of conscience.

"Besides," Willie cajoled, "you accepted Lord Grey's invitation. It would be insulting and dishonorable to leave before his party begins."

Chris made up his mind. "All right. I'll stay. But Willie? At the first threat of compromise, I'll take to my heels and run!"

"Fair enough!" Willie clapped him on the shoulder. "Who knows? You just might have a good time at this event! One thing is certain. You'll see some fine horseflesh."

Chris smiled faintly.

"And now," his younger brother said, beaming, "let us have some luncheon!"

5

Cloaked in mortification, Letitia toyed with her meal and hoped that no one was paying attention to her. The luncheon was miserable. Not the food, of course, for Cook had truly outdone herself in taking the simple type of repast that Lord Grey preferred and turning it into something special. The individual chicken pies were rich and creamy with an incredibly flaky crust. The breads were hot from the oven and light as a feather. The fresh garden vegetables were snapping crisp. Letitia wished she could have enjoyed it, for this was also her favored style of fare, but she didn't have the heart, or the appetite, to indulge. No, the atmosphere was just too stiff, too strained, too perfectly awful.

With the exception of the bright bursts of repartee between Julianne and Lord Brerely's brother, conversation was desultory. The earl had retreated into silence, speaking only when spoken to, and then merely replying in polite, stilted phrases. Perhaps that was just his way. Maybe he was actually very dull. His intellect might even be wanting. But Letitia didn't think so, not after the sharp dialogue in his chamber. Probably he was being so reticent because he felt ill-used. If that was so, he must be a terribly vindictive man. With the raccoon debacle over and done with, and no real harm having occurred, his attitude was decidedly irritating.

Certainly she must admit, however, that she herself wasn't contributing to the entertainment. She was still too disturbed over the impression she must have made. Her mother shouldn't have compelled her to leave her chamber. With a bit more time, she could have risen to the challenge, and at least the redness would have faded from her eyes. As it was, she was not only embarrassed by the horrible event, but by her appearance as well.

"Letitia," Lady Grey said with contrived pleasantness, "perhaps you could tell us of your morning ride."

"It was agreeable," she replied blandly.

When she didn't continue, her father filled the awkward lull. "Letitia is training a most promising young horse," he explained. "He went rather well today, didn't he, dear?"

"Yes. He did." She took a bite of chicken pie, which seemed so dry that she was forced to reach hurriedly for her glass of wine to wash it down.

"Both of my daughters are excellent horsewomen," Lord Grey boasted.

Julianne half-choked, quickly hiding her coughing behind her napkin.

Her father ignored her. "Letitia, I believe, is the more skillful. She has a way with animals."

Letitia stole a quick glance at Lord Brerely. The corner of his mouth was twitching slightly. There was a quick flash of humor in his brown eyes as he met her gaze. She quickly looked back at her plate. He was laughing at her, *the brute!*

Her temper flared. Why should she feel ashamed? No one would have responded the way that they had if it had been a dog or cat in Lord Brerely's bedroom. It was because it was Racky, because he was strange and unusual. A pox on them all!

"In fact," her father continued, "Letitia is a better rider than many men I've seen."

She looked up, squarely eyeing Lord Brerely. This time there was challenge in those eloquent eyes. She proudly lifted her chin in acknowledgment.

"I find it hard to believe, sir," the earl drawled. "I have yet to see a lady ride better than one man, let alone many."

"Perhaps you have seen it, but have refused to admit it, my lord," Letitia said sweetly.

A condescending smile briefly curved his lips. "I doubt it. I am considered to be a fair man."

"Are you indeed?" she murmured.

"Come now, Chris," his brother chuckled. "You've always said that Allesandra and Ellen were excellent riders."

"For *ladies*, yes. I cannot think, however, that they are capable of outdoing a man."

Lord William shook his head. "To decide the winner of this debate, we have no other choice, Lord Grey, but to witness Miss Grey's expertise. I shall look forward to it." He bowed his head to Julianne. "And also to riding with you, Miss Julianne."

Julianne looked at him with wide-eyed dismay. "My father exaggerates my abilities, sir. My talents as an equestrienne cannot compare to those of my sister."

He smiled. "You needn't be modest with us."

"I'm not!" she gasped. "I . . ."

"Julianne's greater talents lie elsewhere," Lady Grey smoothly cut in. "She is particularly accomplished in needlework and on the pianoforte. She has a love of horses, of course. It runs in the family! But she is not quite as good a rider as Letitia. Conversely, Letitia does not excel quite so superbly in those other attributes. Both of my daughters are exceptional in all they attempt. I suppose that it all boils down to what one spends the most time perfecting."

"Yes, ma'am," Lord William agreed.

"I thought to show our guests the stables after lunch," Lord Grey announced. "Letitia, would you care to accompany us? Perhaps you might like to put your young horse through his paces and show these gentlemen that I am correct in my assessment of your abilities."

"I'm sorry, Papa," she murmured. "I fear I must be occupied elsewhere this afternoon."

"Where?" he demanded.

"Papa . . ."

She could feel the bright spots of color staining her cheeks. Why couldn't everyone leave her alone? Had no one else ever experienced the pain of mortification? Racky had created enough havoc with her sensibilities. Must her father do the same in proclaiming her to be some sort of female centaur? This party was awful. Not only would Society laugh about Lord Grey's private Marriage Mart, they would chuckle about his bizarre daughter as well. She could have quietly, without fanfare, demonstrated her skill to the gentlemen. Why must such a great issue be made of it?

"Surely the gel has no duties to perform," her father persisted, "not while we are entertaining visitors."

"Of course she does not!" Lady Grey assured him. "No doubt Letitia believes that she should be present to assist me in welcoming our other guests. It isn't necessary, Letitia. Julianne is more than capable. After all, this is a simple country party. We needn't stand on city ceremony."

"Very well, then," Lord Grey said triumphantly, and proceeded to clean his plate with gusto.

Letitia gazed woodenly as a footman removed her scarcely touched portion and began to serve the dessert. Refusing the cake, she accepted only a small bowl of fruit. Sadly she wondered if she'd have it all back up before the afternoon was over. The very thought of performing before the gentlemen made her body tense all over.

They would be watching her, discussing her, *judging* her! She could almost picture the cynical speculation in Lord Brerely's eloquent eyes. She could visualize the little twitch at the corner of his mouth if she made the slightest error. Oh, yes, he would be a ruthless critic! She would never be able to gain his good opinion.

But fiddlesticks! Who wanted it? He wasn't the man for her! He was much too arrogant and conceited. He wasn't a good sportsman. And he didn't like her.

"Wine, miss?" asked the footman at her elbow.

She looked with surprise at her empty glass. "Yes, thank you."

When and where had her wine disappeared? She must have finished it without even noticing. Goodness, she must get her wits about her! She might not care what Lord Brerely thought of her, but her young horse deserved an attentive rider. Mentally chiding herself, she forced her mind to return to the meal and the stiff conversation.

Surreptitiously, Chris studied Miss Grey as she walked slightly ahead of them toward the stables. He was rather surprised by her choice of riding habit. He had expected her to be clad in a costume of style and flair, as was the custom of ladies of fashion. But there were no epaulets, ruffles, or flowing plumes on Miss Grey's attire. Her dull-gold habit was well-cut, and it showed her slim figure to advantage, but it was plain and unadorned without any of the frills designed to catch a gentleman's eye. In fact, it was, well, business-like. If she wanted to trap a man, she should have a plume dancing over that dainty shoulder.

Then again, perhaps she didn't think she needed it. With those beckoning hips that swayed so nicely when she walked, and with that tiny waist, she could attract plenty of attention without resorting to modish subterfuge. Gad, but she was graceful! She moved with all the liquid agility and assurance of the finest thoroughbred. She would be light as a feather in a man's arms on the dance floor.

Chris felt a very masculine twinge in the region of his groin. That derriere! He couldn't have taken his gaze from it if the King himself demanded. The Greys didn't need to design a mantrap. They'd already done so when they begat this little beauty. Which of the guests would succumb to the lure of her delicious curves? Which man would take home this Grey filly? He took a deep breath. It wouldn't be him.

As if she felt him staring at her, Miss Grey glanced back over her shoulder. Briefly, her eyes met his, and her cheeks bloomed with a deeper shade of pink. With an infinitesimal lift of her chin, she looked away.

He stifled a grin. Despite her abject embarrassment over the antics of her devilish raccoon, the lady had spirit. That had become obvious at lunch, when she had overcome her humiliation to toss him her little challenges. It was too bad that the situation was so potentially dangerous or he might have enjoyed a flirtation with her. But as it was, he must take care to show no particular interest in her, and definitely to keep her at arm's length, preferably a room's length, away.

"My father constructed this quadrangle. Here I keep the carriages and equipment, the stallions, the horses in training, and the personal horses." Lord Grey broke the silence, pausing at the arched entrance to the main stable area. He waved a hand toward the numerous smaller brick barns which skirted the structure. "I added the other buildings to house the brood mares and the younger stock."

Willie whistled softly. "Impressive."

The viscount beamed. He pointed down a neat brick road which curved past the stable and disappeared into a cluster of trees. "My kennels are located there. I also keep a pack of foxhounds, you know. Are you gentlemen interested in dogs?"

"I'm interested in all facets of equine sport," Willie breathed. "Including the fine hounds that lead the hunt."

"Then we'll tour that, too," he promised, "but we'll do it another day. Now . . ." He led the way into the enclosed courtyard.

Chris could scarcely conceal his amazement at Lord Grey's facility. It was, in truth, even larger than it had appeared from the road. In fact, it was the biggest, most magnificent stable he had ever seen. He wished his friends had been invited to Greywood Manor. They would have been astounded.

The two-story, front-entry side of the square was apparently the service area of the complex. Open doors revealed a superb collection of deeply lacquered, highly polished carriages, curricles, and vehicles of all types, even two gaily painted sleighs. Closed doors probably concealed tack rooms, feed storage, and living quarters for the viscount's employees.

The other three legs of the building were lined with smooth, varnished box stalls. Many had their own engraved brass nameplates. Several horses stood looking out over the opened half-doors.

"It's magnificent!" Willie blurted. "I'd give an arm and a leg for a place like this! And for horses of the quality to occupy it," he added worshipfully. "We knew of your reputation for fine blood stock, Lord Grey, but I never expected anything so . . . so grand!"

The viscount smiled and eyed Chris expectantly.

"This has to be the finest facility in England. It's certainly the best I've ever seen," he said slowly. "You must be very proud, sir."

"It's my life," Lord Grey admitted quietly. He looked, almost apologetically, at his daughter. "Perhaps I have neglected other things in building and maintaining my little empire, but I hope I've carved my niche in the annals of sport."

"You certainly have!" Willie exclaimed. "You're already a veritable legend!"

Chris noted the subtle exchange of speaking glances between the viscount and his daughter. The man must be seeking her pardon for slighting his family in favor of his horses, and with her soft smile, she was forgiving him. Idly, he wondered how Lady Grey felt about her husband's complete absorption with his hobby. Was this why the two girls of marriageable age had never been brought to London for their Seasons? Why hadn't the viscountess done it herself?

As Lord Grey moved toward a row of box stalls with William matching his stride, Chris found himself following behind with Miss Grey.

"Your father is certainly a dedicated horseman," he remarked casually, wondering exactly how much she shared his interest.

"Indeed he is," she simply replied.

"Apparently you, too, are an avid equestrienne."

"I enjoy the sport very much, my lord," she answered evasively.

"Only 'enjoy'?" he prodded. "At luncheon Lord Grey gave us to believe that equine activities are of much greater importance to you than that."

She looked him in the eye, her gaze narrowing. "Do you question my father's sincerity, sir?" she asked flatly. "Or are you merely prying?"

Flushing, Chris stiffened his shoulders. "My apologies, Miss Grey. I only intended to engage in polite conversation."

It was her turn to color. "I am sorry, Lord Brerely. I must admit to being rather testy today. Do forgive me."

"Of course."

They paused to examine a fine stallion in an immaculate stall. Tuning out William's effusive compliments, Chris concentrated on Miss Grey. It was probable that the chit was still absolutely mortified over the incident with that strange, pesky beast from America. What young lady wouldn't be horrified at disturbing such a prize target on the Marriage Mart as he? The ordinary female would have reacted with tears and bemoanings, but an original, such as Miss Grey must be, would dart through an entire gamut of emotional expression. In his room, she had been distressed. Now she was impudent and irritable. In her way, she was rather fascinating. Changing his former decision to avoid her, he now determined to know her better. Surely he could do that without endangering his peace and freedom!

"Miss Grey," he began again, as they strolled on toward the next stall, "I am curious to know why we have never seen you in London. I know I would remember should you have had a Season there, for I am sure I would have seen such a horsewoman as you, riding in the park in the early morning."

She shrugged evasively.

"I like to ride at that time of day, when the company is thin," he continued, "but only those ladies serious about their horsemanship will appear at that unfashionable hour."

She stopped dead in her tracks, halfway turning to face him. "Lord Brerely," she said, her voice raising a notch, "if you must know, I have never spent an appreciable time in the city. Nor have I had a Season, and it is immaterial to me if I ever do so. I much prefer my life in the country to the false entertainments of the *ton*."

He raised an eyebrow, suppressing a grin.

"Furthermore," she added indignantly, "I find your prying into my personal life to be both impertinent and arrogant. You are my father's guest. As such, I must assume that you have come here to see his horses and his stable. Go and look at them, and leave me in peace!" she snapped, flouncing away after Lord Grey and Willie, twitching her derriere in an even more provocative manner than she had before.

"Miss Grey!" Quickly he caught up with her. "Once again, I must apologize. I was only attempting to make—"

"Polite conversation, I assume." She gritted her teeth. "No, Lord Brerely, it won't do. You are deliberately trying to unsettle me so that I will perform poorly and make a mockery of my father's boast about my riding skill."

"That was *not* my intention."

"No? Excellent! Then you will have no difficulty in taking your conversation elsewhere. I haven't an interest in it."

With that, she strode more briskly toward her father and defensively slipped her arm through his, leaving Chris to wonder if he had gone way too far with his probing.

It was going to be disastrous. Letitia knew it as soon as she had ridden the young thoroughbred through the gate and into the training enclosure. The gelding moved stiffly beneath her, his tautly bunched muscles and his choppy gait providing no uncertain evidence of his inner tension.

Though fully aware of the poor quality of the performance, there was nothing Letitia could do about it. Her nerves were so frazzled and her irritability so high that she had unavoidably communicated her mental turmoil to the horse, who had responded accordingly. All she could do was to carry on this sham of a display, and hope that neither she nor the animal came to grief over it.

"Perhaps a series of circles will loosen him up!" Lord Grey called as she passed the three men.

Clenching her teeth, Letitia obeyed, but the gelding threw his shoulder inward and refused to round himself to the circumference of the sphere

"Dammit," she said under her breath, and applied a stronger rein, shifting her crop to her other hand and lightly tapping the animal's offending shoulder. The horse ignored her. Frustrated, she drew up in front of the onlookers.

"I'm sorry, Papa." She forced a smile. "Things aren't going well today. Perhaps another time?"

He frowned unhappily. "I can't understand it. This horse has been progressing so rapidly."

Letitia felt Lord Brerely's brown-eyed gaze boring into her. Glancing surreptitiously at him, she saw a faint, bemused smile curve the corners of his lips. He reached out to touch the thoroughbred's shoulder.

"The animal is extremely tense," he observed.

"The audience is rather disconcerting," she explained coldly.

"Of course," he agreed with questionable sympathy. "When one has been tucked away in the country, it must be very difficult to perform in front of others."

Letitia took a deep, quick breath to stop herself from delivering a scorching retort. The nerve of the man! To talk to her thus in the very presence of her father! Most gentlemen would blame the horse in order to save the lady's feelings. Not Lord Brerely! The arrogant earl was placing the fault exactly where it belonged. On her shoulders. She eyed her father.

Lord Grey had missed the significance of the man's remark.

He shook his head, considering.

"No, Letitia has ridden in the company of others before. She is a regular participant in the hunt field. It can't be that. The horse is green. It's simply just a bad day for him."

Lord Brerely stroked the gelding's smooth, sinewy muscles. "Might I try?"

"In my sidesaddle?" Letitia blurted. "And you are not dressed for riding!"

He shrugged.

"The saddle can soon be changed." Lord Grey beckoned to a nearby groom.

"When it comes to riding, Chris never cares about his clothes." Lord William grinned.

"The horse is apparently in your charge, Miss Grey." The earl looked up at her in appeal. "Might I ride him?"

"Certainly, my lord," she said shortly, inwardly seething. "If you wish to soil your attire, it is naught to me."

She looked to her father to help her down, but he remained fixedly in place, forcing her to accept assistance from Lord Brerely. She laid her hands on his broad shoulders, hoping that her gloves would leave equine sweat stains on his lordship's fine blue coat. Lightly, he lifted her down.

"Thank you," she muttered, letting go of him the second her feet touched the ground. Her fingers and palms seemed to burn. In that brief moment, she had discovered that Lord Brerely's athletic appearance was not a mere illusion. His straight, hard-muscled shoulders were just as real as they looked. He was magnificent. She almost sighed with disappointment. It was too bad that such a fine figure of a man was so insufferable.

The saddles were changed, and Lord Brerely slipped his fingers under the girth to check its security.

"My father's grooms do not make mistakes," Letitia commented irritably.

"That may be, but if there was a slipup, I would be the victim of it," he said, casually adjusting the reins.

"It seems insulting."

"No, no, he's right," Lord Grey hastily interjected. "Listen, observe, and learn, Tish. There will be many excellent horsemen attending our party. You may gain some pointers from them."

Traitor, she thought, biting the inside of her lip. Why must her father take *his* side? Did men naturally bond together into some sort of macabre fraternity designed to put women in their place? If so, she would hide in her room and slide the dresser across the door for the remainder of the party. Not even her mother could force her to remove that barricade!

Bitterly, she watched Lord Brerely swing into the saddle and ride away. He possessed none of her nervousness, so it wasn't long before the gelding relaxed and began performing his paces with ease. She clenched her fists as the horse pliably bent himself around a series of circles, first at the trot and then at the canter.

"Well done!" Lord Grey applauded as the earl skimmed gracefully over a small practice jump in the center of the paddock.

"Chris is very talented," Lord William said with pride.

"I can do that," Letitia whispered in frustration.

The earl's brother heard her. "Of course you can." He smiled kindly. "But you see, Chris has always been such a natural rider. He's one with the horse, and the animal knows it."

Lord Brerely trotted over to them and drew to a halt. "He's very agreeable, sir," he said to Lord Grey, but his gaze was on Letitia.

"Yes," she murmured, "I know."

She turned to her father. "You must excuse me now. I am certain that Mother is desirous of my presence, and you have no need of me here."

Without waiting for his reply, she turned on her heel and hurriedly left the stable area.

6

Letitia entered the house by the rear door to Lord Grey's estate office. Momentarily pausing to regain her wits, she leaned against her father's desk and gazed at the oil painting of Sir Righteous, the viscount's premier stud, which hung over the mantel. The sight of the magnificent stallion only served to addle her further. The majestic Sir Righteous was the sire of the young gelding on which she had performed so poorly and that Lord Brerely had ridden so well. A pox on the man! Why couldn't he have achieved merely a mediocre demonstration? After all, he was riding a strange horse, and he wasn't even dressed for the sport. But no, he *would* have to excel, and show her up to be a perfect simpleton. She ground her teeth.

Although Sir Righteous was riderless in the portrait, Letitia couldn't help visualizing Lord Brerely atop the racehorse's sleek back. The sight would be breathtaking. His lordship sat a horse better than any man she'd ever seen. His seat was graceful, yet powerful, like the tautly restrained might of the stallion himself, a delicate balance of strength and control. His hands were commanding, too, yet he communicated with the horse in a gentle and tactful fashion. He asked rather than demanded, and the animal was pleased to comply.

Letitia sighed, begrudgingly admitting to herself that Lord Brerely, as his brother had claimed, was a natural talent. But hadn't her father always said the same about her? Unfortunately, she had allowed her emotions to get in the way of proving it. Instead of informing the gelding of her compassionate authority, as the earl had done, she had instilled her nervousness in him. He had reacted as would be expected, with anxiety and fear. Her father must be terribly disappointed in her.

And what did Lord Brerely and his brother think? First impressions were lasting ones. From now on, no matter how well she rode, she would probably never redeem herself in their eyes. But what did it matter anyway? The earl didn't care for her, and she didn't like him.

With a small shrug, she straightened her shoulders and left the room. She would indulge in a long, luxurious bath, then dress in one of her pretty new afternoon gowns. She would meet the other guests, and hopefully, her father would not boast to them about her outstanding skill as an equestrienne.

Entering her bedroom, she was surprised to see Julianne reclining in the window seat, with a sleeping Racky in her lap.

"How was your ride?" her sister asked breathlessly. "I wanted to come so badly, but I was afraid that Papa would force me onto a horse."

Letitia evaded the question. "Haven't any other guests arrived?"

"No. Not yet. Mama said she'd send for me when they did. Tell me, Tish! Did you impress the earl or . . . or Lord William?"

Bleakly, Letitia shook her head. "I was awful."

"Awful?" Julianne cried in disbelief. "Letitia! How could you ever ride poorly?"

"I just . . . did." She sat down on the edge of the bed. "I was nervous, of course, because of Papa's bragging, and Lord Brerely didn't make it any better."

"What did he do?" Julianne probed.

"He was snide and absolutely abhorrent. He made me the victim of his ridicule. He is arrogant, overbearing, pompous . . ."

"Are you sure?" Julianne asked narrowing her eyes suspiciously.

"Yes!" snapped Letitia.

Her sister waved a nonchalant hand. "I understand. He attempted to flirt with you."

"He did not! He belittled me. He made me feel as if I were the most provincial ninny in God's creation!" she shrilled. "He actually made fun of me for never having had a Season in London. As if I even cared! Oh, he is so infuriating!"

Julianne smiled knowingly. "I believe that you are enormously attracted to him."

"I am not! I *hate* him!"

The vehemence of her remark awakened the raccoon. He crawled from Julianne's lap and scurried across the room, shinnying up the bedpost. Taking a perch on the canopy, he chattered in scolding tones.

"He doesn't like you either, Racky," Letitia said to the little beast. "Lord Brerely doesn't like anyone but himself. He is so puffed up with his own consequence that I could just . . . just . . . Oh, how I would like to take him down a peg or two! Yes, I shall set my mind to the matter!"

"Please don't be malicious," Julianne begged. "I do so like his brother."

"Well . . ." Letitia said consideringly.

"Lord William isn't at all as you envision Lord Brerely," her sister said hastily. "He is sweet, and kind, and amiable. He is all that I have ever imagined a gentleman to be. Oh, please, Tish, do not ruin my chances with him!"

Letitia rolled her eyes heavenward. "Goodness, Julie," she scoffed, "you scarcely know the man. How can you conjure up such truths about him?"

"I *know*," she fervently proclaimed. "I inwardly sense his stature. I want to marry him. I've made my decision."

"Ridiculous!" cried Letitia, horrified. "Outside the neighborhood boys, he's the first young man you've ever laid eyes on!"

"I don't care. He is the one I want."

"But you don't *know* him!"

Julianne adamantly shook her head. "I know what I want. Lord William will be my husband. I shall be his lady, and we'll be happy for the rest of our lives."

Letitia groaned. "I cannot believe you are spouting such nonsense. For one thing, Papa will not allow it. Lord William is too young. Papa invited him here only because of his elder brother. I am certain that he is not on Papa's list of possibilities."

"Papa will permit it," her sister said airily, "because Mama will force him to."

"The earl would not condone it, and their father, the marquess, would probably have a conniption fit. Use common sense. Lord William could probably not support a wife."

"Then we shall live on my dowry!"

"That won't last forever."

"I'm sure that Papa will gift my husband with many fine thoroughbreds. In fact, I'll ask him to. If I show an interest in horses, he will be only too happy to accede." Julianne sighed. "I cannot understand why you are not ecstatic for me, Letitia. Our finding husbands is the purpose of Papa's private Marriage Mart. I have succeeded! I have found the very best man of all."

Letitia flopped back on the bed. "He hasn't even asked you. My goodness, you're being so silly!"

"You are just jealous," Julianne stated, piqued.

Letitia began to laugh. "Jealous?" Her giggles increased.

"Yes, you are! You are envious because you are afraid that you will end up being an old maid, and you are further resentful because you are not as adept as I at catching a gentleman's attention! Do you know what I think?"

"I once thought I did!"

"I think you should turn your concentration away from horses and begin to improve yourself in ways which will make you pleasing to the opposite sex. Just look at you! You are almost brown from outdoor exposure. If you do not have a care, your skin will become as leathery as a saddle! And that ugly old riding habit . . . What gentleman would give you a second glance?"

"This habit isn't old! I had it made while we were in London!"

"But it's so dull."

Letitia sat up, her laughter fading. "It is not dull! It is tasteful and workmanlike!" she protested.

"If a gentleman wanted a woman who was workmanlike, he'd wed a dairymaid," Julianne expounded. "You should allow me to advise you, Tish. Really you should. After all, I have caught my prize."

"You haven't caught anything but a case of mental derangement. Cut line, Julie! Don't you know how absurd you sound?"

"I am only speaking the truth." She fervently leaned forward. "You are my sister, and I love you dearly. Please take my advice. Turn your mind from animals and engage in more feminine pursuits!"

"Very well. For the moment, I shall obey," she said in a mockingly meek voice, rising up off the bed to tug the bell rope. "I shall have a bath and dress in one of my prettiest gowns, so that I will be ready to greet the guests."

Julianne nodded emphatically. "That's the spirit. And forget all about animals for the rest of the day!"

Letitia smiled conciliatingly and reached up to the canopy. "But I couldn't forget about you, could I, Racky?" She paused, green eyes widening. "Racky?"

The raccoon had left his perch and was no longer in view. Letitia's horrified gaze met that of her sister. Quickly, she knelt to look under the bed.

"Where can he be, Julie? He was here just a moment ago!"

"You left the door open!" Julianne gasped.

"I did not! I'm sure I closed it!" she wailed.

"It's open now. Oh, Letitia, if Mama finds out . . ."

"He *cannot* have escaped again!"

Together, the girls fruitlessly searched the room.

"He's gone," Julianne moaned. "He's sure to be up to mischief."

"Let us hope that we can find him before anyone else does," Letitia murmured worriedly. "So much for turning my mind from animals! Hurry! Let's find him!"

Dashing out the door, the sisters nearly collided with a footman.

"Have you seen Racky, Paul?" Letitia exclaimed.

"No, miss. Lady Grey sent me to inform you that other guests have arrived."

"Oh, dear." She turned to Julianne. "Placate Mama. Tell her that I shall join them shortly. And don't say anything about Racky!"

"I won't!" The girl darted off toward the stairs.

"Paul," Letitia implored, "see that a bath is immediately prepared for me, and inform all the servants of Racky's escape. Have them begin the search. And please, *please*, don't let Mama get wind of this!"

"As you wish, miss." He quickly departed down the hall.

"Balderdash!" she swore to herself. "Where can he be?"

She looked hurriedly in all directions. Thank heavens! The doors, including that of Lord Brerely, appeared to be closed securely. At least the raccoon had not invaded the bedchambers. But where could he have gone? Grimly, Letitia began the quest.

"What is this?" Chris mused aloud, pushing open his unlatched bedroom door and entering. His valet was not present. Nor were any of the Grey servants. He knew he had firmly closed the door when he had left for the tour of the stables.

"*Chit—chit—chit—chit—chit.*"

His gaze shifted to the bed. In the very center of the white coverlet lay that pesky raccoon. The beast grinned at him and playfully rolled over on its back, clutching a mint in its tiny hands.

"Racky!" Chris groaned. "How the hell did you get in here again?"

"*Chit—chit.*"

Miss Grey must have done it. She must have put the bothersome little demon into his chamber in order to get even with him. Damn! Now what? He'd have to pick up the creature, risk getting bit, and either return it to her or set it out into the hall to continue on its mischievous way. He decided to return it. In all conscientiousness, he couldn't simply turn it loose upon the unsuspecting household.

"Come here, Racky."

The little animal came willingly enough into his arms and proceeded to untie his neckcloth.

"What are you? The embodiment of some deceased valet?" he asked.

The raccoon planted a damp, sticky kiss on Chris's cheek.

"Stop that."

Miss Grey might enjoy the rascal's caresses, but he did not. Grinning, he wondered if the only kisses she had ever received had come from her pets. She could be so prickly that any normal man would hesitate to attempt to embrace her. He could picture what would happen if he swept her suddenly into a passionate embrace. It would almost be worth it to see her outrage. Then again, she'd probably slap his face, and, given her preference for active, outdoor activities, she'd likely knock him off his feet. No, Miss Grey was definitely not cut out for a sophisticated, discriminating gentleman. She'd be better off as the quarry for some blustering, red-faced squire.

Chuckling, he carried Racky into the hall and turned toward Miss Grey's room. No one answered to his light rap. Pressing his ear to the door, he could discern no movement or conversation from within. He turned the knob and bent down, intending to push the raccoon through the crack.

"*Lord Brerely!*"

He quickly straightened.

"What *do* you think you are doing?" Miss Grey cried, shocked. "Oh." Seeing the furry bundle in his arms, she answered her own question. "There he is, the little scoundrel!"

"Escaped again?" he asked cynically.

She narrowed her eyes. "I fear he did."

"It seems highly unusual that he should sneak away so frequently."

"He seems to have become an artist of deceit." She lifted her delicate chin and pushed open the door behind him. "I cannot imagine how he continues to elude me."

"Perhaps because you wish it?" he accused her.

"*I?*" she shrilled. "Do you believe that *I* enjoy chasing him?"

"Miss Grey, I have been at Greywood Manor for only a scarce few hours, and already he has been in my room twice."

"Are you implying that I *put* him there? Really, Lord Brerely, that is outside of enough! How dare you, sir! How dare you . . ."

Lady Grey's voice, and those of several gentlemen, echoed from the stairway.

"Oh, dear heavens!" Miss Grey gasped. "If she finds that Racky has been causing trouble again . . ." Hastily, she shoved Chris and Racky into her room and closed the door, turning the key in the lock.

"*Miss Grey!*" he exploded.

"Shh!" she begged. "Oh, please, be quiet! If she finds out . . ."

"Indeed so!" Chris exclaimed, but he lowered his voice to a whisper. "If she finds out that I am in your room, there'll be hell to pay!"

"Oh, my God," she wailed. "I didn't think of how this might appear! I'm so sorry, Lord Brerely."

Chris fought against his rising panic. He was trapped in a very neat compromise. Was it planned?

His first impulse was to bolt right through the door and never stop running until he reached the Continent. His next was to grab Miss Grey around the throat and throttle her. His third was to leap to his death from the window.

She grasped his forearm. "Please, Lord Brerely," she implored, "do not tell a single soul!"

"You have my word on that!"

"You won't tattle?"

"Hell, no!" he exclaimed. "You little ninny! Don't you realize what would happen if I did?"

Her eyes grew very wide. "Oh, my God, we'd have to wed!"

"Exactly," he said sarcastically. "Do you want a husband, Miss Grey? You have snared yourself one. All you have to do is call out to your mama."

"Marry *you?*" she retorted. "I'd rather marry Racky."

Wed a raccoon instead of him? Her comment was absolutely infuriating. To make matters worse, the raccoon, hearing his name, began to chitter loudly and pinch Chris's cheek.

"Shut up," he growled, and set the beast on the floor.

"This is my room," Miss Grey snarled. "I don't have to be silent unless I want to!"

"You'd better be still," Chris hissed as footsteps paused outside the door.

Once more her expression shifted from anger to alarm. "What shall we do?" she whispered, wringing her hands.

"Hush." He knelt down and pressed his ear to the door.

Apparently several guests had arrived, and Lady Grey herself was showing them to their chambers. They had hesitated outside Miss Grey's door for an affable chat. Dammit! Why couldn't they go on about their business?

Eavesdropping, he heard the names of Lords Morley and Rotham and that of Michael Warden, all three noted horsemen and members of his club. Damme! If any of them discovered where he was, they'd never stop laughing and recounting the tale of his ensnarement. He'd be wed to Miss Grey in a thrice, and the rest of his life would be pure hell.

"What are they doing?" she breathed.

"Standing there, talking." He rose and drew her toward the window, safely away from the door. "If anyone knocks, I'll hide under the bed."

She nodded anxiously.

"Maybe I'd better get under there anyway."

She nodded again.

"Remember," he warned her, dropping down to the floor, "you must play your part in this and behave as if nothing unusual is happening. Otherwise, we'll find ourselves married. And we don't want that, do we?"

"No." She shook her head violently. "No, we don't."

"Don't forget." He slipped under the dust ruffle.

"Lord Brerely?" She poked her head beneath the fabric.

"What now?" he asked irritably.

"When will you get out?"

"Just as soon as I can!" he assured her crossly. "Listen at the door. When you think they've gone away, peek out and make sure. As soon as it is safe, I'll make a run for it."

"All right," she agreed, and disappeared.

He soon discovered that the servants were dreadfully lax about cleaning under Miss Grey's bed. The floor was littered with dust curls, or perhaps it was raccoon hair. Whatever the composition, it was giving Chris a powerful urge to sneeze. Desperate for fresh air, he rotated onto his back and stared at the woven ropes above. Idly he noticed that Lord Grey's employees had been careless in their maintenance, too. The cords should be pulled more tightly. As it was, the bed would dip to the middle. If Miss Grey ever shared it with a husband, they would be pitched together in a small cocoon.

The image of it made his body flood with warmth. She was quite a beautiful and enigmatic little nuisance. With her mercurial, passionate temperament, she'd be quite a handful under the sheets. He caught his breath as his virility responded. He'd best get his mind off such things. Letitia Grey was trouble enough to give a man a brilliant headache.

"*Chit—chit.*"

Goddam, he thought. Turning his head sideways, he saw that nightmarish masked face as Racky joined him under the bed. Why had he ever let Willie talk him into coming to Greywood Manor? He would leave tomorrow. In a matter of hours, he had already been plunged in the suds. To stay another single day might mean certain disaster. He would conjure up some excuse and leave first thing in the morning.

Racky crawled up onto Chris's stomach and proceeded to bed down, his head on the earl's breastbone. Thank God. At least the vexatious beast wasn't in the mood for kisses and fondling. Chris stiffened as a scratch softly echoed on the chamber door. What now? Discovery? He prayed that Miss Grey kept her wits about her.

"Who is it?" he heard her demand.

There was a muffled reply.

"Just a minute." Her pretty face appeared beneath the dust ruffle. "It's the servants with my bath," she murmured. "What shall I do?"

"Let them in," he told her.

"How can I?" she gasped. "I can't take a bath in front of you!"

"You're not in front of me. I'm under here," he reminded her.

"I can't take off my clothes with you in the room," she told him severely.

"If you don't carry on as usual, you'll be taking off your clothes with me in the room for the rest of your life," he threatened.

"Oh, my God!" She drew back, but not before he had seen her face flush scarlet.

He heard a shuffling of feet as she opened the door and allowed the servants to enter.

"No, Maudie," she stated firmly. "I do not require your assistance."

"But miss . . ."

"Let me alone!" she wailed. "I want to be alone!"

"Are you all right, miss?" the abigail questioned suspiciously.

"Yes, I am. I . . . I wish to meditate. To engage in meditation, one must be alone!"

The maid snickered. "Thinkin' about that Lord Brerely, are you? A handsome devil, he is!"

"That's enough, Maudie," she said stiffly. "Go along now. I shall ring for you when I've finished my bath and am ready to dress."

"Very well, miss. About that raccoon . . . The servants can't find him."

"It's all right. I have him back."

Chris heard the door snap shut and the key turn in the lock. He exhaled a pent-up breath. He had eluded detection.

"Lord Brerely?" The lady lifted the dust ruffle and peered at him. "There was no one else in the hall. As soon as the servants are safely gone, you may hurry away."

"With pleasure, Miss Grey." He dumped Racky from his lap, slipped from under the bed, and stood. "Not only shall I hurry away from your room, but I shall hurry away from Greywood Manor, just as soon as possible!"

"How insulting!" she snapped. "You will hurt Mama's feelings. She is trying so hard to be a good hostess, and she seldom gets the chance!"

He looked at her inflamed countenance. "Well . . . we'll see."

"I assure you that I shall be able to put up with you for the duration of this house party."

"Put up with me?"

She nodded vigorously. "I know I'll succeed at it. Once I had the influenza and had to stay in bed ever so long. I was able to put up with that, so I know I'll be able to put up with you," she said maliciously.

"You little . . ." Chris began.

"Hurry away!" she urged. "Before someone else comes along!"

Before he could come up with a blistering rejoinder, she had shunted him into the hall and closed the door in his face. Damn, but she was infuriating! But so utterly, amazingly fascinating. Who really was Miss Letitia Grey, under all her flutters and foibles? What motivated her? Perhaps he would stay a bit longer at Greywood Manor, just to find out. Besides, he was a gentleman, and he had no desire to wound his hostess's sensibilities. Nor did he want to disappoint his brother.

7

Her gaze resting modestly on her folded hands, Letitia sat demurely in the salon as the guests assembled before dinner. All those who had dared to accept the invitation to Lord Grey's house party had arrived by late afternoon and were now settled into Greywood Manor. Due to her mortifying experience with Racky and Lord Brerely, Letitia hadn't met every gentleman, and at present, she didn't care if she ever did. She was still much too shaken from that dreadful encounter in her bedchamber to think coherently, let alone to attempt to engage in sparkling conversation. If the men thought her dull, it was just too bad.

Twice in one day! What a ghastly calamity! What if Racky disturbed Lord Brerely again? The man would definitely leave posthaste! He wouldn't hesitate as he had today. He would flee, and when she learned the reason for his rapid departure, Lady Grey would be furious! What if it happened to other gentlemen? Letitia knew she would simply perish, right on the spot! How was the pesky raccoon escaping her room? She must discover his method as soon as possible and put an immediate halt to it. If Lady Grey was correct, Lord Grey's Marriage Mart was already making the family a laughingstock among the *ton.* If tales of Racky's antics were to leak out, they would be even more humiliated. Lady Grey would be devastated. Julianne would be perfectly miserable.

Letitia herself wouldn't mind. In the future, if she were to enter the social world, she would be certain to see Lord Brerely on numerous occasions. And every time she was in his presence, she would remember him crawling under her bed. It was just too embarrassing for words. If she ever married, she would make sure that she wed a man who preferred to remain in the country and never, *ever* would wish to go to London.

The three gentlemen whose arrival had forced Lord Brerely into hiding entered the room and were greeted by her parents. Although realizing that she must appear boring, she continued to keep her eyes downcast throughout the introductions. Despite her mother's nudging elbow in her ribs, she just didn't care.

Immaculate in their fashionable evening attire, Lord Brerely and his brother strolled in. Surreptitiously peeking through her long lashes, Letitia saw Julianne brighten and begin to flirt. The silly goose! If she wanted a husband, why didn't she exercise her charms on the older, more eligible bachelors? Her ridiculous crush on young Lord William would never bear fruit. She'd be far better off setting her sights on the earl.

A small stab of panic twisted Letitia's stomach at the thought of a match between Julianne and Lord Brerely. Goodness! What a tangle that would create within the family! Thank heavens he showed little interest in her sister. He merely exchanged pleasantries with her and began to move about the room, talking with the other gentlemen. She closed her eyes in silent thanksgiving. When would supper be called, ending this awful gathering?

"Rather quiet this evening, Miss Grey," a deep voice observed from over her shoulder.

Letitia started. Where had he come from? She'd last seen him chatting with the other men.

Lord Brerely sat down beside her on the sofa. "Struck with sudden shyness? Silenced by remorse for your torment of me?"

"You know I had no intentions of disturbing your peace, my lord," she answered tightly, her gaze remaining on her hands. "How can you hold me responsible for the unfortunate actions of my pet?"

"Are you not the one in control of that bothersome beast?" he drawled, leaning toward her. "Ah, but lovely young ladies tend to be timid and mollifying, so it's no surprise you've lost the upper hand with your animals. Retaining command of oneself and one's animal is such a simple matter, really. Insofar as riding is concerned . . ."

Letitia trembled, struggling to remain placid. "That is quite enough, Lord Brerely," she managed in a neutral tone.

"A young horse requires calm, relaxed handling," he went on. "You were sitting him much too stiffly, and your hands . . ."

Abruptly she stood up. "I shall not suffer your criticism, sir. Please excuse me. I find I have no appetite for the meal, so I believe I shall retire to my chamber for the evening."

"Running away again? Like you did from the paddock this afternoon?" he teasingly asked, rising also.

"I did not run from the paddock! I simply realized that it was time for me to assist my mother," she stated, glaring at him.

Lord Brerely grinned. "You were running away because I rode *your* horse better than you did."

Letitia's temper soared. She clenched her hands, wishing that she could plant her fist right in the midst of his arrogant smirk. How despicable he was! How conceited! How loathsome! How devilish!

Taking a deep breath, she turned toward the door and caught sight of her mother. Lady Grey was frowning severely at her. Others were staring at her too, their expressions full of avid curiosity. She suddenly realized what a scene she was making. It didn't matter that it was Lord Brerely's fault. She was the one who would be blamed for it. Angrily, she flounced back down on the settee.

The earl joined her once more. "Change your mind?"

"Why are you doing this?" she demanded.

"Doing what?" he asked innocently.

"You are deliberately provoking me!"

"Whyever should I do that?" he queried mildly, eyes dancing.

"I do not know. I've done nothing to you," she heatedly told him.

"Oh, no?" He chuckled. "You've set out to disturb me from the moment I set foot in this house! Am I your quarry? I must admit that I was surprised when you didn't spring the trap once you had me in your bedroom. You could have had me for a husband, Miss Grey."

"Who would want you for a husband?" she hissed. "Not I. Most certainly not!"

"Because I ride better than you do?"

She barely caught herself before she leaped to her feet again. "I do not believe that. My poor performance this afternoon was due to my nervousness. You are no better a rider than I am. I can ride just as well as any man in this room!" she recklessly proclaimed.

He laughed again. "A woman? Oh, Miss Grey, you are the most misguided female I have ever met! Assembled here are some of the best horsemen in England. And you think you can ride as well as they? Good God, I don't think I've ever heard anything so comical!"

Letitia tossed her head. "Think what you wish, Lord Brerely, but you are wrong."

"Never! Dear me, I believe I'll have to have another drink to restore my senses. I'm sure I'm hearing things." He stood, bent over her hand, and lithely strode toward the sideboard.

She sighed with relief, which was short-lived, because her mother quickly took his place.

"What do you think you are doing, Letitia?" Lady Grey demanded. "Your deportment is most unbecoming. First you behave as a dullard, then as a veritable shrew! And with Lord Brerely, of all people! I am most displeased!"

"I'm sorry, Mama. I cannot bear the man! Moreover, I despise this entire farce!"

"That is just too bad! You will conduct yourself as a lady, and there's an end to it! My goodness! I've a notion to send you to your room!"

"I wish you would," Letitia implored. "It would end my misery."

Lady Grey pressed her lips together to form a tight line. "For that reason, I shall not! No, young lady, you will use this opportunity to learn to exercise some self-control. You will be pleasant with our guests, and you will conceal whatever illogical emotions you are suffering."

"My feelings are not irrational! Lord Brerely was deliberately harassing me!"

"No doubt he was merely flirting with you. He was smiling, laughing, *teasing* you."

"Because he knew that would offend me further! Mama, he was administering set-down after set-down! He is a most obnoxious, contemptuous man! He is scornful and cavalier, and I hate him!"

"Lower your voice, you silly gel," Lady Grey warned. "It is obvious that you do not recognize when a man is attempting to carry on a flirtation. Lord Brerely is a prize catch! You will be sweet to him."

"I will not!" Letitia sputtered. "I will give him back what he deserves!"

"You will treat him as an honored guest in your father's home. If you have no respect for Lord Brerely, at least you may show some for your poor papa."

"All right," Letitia grumbled.

Her mother was right, and she knew it. Her behavior was outrageous. No matter what she thought of Lord Brerely, or any of the other gentlemen, it was her place to treat them with respect. Also, she owed it to her sister to help make the guests' stay a congenial one. Under so much male attention, Julianne was positively glowing with charm. Despite the girl's ill-fated preference for Lord William, she might end up with one of the others for a husband. Letitia couldn't allow her own emotions to spoil her sister's chances.

How long was the house party? Only two weeks? Surely she could force a smile and carry on agreeable conversation for that amount of time. Yes, she could do it, even if Lord Brerely set out to addle her wits entirely. A serene, affable countenance would certainly spike his guns!

Dinner passed without further incident, and the ladies withdrew to the salon while the gentlemen shared bottles of Lord Grey's finest port. Letitia was proud of herself. She had chatted genially with the gentlemen on either side of her, thus earning her mother's smile of approval. Now she could surely survive the remainder of the evening. She would keep a low profile and definitely contrive to avoid

Lord Brerely. After all, he was the only one who would intentionally set out to agitate her.

With much laughter and conviviality, the gentlemen entered the room. Letitia wondered what they had been talking about. Horses, no doubt. She hoped that her father hadn't boasted of her and her sister's notable horsemanship. If he had, his remarks would definitely stir Lord Brerely to renew his attack on her riding skill. She held her breath.

The earl graciously accepted tea from Lady Grey and turned in her direction. Luckily, he merely nodded to her, though his eyes sparkled with deviltry as he moved off toward the group surrounding her father. Letitia relaxed.

Finished serving the warm brew, Lady Grey announced that they would have piano music. "Letitia," she asked, "will you commence?"

Her stomach coiled with dread. This was certainly unexpected. Why hadn't her mother bade Julianne to play? Her sister was a mistress of the art. Her own playing bordered on the deplorable.

"Letitia?" Lady Grey gently prodded.

She forced a smile. "Surely our guests would prefer to hear Julianne, Mama. Her music is so exquisite."

"Both of you may delight us, my dear," her mother said serenely. "Why don't you play that little country song you've been practicing? I do enjoy it so."

Country song? Letitia's mind went blank. What could her mama mean? She hadn't played the pianoforte in months!

"The one you practiced last winter," a sympathetic Julianne reminded her.

"Oh," she replied woodenly, the blood pounding through her veins. Last winter, sheer boredom had sent her to the pianoforte when it was too snowy to be outside. She'd picked up a sheet of what seemed to be a simple composition and had lackadaisically played it. She hadn't performed well then. She would be infinitely worse at it now.

"Play for us, dear," Lady Grey urged.

"Mama, I . . ."

All attention was upon her. The gentlemen smiled expectantly. Her father beamed with pride.

"Don't be shy, Letitia," Lord Grey said jovially.

She was trapped. If she fled the room, her mother would be angry, and Lord Brerely would seize the first chance to deride her. Fearfully, she rose and approached the instrument. Seating herself, she began sorting through the sheets of music. Unfortunately, she easily found the piece. Dear Lord, it looked so difficult! The notes seemed to blend together in an unfathomable black mass. Had it seemed this formidable last winter?

"May I assist?" Lord Brerely inquired.

"I suppose you play the pianoforte with distinction," she said irritably.

"No, I don't play at all. I am simply offering to turn the pages."

"If you must." Letitia lay quivering fingers on the keys, took a deep breath, and began to play.

She accomplished the first page with only a few crashingly sour notes. On the second, she lost her place, distracted by Lord Brerely's long, slender fingers and immaculately manicured nails. From then on, matters became worse. She was so acutely conscious of the handsome, powerful gentleman beside her that every key she struck seemed to be the wrong one. By the time she finished, she could scarcely see the notes through a blur of unshed tears.

"That was horrible," she murmured.

Lord Brerely did not dispute it. "Perhaps it was due to nervousness," he suggested.

She did not reply, and did not even look at him. If she saw his supremely disdainful face, she knew she would burst out crying. Blinking rapidly, she hurried back to her seat amid scant, but polite, applause.

Julianne took her place. Soon rich, mellow chords filled the room as her sister displayed her consummate achievement. The girl was gifted, and the gentlemen responded with exuberant, unadulterated praise.

Applauding along with the others, Letitia did not begrudge her sister this triumph. Julianne practiced long and hard. It was her just due to receive the gentlemen's adulation.

As Julianne commenced a sonata, Letitia covertly withdrew her handkerchief and dabbed the remaining tears from her eyes. Why had her mother ever requested that she play? She should have called upon her sister from the very beginning. Her parents seemed to think that their offspring could credibly perform a multitude of things. How sadly mistaken they were! Julianne was accomplished in ladylike, indoor pursuits, and Letitia was talented in equine activities, and in her rapport with animals. Or was she?

Racky had made a perfect fool of her with his mischievous antics. She had made a dolt of herself on her horse. Perhaps Lord Brerely was right. Maybe she was only deceiving herself in believing that she was skilled in anything at all. Probably, in cold, clear truth, Letitia Grey was merely an inept buffoon.

Once again, tears prickled her eyelids. She was in error when she had condemned Lord Brerely to her mother. She actually wanted to impress him. Despite his arrogant self-assurance, he was the most handsome man she had ever seen. He was perfect.

She wiped her eyes. Thankfully, the composition Julianne was playing was a sad one. If the guests saw her tears, they would think that she was moved by the music. They wouldn't guess that her heart was breaking. She bit her lip to still her inner turmoil. Just a little while longer, she told herself. Surely the evening would soon be ending.

As the Greys and their guests sought their beds, William followed Chris into his room. "Might I have a word with you, brother?" he entreated earnestly. "I need your advice."

The earl sighed, his glance flicking around the room to make certain that it had not been invaded by Miss Grey's vexatious raccoon. All seemed normal. The mints on the bedside table were undisturbed, and there was no fluffy-furred creature to chitter a welcome. Satisfied, he began to remove his neckcloth.

"What is it, Willie? I'm rather tired from today's events." He yawned mightily.

The young man waited until the valet had assisted his brother from his coat and retreated to the dressing room.

"She was magnificent tonight, wasn't she, Chris?"

"Who was?"

William's eyes widened with disbelief. "Miss Julianne, of course! What's the matter with you? Are you blind? Deaf?"

"The young lady is attractive, and, yes, she is a gifted pianist," he answered wearily.

"You don't seem very enthusiastic."

"What do you want me to do?" Chris snapped. "Fall down in worship at her feet?"

His brother bristled. "You can admit that she is a flawless Incomparable!"

"Don't be ridiculous." The earl sat down to take off his shoes. "Miss Julianne is pretty, but she is too young to invoke such superlatives from me. A girl fresh from the schoolroom is hardly old enough to be considered magnificent."

"Perhaps you prefer Miss Grey," Willie surmised.

"I don't *prefer* either! Good God, Willie, you act as though I must choose between them! I didn't come here to select a wife. And neither did you."

"Perhaps not. But I've found one," he murmured reverently.

Chris groaned. "Get to the point, so that I may go to bed. What did you wish to ask me about?"

"The competition. I can see that I'll face stiff rivalry for Miss Julianne's hand."

"From this bunch of confirmed bachelors?" He grinned. "I doubt it, brother."

"I wish I could be so sure." Willie shook his head. "I *think* she prefers me, but how can I be sure? And what about her father?"

"You're being precipitous," Chris advised. "You're too young to be considering such a great step. You should wait a few years before marrying."

"By then she'll be taken! I can't just stand by and let her go! I must make my move now!" He dragged up a chair and sat down. "What shall I do, Chris? You've got to help me! That's what brothers are for."

Chris rolled his eyes heavenward. "I don't know of anything you can do, other than what you have been doing. You're showing her the greatest attention." He yawned again. "But you should think it over very long, and very thoroughly, before making an offer."

"I already have, and I've made my decision. I wish to spend the rest of my life with Miss Julianne," he announced firmly. "I know you think I'm too young, but what's true for you may not be true for me. I'd be a good husband, Chris. Just you wait and see. I'll love her, and cherish her, and . . ."

The earl held up a hand. "Spare me the platitudes, please! All right, Willie, if she is your choice, I wish you luck. I can do little more than that."

"You'll intercede with Father if it's necessary?" he asked hastily. "And you'll put in a good word for me with Lord Grey?"

Chris nodded.

"Thank you." He rose and started toward the door, then turned. "Chris? What was going on between you and Miss Grey this evening?"

"What do you mean?"

"She seemed so overset when you were talking with her before dinner, and, when she left the piano, there were tears in her eyes."

"If you had performed so poorly, wouldn't there be tears in your eyes, too?" he asked jokingly.

William scowled. "She was nervous."

"She was inept."

"I think you disturbed her," his brother accused.

"I merely teased her a bit," Chris defended himself. "It really isn't your business, Willie."

"What affects the Greys affects me," he proclaimed. "I won't have you treating my future sister-in-law shamefully."

"*You won't have . . .*" He chuckled. "Go to bed. You obviously need a good night's sleep!"

"Remember what I've said," William cautioned. "I won't allow you to overset Miss Grey."

"Just what are you going to do about it?" Chris said as the door closed behind the young man.

He leaned back his head and stared upward at the ceiling. Tears in Miss Grey's expressive green eyes? Standing above her, he hadn't noticed. Of course, he did know that he'd aggravated her earlier. But Miss Grey was too overconfident in her own abilities. She'd needed her comeuppance. But tears? Well, it wasn't his fault. He'd done nothing to distress her to that extent. He had made her angry, and that was all. Certainly he had done nothing to make her cry.

Rising, he walked to the dressing room, unfastening the studs on his shirt. Perhaps he had been too harsh with her. He'd given in to an overwhelming urge to take her down a notch. Well, he would make it up to her tomorrow. He'd find some way to compliment her. That should restore her spirits. After all, he was a gentlemen. Far be it from him to cause a lady to cry!

Satisfied, he gave himself up to the ministrations of his valet and finished preparing for bed. Slipping between the cool sheets, he bade Nickerson good night and blew out the candle. He closed his eyes, but, weary though he was, he couldn't fall asleep. He couldn't keep from thinking of Miss Letitia Grey.

She was an enigmatic little minx. She was beautiful, certainly, with that thick, rich brown hair and those flashing green eyes, but Chris had seen countless lovely women. It was her mercurial personality that was barring him from his slumber. He couldn't quite figure her out. He'd always been able to guess what a female was thinking, and to gauge her probable reactions. But he was at a loss with Miss Grey, and it was a totally new, and most unsettling, experience.

He sighed, rolling over onto his stomach. Tomorrow he would explore her mystique more fully, but he must watch his step. A puzzling lady like Miss Letitia Grey could be frightfully dangerous to a man's equilibrium.

8

The morning mist was still thick, dampening Letitia's face as she made her way to the stable. She had awakened early after a troubled night's sleep, during which she had dreamed, over and over, of her inept ride in the paddock, her ghastly performance at the piano, and her mortification over Racky's escapades. In each nightmarish episode, Lord Brerely's handsome face had loomed large in all its guises of anger, arrogance, and censure. She'd arisen fearful that she was, and always would be, a complete failure at whatever she attempted, that she must be an embarrassment to her family, and that no man would ever love her. It was an appalling thought.

However, after she'd had a rejuvenating cup of tea, served to her by a drowsy Maudie, she'd felt her spirits rise. She couldn't be nearly so awful as she imagined. She'd merely had a bad day, made worse by her nervousness, which had been sparked by the intimidating presence of Lord Brerely. No one could be at one's best at all times. Even the suave earl must have been less than perfect at least once or twice during his life. She could overcome this setback. She was determined to do so.

First, she would prove to herself that she was, beyond a doubt, an accomplished horsewoman. She would take her young thoroughbred for an invigorating ride across the estate, leaping fences and walls, and thus restoring her confidence in herself. Then, the next time Lord Brerely saw her on horseback, she would be calm, collected, and in control. After that, she would examine her other dilemmas.

Entering the stable, she called a cheerful good morning to the busy staff and proceeded to her horse's stall, where a groom assisted her in readying him for the ride.

"I won't be needing you today, Lyle," she brightly told the man. "It's early yet. No brigand will even see me, let alone accost me. As if they ever would," she added with a chortle.

The man hesitated, well aware that Lord Grey always wished an escort to accompany his daughter.

"I shall be fine," Letitia assured him, "and I'll be back before anyone misses me. Don't worry. If Papa should somehow find out, I shall take all the blame. I won't allow him to dismiss you."

"Very well, miss," he said uncomfortably, giving her a leg up. "If you insist."

"I do. My father was up late last night. He won't be awake before I return. I really do wish to be alone."

"Yes, miss, but . . ."

"I'll be fine!"

With a jaunty wave of her crop, Letitia rode through the arch and across the brick drive, heading toward the distant woods. As usual, she took great pains to warm the gelding properly, walking and jogging him for some time before she set him into a canter. The gelding performed so well that it didn't take her long to reassure herself that it had been anxiety, indeed, that had caused her unfortunate showing the day before. Though she was honest enough to admit that her frazzled nerves had nothing to do with Racky's mischief, and had little effect on her unpracticed piano playing, she knew they had definitely disturbed her ease with her horse. Free of Lord Brerely's censorious gaze, she rode proficiently once again.

Heart soaring, she urged the thoroughbred to a gallop. The animal responded with perfect, liquid grace. He was attentive to her, unruffled, and eager to do her bidding. She was fully in command. Together, they sailed smoothly over a low wall.

"Bravo!" came a hearty male shout.

Letitia gasped, abruptly pulling up. "You!" she cried.

Lord Brerely touched his hat, bowed, and trotted forward.

"No one told me that you were out riding!" she sputtered, feeling her body tense.

He shrugged negligently. "Whenever possible, I take a morning ride."

Letitia eyed him suspiciously. "Are you sure you didn't come out to spy on me?"

His eloquent brown eyes displayed innocence. "Miss Grey," he drawled, "why should I do that?"

"I . . . I don't know." Shaken, she lowered her gaze, fingering the gelding's mane with a quivering hand. "To unsettle me?"

"I repeat, why should I wish to do that?" Lord Brerely brought his horse up so close that his knee almost touched hers. "Shall we continue?"

"Continue what?" she asked uncertainly.

"Our ride. Won't you show me about the estate?"

"I'm not so sure that's a good idea," she murmured tightly.

Her young thoroughbred was already reacting to her tension. He tossed his head and danced sideways, loudly champing the bit. His muscles began to bunch, coiling tautly as springs.

"Loosen up," said Lord Brerely.

"I beg your pardon?" she shrilled, incensed.

"I watched you ride across the pasture. You're very accomplished, but occasionally you're much too stiff. You should . . ."

"How dare you? Just mind your own business!" Angrily, Letitia dug her heel into the gelding's ribs and leaned forward as he leaped into a gallop.

"Miss Grey!" called the earl.

Wind whipped across her face. The grass beneath the horse's hooves became a soft green blur. For a moment, she seemed alone in the heavy fog, but then she suddenly heard the pounding of hoofbeats behind her. Fiddlesticks! He was coming after her!

Letitia urged the gelding to lengthen his stride. He responded with such a breathtaking burst of speed that the sheer exhilaration of it blew away all her anxiety and irritation. Instead of screaming with indignation, she could have shrieked for joy.

Lord Brerely appeared alongside her, his mount matching her horse's gait perfectly. She wished she could feel anger at him for spoiling her solitary outing, but she simply couldn't. The happy thrill of the gallop was just too strong. She glanced at him and saw his grin. He was enjoying it, too, and there was no criticism in his expression of pleasure. Unable to help herself, Letitia turned to him and smiled back.

Side by side, they soared across a small brook and thundered toward the woods. She could see that he was holding back his faster horse to equal her gelding's slightly slower pace. She had to admire his subtle finesse in controlling his mount. Though his animal was filled with restive high spirits, Lord Brerely was able to retain his authority without a struggle. It was a superlative example of excellent horsemanship. The man was more than a natural talent. He was a master of the art.

"Well done!" she exclaimed uninhibitedly as they drew up at the edge of the copse.

"You're wonderful!" he shouted. "I've never seen a lady who could ride so well!"

Breathless, Letitia stared at him in surprise. Though she hadn't been long acquainted with him, she would never, ever have expected such a response, especially after last night's criticism. Her breast seemed ready to explode with elation. He thought she was wonderful! Lord Brerely had actually complimented her! It was unimaginable. It was . . . it was terribly, earth-shatteringly delightful.

He gazed back at her, his expression reflecting a similar amazement. Was he astonished because she had ridden so well? Or was he baffled by his own outburst?

He took a deep breath. "We should cool the horses," he said quietly.

"Yes. Let us dismount." Letitia started to slide down on her own, but he motioned her to remain in the saddle.

"Allow me, Miss Grey." He dropped to the ground, looped his reins over his arm, and came to assist her.

Once again, Letitia laid her hands on Lord Brerely's magnificent shoulders, but this time, as he assisted her down, he held her much more closely, and he did not remove his hands so quickly from her waist. A strange, but pleasant, frisson of excitement tingled through her veins. Almost shyly, she looked up at him.

"Shall we walk the horses, my lord?"

"Yes." An expression of confusion briefly crossed his face again. "Shall we enter the woods, or turn back?"

Letitia glanced up at the clearing sky. "I would like to stroll through the woods, but we'd best return home. My father will soon arrive at the stables and find that I've gone out without a groom. He won't be pleased about that."

"No, you shouldn't go out unaccompanied." He grinned. "But then, I am with you."

Who will save me from you? she wondered, heart pounding. Somehow during their gallop, something had happened between them. Letitia didn't understand why, but in that short space of time, she had lost her nervousness of him. Instinctively, she knew that she would never be fearful of riding with him again. The feeling went beyond his marvelous compliment. There, in the field beside him, she had ridden for the pure delight of it. She hadn't tried to prove a thing. She hadn't attempted to impress. Neither had he. They had merely shared a good time.

Leading their horses, they started toward Greywood Manor. The sun had broken through the haze, promising a beautiful day. Letitia felt warm and glorious, both inside and out.

"Have you taken breakfast, my lord?" she asked.

"No, I usually like to have my ride first."

"So do I," she agreed. "And then I am absolutely ravenous! Cook prepares a splendid repast in the mornings. I know you'll savor it."

"I'm sure I shall."

"Ham, bacon, steak-and-kidney pie. Eggs, muffins, loaves hot from the oven, fruit . . ." She broke off, flushing. "I'm chattering too much."

Lord Brerely laughed. "I don't mind that, but your description is making me famished."

"Nothing tastes so good as breakfast in the country," she mused, "especially after a splendid ride."

"I fully agree!"

Letitia fell silent, marveling at their companionable conversation. It *had* been a splendid, indeed a phenomenal, ride to have chased away her strain and his starch. Lord Brerely almost seemed like a normal human being. But not quite.

She cast a sideways glance at him. No man with his appearance could ever be considered ordinary. His form and profile would cast a Greek god into the shade. Even if he were not a wealthy lord, he would turn the heads of women and incite the envy of men wherever he went. Probably, it was only right that he was a bit spoiled and arrogant.

Also, it was no wonder that he and she had started off on the wrong foot together. From his point of view, it must seem as if she had deliberately set out to distress him. Even if the incidents with Racky had not occurred, she had not made his stay a pleasant one. She had been nasty with him and challenged his male vanity. Of course, he had brought a great deal of it upon himself. But in her new, charitable mood, she was quite willing to take the blame.

Lord Brerely turned his head and caught her looking at him. Letitia blushed and stumbled on an uneven patch of soil. He caught her arm, smiling faintly.

"Perhaps you would rather ride," he suggested.

She shook her head. "It will cool the horse much faster if I don't. I do dislike bringing a terribly warm horse back to the stable. Even though the grooms would do a thorough job of cooling him, it just doesn't seem right."

"Some people wouldn't care."

"That is true, but I could scarcely consider those people good horsemen . . . or horsewomen."

He nodded.

"I always bring back my horse prepared for his bath, so that the groom does not have to walk him first. Papa believes that horses should be sponged after every ride, not just rubbed down," she continued. "If the horse is too hot, the cold water could be an unpleasant shock to him."

"Indeed."

"Yes. Just put yourself in the animal's place," she rattled on. "If you were extremely hot and sweaty, a plunge in cold water would be horribly displeasing. It would take your breath away, bunch up your muscles, and . . ." She caught herself, flushing deeply.

Lord Brerely's brown eyes twinkled. "And?"

"And . . . uh . . . it would be quite uncomfortable." She nervously nibbled her lower lip. "Forgive me, Lord Brerely. When I talk of horses, I often get carried away."

"I find it refreshing," he assured her. "I have met few ladies who express their opinions so colorfully."

She quickly eyed him. Was he laughing at her? There was a small twitch at one corner of his lips, and his eyes were sparkling mirthfully. He probably thought that she was the most naive chit in all Christendom. Damn! She had been doing so well. Why had she allowed her tongue to get away from her? Lord, but her mother would be shocked!

"Please recommence, Miss Grey," he invited. "Your father is one of the premier horsemen in England. Since you were trained by him, I am confident that what you have to say would be of interest to all of us who love horses."

"I think I've said enough," she murmured stiffly, and walked the rest of the way in silence.

Breakfast at Greywood Manor, as at most country homes, was an informal meal, the family and guests arising when they pleased and proceeding to the dining room to help themselves to a buffet laden with a large array of delicious victuals.

Here, however, the meal reached the ultimate in casual, in that Lord Grey had proclaimed that early-morning riders need not change their attire before partaking. Though Miss Grey assured him that he could go at once to the table, Chris could not bring himself to sit down smelling of horses and leather. He went to his chamber to freshen up, and she did the same.

Entering the dining room, he was surprised to see that she had arrived before he did. Once again, he was amazed by her. The ladies he knew would have taken much, much longer to prepare themselves. She was unusual. That was certain! And he had to admit to himself that he was fascinated. He filled his plate and sat down across from her to watch her.

Observing her was easy, for Lord Grey, William, and several of the guests were already at the table, dominating the conversation. Chris listened with half an ear and concentrated on Miss Grey. She had a full plate of food, again a departure from the normal. Most ladies ate like birds, but not Letitia Grey. She wasn't deceiving him when she'd said she was ravenous.

"Brerely? Oh, Brerely?"

"Chris!" William jabbed him with his elbow.

Chris started. "I beg your pardon?"

His brother laughed. "Lord Grey was speaking to you."

"I'm sorry." He flushed.

Across the table, Miss Grey dabbled at her mouth with her napkin to hide a simper.

"I heard that you and Letitia enjoyed a fine ride this morning." Lord Grey grinned.

"Yes," he replied, "it was very nice."

Dammit! Why had the viscount said anything about it? Now all the bachelors were smirking and speculating. There would be talk of Marriage Marts, and grey mares, and Brerely, the stud. Chris set his jaw. He would be a laughingstock.

"I hope that the two of you will join us for an afternoon trek," Lord Grey went on. "Since your horses have already had an outing, I'll mount you on others."

"Thank you, sir," Chris graciously accepted, wishing, however, that he could strangle the man. *The two of you!* Lord Grey had neatly paired them up. The man was trying to spring a trap.

"Papa, you know I would never turn down a ride," Miss Grey responded. "You must mount Lord Brerely well. He is a magnificent rider. Perhaps he could ride Sir Righteous? The stallion could stand the exercise," she added lightly, seemingly oblivious to the dangerous undercurrents in the room.

There were several low chuckles. Miss Grey frowned slightly. She glanced innocently at the guests, as if waiting for someone to clarify the reason for the humor.

"Sir Righteous it shall be!" Lord Grey readily agreed. "If that is acceptable to you, my lord?"

Chris gritted his teeth at the mirth of his fellow bachelors. Damn them all! He'd show them that their snide mockery had no effect on him!

"That would be more than acceptable, sir. Indeed, it would be an honor. Sir Righteous must be one of the finest thoroughbreds in the land." He arrogantly lifted his chin, offering them challenge. "Eat your hearts out, gentlemen!"

Raising an eyebrow, Lord Morley accepted the dare. "You must be the chosen one, Brerely."

Chris took a sip of tea. "Excellence always stands out above the mediocre, Morley."

"Indeed? Would you care to . . ."

"Enough, gentlemen!" Lord Grey laughingly interrupted. "Before the party's ended, each of you may ride whichever of my horses you choose!

Damme! You do me great tribute in placing such importance on my humble stable!"

"You deserve it, sir," William said reverently. "You are the finest horseman in England. And your stable is scarcely humble. It's . . . why, it's the most superior collection of horses that I have ever been privileged to see!"

"Thank you, m'boy." The viscount bowed. "But I've done nothing more than any man could."

"Oh, no, my lord! You are an absolute magician when it comes to horseflesh! A virtuoso! A veritable . . ."

Lord Rotham suspended William's string of superlatives with a pointed question on a variety of oat.

"Coming it too strong, Willie," Chris whispered to his brother.

"Was I?" he asked anxiously.

"You can be appreciative without toadying."

"Chris, I . . ." William's mouth fell open as Miss Julianne glided into the room. "Oh-h-h-h . . ."

Now it was Chris who jabbed Willie in the ribs with his elbow. "For God's sake!"

The gentlemen rose as the lady seated herself at the table. A footman served her a cup of tea and a small plate containing a single muffin. Obviously, the young lady's appetite did not equal her sister's.

"Good morning." Her smile encompassed all of them, but lingered somewhat longer on Willie.

"G-g-good morning," he responded, as the others added polite greetings.

From that moment forward, William was lost. He ignored his food. He disregarded all conversation, unless it originated from Miss Julianne. He behaved like a lovesick mooncalf. Chris could have throttled him.

The young lady was just as distracted. She barely nibbled at her muffin. She had eyes for no one but William. Obviously she thought she was in love with him. It was utterly ridiculous.

Her father finally gained her attention. "You'll be riding with us this afternoon, Julianne."

The girl blanched. She dropped her bite of muffin to the floor. "Oh, but . . ."

"No 'buts,' my dear," Lord Grey insisted. "We shall be very disappointed if you are not present to exhibit your expertise."

"Yes, we will!" Willie said fervently.

"Well, then . . ." She quickly glanced at her sister. "All right," she breathed, once more seeking Miss Grey's eyes.

Chris watched the interplay with interest. Something was wrong here. Didn't Miss Julianne ride as well as her father had proclaimed?

Perusing the ladies, he almost missed seeing the flash of gray fur and ringed tail darting from under the buffet to pick up the fallen bit of muffin. There was an uninvited guest in the dining room. Racky had escaped again. Or did Miss Grey set him loose to gain attention? Chris wondered.

"What am I going to do?" Julianne wailed, entering her sister's bedchamber. "Oh, Tish, how could he?"

"You knew he would want you to ride," Letitia returned sympathetically. "Just as I should have known that Mama would ask me to play the piano."

"But he *knows* that I am perfectly awful at the sport!"

"Our parents think we excel at everything," Letitia bemoaned, "or perhaps they believe in miracles."

Julianne flounced unhappily down on the bed. "I'll make a fool of myself. Everyone will want

to gallop and jump, won't they? You know how
I hate to ride fast! And it terrifies me whenever
I see an obstacle! What shall I do? Everyone will
laugh!"

"Then you must laugh back."

Julianne snorted. "You certainly didn't do that
yesterday."

"No." She sighed. "I didn't."

"What shall I do?" her sister repeated.

Letitia considered. "I know!"

"Tell me!"

She caught Julianne's hand and propelled her
into the dressing room, pushing her in front of the
mirror. "Look at you."

Julianne wrinkled her nose. "So?"

"So? You are absolutely beautiful in your scarlet
riding habit. That color against your mare's black
coat will be perfectly stunning!"

"I still don't understand . . ."

"Lord William will be so staggered by the picture you present that he will wish to remain at
your side, *talking*. Now do you see? He won't want
to go above a walk! You can do that, Julie," she
encouraged. "You can walk a horse and appear
comfortably at home in the saddle!"

"Yes," she answered slowly. "Yes, I can do that."

"You'll be perfection itself!"

"You're right, Tish!" she cried, the bloom returning to her cheeks. "I *can* do that!"

There was a scratch at the door.

"Come in!" Letitia called.

The door swung open to reveal the butler,
Formby, holding Racky aloft by the scruff of his
neck.

"Oh, no!" Letitia cried, hurrying forward to
retrieve her pet.

"In the dining room, miss," he said with stilted
disapproval. "*Again*."

"Goodness! I hope no one saw him!" She clasped the raccoon to her shoulder. "I cannot imagine how he is escaping!"

"Neither can I," Formby stated in disparaging tones, then turned on his heel and stalked away.

Letitia exchanged worried looks with Julianne. "I have taken extra pains to shut the door firmly, and I've cautioned the servants to do the same. I must discover his means of departure before he gets up to any more mischief! I simply *must*, or Mama will banish him to the stable! And he would be so unhappy there."

9

Letitia wanted to keep an eye on Julianne, and, also, to watch Lord Brerely on Sir Righteous, but she found she had her hands full with the mount her father had selected for her. Once again, she was astounded by his decision. Lord Grey had put her up on Righteous Flash, a youngster destined for the racetrack, with a mind full of running and an utter disdain for remaining at the rear of the procession, where she was attempting to keep him. She had never ridden the young stallion before; he could never, by any stretch of the imagination, be considered a lady's mount, and he had no business going out for a hack in the country. At least she had no time to be nervous about the gentlemen observing her skill. She was far too busy keeping her seat on the fractious colt.

"Do you wish to exchange horses?" Lord Brerely asked sympathetically, dropping back to ride beside her.

"No," she answered irritably, as Flash lunged and bit at the seasoned Sir Righteous. "I wouldn't want to inflict this animal upon you."

"Hardly the horse for a pleasure ride," he observed.

"Papa must have lost his wits!" She gritted her teeth as her tailbone came into sharp contact with the saddle after a particularly rowdy buck by the

110

young thoroughbred. By the time they returned, she'd be lucky to be able to sit down.

"Miss Grey, I must insist," he persisted. "Allow me to ride him."

"No!" she stubbornly refused. "Papa wanted me to ride him, and ride him I shall!"

"Hardheaded wench," he muttered under his breath. "When this group starts to canter . . ."

"I'll leave them behind, in a cloud of dust," she finished shortly. "I know, my lord, that I won't be able to hold him back, but I won't fall off. It's easy to ride a running horse. At least he won't be bucking and jigging," she added ruefully.

"Very well, Miss Grey, have it your way." He turned Sir Righteous to the left into Flash's shoulder, forcing the younger, smaller stallion out of the gathering. "But we'll go in *my* direction."

Separated from the others, the colt settled a great deal, especially if Sir Righteous's head remained back by his shoulder. His walk was hurried, and he continued to fret at the bit, but he ceased his frenzied dancing. Letitia was able to relax a little.

"This was a good idea, Lord Brerely," she admitted, then shook her head. "I cannot imagine why Papa would have ordered Flash for a ride such as this."

"He probably wished to show off your skill."

She beamed, confident now in her own ability. "I have nothing to prove."

He grinned. "Did you feel like that yesterday?"

Letitia's smile faded.

"I'm sorry," he said hurriedly. "I shouldn't have mentioned that."

She stroked Flash's perspiring neck, unmindful of the lather collecting on her gloves. The whole party was such a farce. Lord Brerely was not a fool. He knew that Lord Grey was using horses as an excuse to introduce his daughters to the cream of

English horsemen, and to impress them. He must also be aware that Lady Grey was striving to make Letitia and Julianne seem as accomplished as possible in the womanly arts. He probably recognized that both of her parents were trying entirely too hard, to the point of absurdity. The entire scheme of things might have overset Letitia the day before, but now it seemed vastly amusing. She began to laugh.

"Miss Grey?" Lord Brerely inquired uncertainly.

"I was thinking of the events of yesterday." She giggled, nearly bending double over the pommel. "I cannot remember when I have had a worse day!"

He raised an eloquent eyebrow.

"First, there was Racky and his mischief. Then I was so nervous when I rode. I must have looked like disaster personified! And when I played the pianoforte . . ." She was laughing too hard to continue. Tears of mirth streamed down her cheeks. Her shoulders shook with merriment.

Lord Brerely eyed her as if she'd taken leave of her senses.

"Don't you see?" Letitia gurgled. "Yesterday I was so utterly distressed, but actually, it was truly, terribly funny!"

"I suppose," he mumbled.

"When I recall . . ." she began, just as Flash, sensing her momentary lack of attention and control, bounded forward and bucked. Ill-prepared for his high jinks, Letitia flew into the air and plopped to the ground. Snorting, the young thoroughbred kicked up his heels and galloped toward the stable.

"Miss Grey? Letitia!" Lord Brerely leaped from his horse and was beside her in a moment.

Stunned only briefly, she glimpsed his horrified face and broke out into renewed gales of laughter, burying her face in the fabric covering her knees.

"Letitia!" He gathered her into his arms. "Are you injured? Don't cry."

He thought she was hurt. He thought she was weeping. She tried to shake her head, but he was holding her too tightly.

"Letitia!"

She took several gasping breaths. "I'm fine," she croaked.

"Are you certain?" he demanded anxiously.

Oh, yes, she was certain! How could anyone, held so closely in Lord Brerely's embrace, be anything but perfect? Her hysterical amusement waned as she inhaled deeply of the scent of horses and leather, and the faint fragrance of the spicy, masculine cologne he wore. This was how a man should smell. She leaned against his shoulder and basked in the wonder of it.

"Letitia?"

She mentally grappled to regain her senses, thrilling at the sound of her first name on his lips. "I wasn't paying attention to what I was doing, was I?" she murmured shyly, her laughter set aside.

"No, you were not."

She lifted her head, gazing up at his handsome face. "Will you tattle?"

He smiled faintly, nodding toward the distant profile of the running Flash. "I believe that your horse is going to do that."

Letitia groaned. "Goodness, that's true! I shall be a laughingstock."

"Not so much as I," he said grimly, standing up and drawing her to her feet.

"You? Why should you be an object of amusement?"

He sighed. "You don't understand, do you?"

"No." She shrugged, wishing he had held her for just a little while longer. "I suppose I do not."

"We separated ourselves from the others."

"So?"

Lord Brerely frowned slightly. "I shouldn't have initiated that," he muttered, almost to himself.

"Why not? Actually, it was the sensible thing to do," Letitia stated, shaking the dust and bits of brush from her skirt. "Sooner or later, Flash would have disturbed everyone. He would have disrupted the entire ride."

"Yes, you're right, of course. Let us go back." Abruptly, he turned and strode toward Sir Righteous, who was restlessly cropping grass nearby.

"That horse can be flighty!" Letitia advised. "Approach cautiously and . . ."

Her warning came too late. The stallion shied and stepped on his reins, breaking the straps neatly in two. With a loud neigh, he plunged into a gallop and dashed for home at a pace that would have delighted his bettors at Newmarket.

"Dammit!" cried Lord Brerely.

"It's all right," Letitia soothed, walking up beside him. "He knows his way back to the stable."

"It is *not* all right!" he roared. "I've broken equipment, and I've let loose the best racehorse in England!"

"The best? I'm not so sure. If it's any consolation, I believe that Flash is going to be the faster of the two," she offered. "People will soon forget Sir Righteous when they see Flash on the track."

"Not me! I shall always remember my incompetence!"

"Now, now, Lord Brerely. After all, there *were* extenuating circumstances. Come, let us start for home." She patted his arm. "Besides, I have learned that one can't always be at one's best!"

The earl mumbled unintelligibly. Letitia decided that it might be wise not to ask him to repeat it. He was awfully aggravated. If he was anything like her father, it would be better to leave him alone until his mood improved. She didn't mind. If anything, the whole incident only served to make him seem more human. And more desirable. Savoring the memory of his embrace, she silently fell in step with him as they walked toward the faraway cluster of buildings.

Chris paused at the doorway to the billiard room. After the incident on the afternoon ride, he wasn't anxious to face his fellow bachelors, but he wanted to get it over with before dinner. There was no point in ruining a good meal by listening to covert jests and sly innuendoes. He'd let them get it out of their systems now. Hopefully, then, they would leave him in peace.

Why had he ever come to Greywood Manor? It had been disastrous from the very beginning. Miss Grey might think it all amusing, but he did not. He had come damned close to being caught in a compromising situation, and, while the lady might have felt especially good in his arms, and though she was an excellent riding companion, he certainly wasn't prepared to marry her or anyone else. Good God, he must watch his step!

He opened the door and quickly surveyed the occupants. All the men seemed to be there, with the exception of Willie and Lord Grey. Damn! Without the viscount's presence, he'd really be ridiculed. He started to back out, but Michael Warden had already seen him.

"Ho, Brerely! Enjoy your ride?"

"What were you *really* doing when the horses ran away?" another guest jeered.

Chris sighed and went to the sideboard, pouring himself a hefty glass of brandy.

"When do you intend to announce your upcoming nuptials?" Lord Morley asked.

He turned, drinking deeply. "Right after you announce *yours*."

"What if I told you I'd already asked for a lady's hand?"

"I wouldn't believe it."

Morley chuckled. "You're right. Lord Grey won't catch me in his private Marriage Mart!"

"Nor me!" Lord Rotham seconded.

There was unanimous vocal agreement and shaking of heads.

"Keep your voices down," Chris cautioned. "Lord Grey might hear you."

"He was called to his office on business. Said he'd be gone at least an hour," Michael Warden told him.

He felt a slight sense of dread. Surely Lord Grey wasn't meeting with Willie. His brother wouldn't ask the viscount's permission to pay his addresses to Miss Julianne without mentioning it to him first, would he?

"Have you seen William?" he asked guardedly.

"Your brother's out walking with Miss Julianne," Michael informed him. "The boy's acting like an absolute mooncalf. Seriously, Chris, you'd better do something about that."

He shrugged. "I've tried; I can't."

"He's caught?" Rotham questioned incredulously. "He's too young for parson's mousetrap!"

"I'm hoping Lord Grey will turn down his suit."

"He won't." Morley shook his head. "When none of us come up to scratch, he'll take whatever he can get. He must feel desperate. You'd better watch out, too, Brerely. You've been alone, twice, with Miss Grey. You're leaving yourself open for compromise."

They didn't know the half of it. If the confirmed bachelors in this room knew that he'd hidden under the lady's bed, they'd fall over in a dead faint.

Then, when they revived, they'd rush to London to spread the gossip.

Rotham's eyes twinkled. "Perhaps Brerely *wants* to be caught."

Chris drained his glass and turned to refill it. "I made a poor decision this afternoon. That's all. The lady's horse was too restive to go along with the group. I was thinking of her safety."

"You'd best think of your own!"

"I know," he said dourly.

"Lord Grey must have known that the horse was unsuitable," Warden mused. "It was probably some kind of a ploy to ensnare one of us."

"That may be." Chris took another hefty sip.

"Probably the lady's fall prevented the trap from being sprung," Michael went on.

The earl couldn't keep from grinning. "You have a hell of an imagination."

"I do indeed. That's why I've managed to escape the yoke these many years! Be careful, Brerely. I think you're Grey's target."

Chris uttered an oath of derision.

"I mean it!" Warden protested. "The man's aiming for you, and you're right here in his house! It boggles the mind to think of the number of ways he can set you up."

He downed his drink. Michael Warden could be right. He thought of all the incidents with Miss Grey, especially those involving that pesky raccoon. The occurrences could have been staged. They might have been traps gone awry.

And yet, when she'd had him squarely caught, right in her very chamber, she hadn't taken advantage of it. She'd helped him hide, helped him escape! Why?

Perhaps it had been a ruse that, because of his actions, had turned in the opposite direction. That might have surprised her, causing her to forget all about the original scheme. No matter what, he was extremely lucky to have emerged unscathed.

Chris shuddered. He reached for the bottle of brandy, but changed his mind. If Michael was right, he needed all his wits about him.

Still, it was difficult to believe that the Greys would be so dishonest. They seemed like pleasant, honorable people, and the daughters were very attractive. They wouldn't have to resort to trickery to find husbands.

His mind was fogged with confusion. Instead of remaining with his acquaintances, he decided to take a nap to attempt to clear his thoughts before meeting the family again. Bidding adieu to the vigilant bachelors, he walked up the stairs to his room and went inside, closing the door behind him.

"*Chit—chit—chit—chit—chit!*"

Chris's heart leaped to his throat. The first sight he saw was Miss Grey, back toward him and standing on his bed in delectable bare feet. Arm outstretched, revealing her shapely bosom, she waved a mint aloft. His next vision was of Racky, peeping over the canopy and chattering merrily. Panic gushed through his veins. A marriage trap! Where was his valet? Good God, where was Lord Grey? Was the viscount really in his office, or was he just outside in the hall, ready to pounce into the chamber to save his daughter's virtue? And why the hell was he himself frozen in place?

"Nickerson!" he bellowed, hoping against hope that his valet was in the dressing room.

Startled, Miss Grey screamed and fell to the mattress with a great flouncing of petticoats, providing him a beautiful view of her long, luscious legs.

"Lord Brerely!" she shrieked. "I thought you were downstairs with the others!"

"What are you trying to do to me?" he shouted.

Sprawled on his bed, she scrambled to draw down her skirts. Her face turning scarlet, she managed to sit up. She pointed wordlessly upward.

Racky trilled, grinning.

"Dammit!" Chris thundered.

"Please, Lord Brerely," she begged. "Please lower your voice. If someone should hear . . ."

"Yes! That's the general idea isn't it?" he demanded. "That someone *will* hear! And that they'll come in here to catch us!"

"I don't know what you're talking about!" she wailed. "Please help me get Racky down!"

"What do you want me to do?" he asked savagely. "Get into bed with you?"

Miss Grey's mouth dropped open. Her distraught expression transformed to one of anger. "No, I do not! I thought you would be a gentleman about this and assist me in removing Racky from your room!" she snapped. "You've been rather pleasant all day, and I'd changed my opinion about your arrogance. Now I can see that I was wrong!"

Racky warbled loudly and slipped over the edge of the canopy, hanging by his hands.

"He's going to fall!" Miss Grey cried, standing up on the bed and reaching unsuccessfully for the furry body. "Help me, Lord Brerely!"

It really did look as if the little animal was struggling. Chris leaped onto the bed and plucked the raccoon from danger. In doing so, he lost his balance and fell forward into Miss Grey, knocking her onto her back, himself on top of her.

"Lord Brerely!"

He looked into her wide green eyes, while Racky wriggled out of his hands and helped himself to the dish of mints.

"Lord Brerely," she breathed.

Mesmerized, he lowered his lips toward hers, then caught himself and stopped short of the mark.

"My God!" Panic-stricken, he sprang off her, off the bed, and across the room to the window.

"Lord Brerely?" Her voice was husky and soft as silk.

"Get out of here," he said thickly. "Just get out of here, and take that damned mischief-maker with you."

Clasping Racky to her shoulder, Letitia fled Lord Brerely's room and scurried to her own chamber. She flung the door shut behind her and leaned against it, inhaling great gasps of air. Dear heavens! He had almost kissed her. Why had he stopped, when she had so desperately wanted him to go on?

She set the raccoon on the floor and nearly staggered across to the bed, collapsing weakly upon it. Her lips still seemed to sizzle from their delicious proximity to his. Her heart continued to race wildly, and she had the worst sense of longing coursing through her veins. Thank God that Maudie or Julianne wasn't in the room to witness her discomposure.

"Lord Brerely," she whispered. "Christopher."

Her mind wiped itself clean of his prior wrath and her sharp retort. All she could remember was the soft look in his eyes and the enticing curve of his mouth. And lying in such a position! Cheeks burning, she rolled onto her stomach and pulled a pillow from under the counterpane, burying her face in the cool linen case.

"Christopher," she murmured again.

Letitia sighed deeply. How long had she been acquainted with him? Scarcely two days, and yet she was threatening to act as foolishly over him as Julianne was over his brother. It was ridiculous. She barely knew him! But surely it was harmless to dream just a little.

Christopher Brerely was perfect. Oh, he had his little touch of conceit, but didn't he have the right? In every other way, he was flawless.

Marriage to him would be completely wonderful. They could have such fun! They could ride together, and build a formidable stable of thoroughbreds. He could kiss her whenever he wanted, without worrying about being a gentleman. She would have to act as his hostess every now and then, but that wouldn't be so bad. Not with him at her side. Smiling, she closed her eyes and visualized their happiness.

A cold nose poked her neck.

"Yes, Racky, he'd have to learn to like you." Letitia giggled, turning onto her side. "I believe he already does. He just isn't accustomed to your mischief."

The raccoon chirped.

"And just maybe, he'll come to love me," she whispered softly. "I think he's feeling the same attraction I do. It shows in his eyes. I wonder if gentlemen engage in dreaming too?"

10

With the exception of performing the required, polite, social civilities, Lord Brerely largely ignored Letitia at dinner and during the pleasant evening following the meal. Disappointingly, he retired early, too, long before any of the others. His coolness did not overly disturb Letitia, however. She had noticed that he'd barely picked at his meal, and he'd scarcely touched his wine. Perhaps he had a headache, or an ailing stomach. Hopefully, he would improve by morning, in time for a ride at daybreak.

The following day, Lord Brerely did not appear at the stable, and Letitia began to be concerned. What if he were seriously ill? She went out for a very brief ride and hurried back to the house. She was relieved to discover him at the breakfast table.

"Good morning," she said brightly to the others, filling her plate and sitting down across from Lord Brerely. "I thought I might have seen you riding this morning, my lord," she told him.

"I overslept." He glanced hastily at her and returned his attention to his meal.

"It was very pleasant outside," she remarked, attempting to draw him into conversation. Apparently, he was feeling well. No one whose plate was heaped as full as Lord Brerely's could be indisposed. His spirits seemed low, however, for a tiny frown faintly creased his brow.

"I'm sure you enjoyed yourself," he remotely declared.

Letitia wished she could say that she'd like to go out again, this time in his company, but she couldn't do that. It would be much too forward. But she could hint.

"Perhaps you will go out later?" she suggested.

"Perhaps." He shrugged noncommittally.

"You should ride Sir Righteous again," she continued. "Yesterday you were rather cheated of the experience."

Several of the company chuckled.

Lord Brerely flushed and stiffened. "I don't think I'll do that, Miss Grey."

"But . . ."

"Sir Righteous has been promised to me," Lord Morley interjected.

"I see." She smiled sweetly at the sophisticated peer. "You wouldn't mind relinquishing him, would you, my lord? After all, Lord Brerely lost his opportunity because of my difficulties."

"Of course not, Miss Grey, but . . ." He cast a quick look at the earl.

"I'd rather Morley rode the horse," Lord Brerely said flatly. " In fact, I don't believe I'll be going with the group at all. I thought to take out my curricle. My team could stand the exercise."

"Oh, I didn't realize you'd brought your curricle!" Letitia's heart skipped a beat. Perhaps he would ask her to go with him! She pictured herself sitting beside him in the close confines of the sporty vehicle as they sped down a shady country lane. It would be heavenly.

"Dash it, Chris!" Lord William exclaimed. "I was going to ask you if I could borrow it!" He amorously eyed Julianne.

"Sorry, Willie. Maybe another time."

The young man shifted his gaze toward his brother and then to Letitia. "Oh! Are you going to take—"

"On second thought, I may not go," Lord Brerely cut in. "If I change my mind, I'll let you know."

"Thank you," Lord William muttered crossly.

"That's a fine-looking team you have, Brerely," Lord Grey observed. "Letitia, you should see it. Pair of matched bays! You've always expressed admiration for that color horse."

"Yes, I have," she agreed. "I do relish blacks and bays. It's strange that we have so many chestnuts, but I suppose that the color dominates Sir Righteous's line. Perhaps the new stallion you bought, Papa, will change matters."

The viscount nodded. "He might accommodate you there. Bays," he repeated. "Smart steppers, I'm sure, my lord! Maybe you could put them through their paces for Letitia."

The earl narrowed his eyes.

"Needless to say, my daughter knows all the roads in the area. She'll be an excellent guide!"

The lines on Lord Brerely's forehead deepened. There was an irritable twitch at the corner of his mouth. He laid down his fork.

"I know she'll be happy to accompany you," Lord Grey persisted.

Letitia blushed with horror at her father's outright manipulating. A twinge of dismay gripped her stomach. It was plain that Lord Brerely resisted her company. Why couldn't Lord Grey hold his tongue? The earl was obviously a man who disliked being pushed.

"Papa," she murmured quietly, "Lord Brerely has informed us that he is not certain that he will go out in his curricle. Perhaps he is weary and wishes to remain inside today."

"Weary?" The viscount chortled. "A young man like Brerely?"

"Papa!" she warned, shocked by his forwardness.

Lord Brerely folded his napkin and laid it beside his plate. "Please excuse me," he said abruptly, standing. With a bow that encompassed all present, he left the room.

Letitia unhappily watched a footman remove the earl's half-eaten plateful of food. He hadn't even been able to finish his breakfast because of her father's hounding. Her parent had effectively driven him from the room with his machinations. Her heart sank to her toes.

She could only hope that Lord Grey hadn't advised his lady of his matchmaking attempts. If her mother became involved, it would surely be disastrous. The two of them might force Lord Brerely to leave Greywood Manor altogether. She would probably never see him again if that unfortunate event occurred.

She must inform her father, in no uncertain terms, to stay out of her affairs. If necessary, she would dictate the same to her mother and to Julianne, for that matter. She couldn't have their interference. The circumstances were far too delicate to risk the smallest disturbance. Quickly finishing her breakfast, she excused herself from the table and went out into the hall to await Lord Grey.

"Papa?" she called when he emerged. Before he had the chance to escape, she caught his arm and drew him into the salon. "I wish a word with you."

"Yes, missy?" His blue eyes twinkled. "Are you going to tell me that Brerely's leading the pack in the race for your hand? You needn't do so. I can see that!"

"A race for my hand? Don't be ridiculous!" she admonished. "I am going to tell you that you must not interfere! You'll drive him away!"

"A bit shy, is he? No matter! He'll come round to the notion."

"Papa, please!" she hissed. "He is not a man to be pushed!"

"Ha! Every man needs a shove now and then," he disagreed cheerfully, "especially in the direction of marriage. Like him, do you, Tish? He's a fine young man. First-rate horseman. Good family, too. You've made an excellent choice."

"I won't have any choice at all if you don't cease your meddling! He couldn't even finish his breakfast because of your goading! How many times must I tell you? He isn't a man to be forced into anything that isn't his idea!"

Lord Grey guffawed. "Since when have you gained such a knowledge of men?" he teased.

"I can sense it! Papa, please," she begged, tears blurring her vision. "Stay out of this. If Lord Brerely is pressured further, he'll bolt. I know he will!"

He sobered, seeing the dampness in her eyes. "Very well," he agreed. "Do you sincerely think he's the one for you?"

Letitia colored. "I like him very much. I scarcely know him, but I think . . . I think I could be happy with him."

Her father nodded. "Very well, then. I'll not interfere! But if you wish me to spur things along, you'll let me know?"

"I promise," she thankfully acceded. "And Papa?"

"Yes?"

"You haven't mentioned any of this to Mama, have you?"

He shook his head. "No. Should I?"

"Please do not! Above all things, I don't want her involved! I shall handle this in my own way."

"All right, Tish." He lovingly tweaked her

ear. "You've always been successful at all your endeavors. I expect nothing less in this."

"I hope so," she whispered, almost prayerfully. "I certainly hope so!"

"And for a wedding present, you know what I'll give you!"

"Horses?" She laughed.

"Indeed! A selection of some of my finest!" He grinned, gleefully wringing his hands in anticipation of the happy event. "All England will be envious of Brerely because of his top-drawer stable. And because of his pretty wife," he added fondly.

"One thing more, Papa," she said urgently. "Don't prompt me to go riding today. If Lord Brerely stays at home, I shall remain behind as well."

"Fine idea, my dear. Keep yourself readily available!" Winking at her, he started toward the door, then paused. "What do you think of young Lord William, Tish? He seems rather taken with Julianne, and she with him."

Letitia hesitated a moment. It was an awkward subject. "Julianne does care for Lord William," she answered slowly. "She told me so. But he seems awfully young for marriage."

"Yes, I would have preferred one of the others, but I doubt that will materialize. She has eyes only for him."

"She has certainly favored him from the start."

Lord Grey exhaled deeply. "I tend to accept it. He *is* youthful, but he seems like an upstanding, eager young man. With guidance from me and your mother, and from his own family of course, I believe that the match could be a happy one. I wish both my daughters to have the men they want. Don't mention what I've said to your sister, though, Tish. I haven't quite yet made up my mind, and I haven't consulted your mother."

"I shall hold my tongue," she vowed as he left the room.

Julianne must now solve her own problems, Letitia surmised, idly crossing the room to peer out the window. She had too much on her own mind to exert further effort assisting her sister. How could she bring Lord Brerely up to scratch? He was like a determined and hesitant colt that was reluctant to accept the bridle. She must think of some way to gentle him, but he must never, ever realize what was happening.

Chris flinched as he stood before his chamber door, wondering what terror awaited him within. Another trap? Lord Grey and his daughter had overtly tried to snare him at the breakfast table, but he had avoided their bait. They were tenacious, however. They wouldn't give up yet. Ready to bolt, he cautiously opened the door and peered inside.

"*Chit—chit—chit!*"

Chris gasped, backing away. He wouldn't enter that room for all the horses in the world! Turning on his heel, he strode down the hall. Let that dratted animal escape and ply its mischief on the whole household! He didn't care. Maybe Lady Grey would catch it and relegate it to the stable!

He tromped downstairs and into the library, leaving open the door so that he could not, under any circumstances, be bagged in a compromising situation. Dammit! He had to leave Greywood Manor just as quickly as he could. But first he had to speak with Willie, and attempt to cajole the young man into accompanying him. Why the hell had his brother gone walking in the garden with Miss Julianne? He needed him. *Now.*

He pulled a book from the shelf to make his presence in the room seem legitimate. He certainly didn't desire a passel of questions on what he was doing. Sitting down on the cozy sofa, he opened the volume and gazed unseeingly at its pages.

"My lord?"

He looked up at the Greys' butler.

"Forgive my intrusion, sir. I was wondering if there was something you might require. A cup of tea, perhaps? A glass of wine?"

His first impulse was to give the servant a blistering set-down for his trespass, but he overcame his irritation. The man was only doing his job.

"A glass of wine would be welcome, thank you," Chris said, then considered. "Also, could you have my curricle brought round? And send my valet to me."

"At once, my lord." He bowed himself out.

Chris nodded to himself. He would be prepared to flee, as soon as he had talked with Willie. No matter what his brother decided, he would depart at once in his curricle, carrying only the necessary changes of clothes. Nickerson could follow in the traveling carriage with his baggage and his riding horse. With any luck, he would be gone from Greywood Manor by noon.

"Sir?" Nickerson appeared, bearing the glass of wine.

Chris thanked him and gave the orders for his departure. "Watch for Lord William," he added as the servant turned to leave. "Send him to me as soon as he returns to the house."

Plans made, he felt a vast sense of relief. He leaned back on the soft cushions, sipped his wine, and stared at the book. Thank God, it would soon be over! It was too bad it had turned out the way it had. He'd rather enjoyed Miss Grey's company and her chameleonic changes of mood. Lord and Lady Grey were affable hosts and kept a fine table. Even little Miss Julianne was sweet and entertaining. How unfortunate that they'd looked on him as nothing but a quarry.

He briefly closed his eyes. Lord Grey was wrong. He *was* weary. He'd lain awake half the night, worrying about what was going to happen to him next. Well, that would soon be over. Comforted by the thought, he dozed.

Where was Racky? Letitia trembled at the thought that her pet might be disturbing Lord Brerely, but she'd heard no lordly bellow. Heart fluttering, she entered the upstairs hall and looked up and down. Lord Brerely's door was open! Cautiously, she approached and peeped in.

She sighed with thanksgiving. Only the valet was present, sorting through his lordship's clothing. He glanced up.

"I'm looking for my raccoon," she explained. "Have you seen him?"

"No, miss, I have not." He returned to his work.

Letitia thanked him and turned down the hall. Every other door was securely closed. Racky must have gone downstairs.

Briefly, she considered enlisting the servants' aid, but she quickly changed her mind. Far too frequently, she had engaged the staff to assist her. It was pure luck that no one had told Lady Grey. If she involved them too often, word would be sure to leak out. Setting her jaw, she began her solitary search.

Racky wasn't in any of the salons. Nor was he in the dining room, hunting for bits of dropped food. Almost ready to give up and beg the servants' help, she spied the open door of the library and hurried in that direction, peeking in.

"*Chit—chit!*"

Letitia reeled against the doorjamb, scarcely daring to believe her eyes. She had found her pet.

But . . . oh, God, what would she do now?

Racky trilled, looking at her with black, beady eyes.

"What have you done?" she groaned quietly.

Lord Brerely lay asleep on the sofa, the raccoon perched beside him. His neckcloth was completely removed. His coat and his shirt were unfastened and lay open, exposing his lordship's magnificently muscled chest. Currently, the fly of his pantaloons was being unbuttoned by dexterous little fingers. Dear Lord in heaven! If anyone should see this . . .

Letitia swiftly entered and closed the door behind her. She knelt down and stretched out her arm. "Come here, Racky," she coaxed, wiggling her fingers.

"*Chit—chit!*"

"Shh," she whispered. "Come, Racky."

He paused, cocking his head back and forth, then continued his scandalous work.

"Racky, please . . ." She dropped to all fours and crawled across the room. *Dear Lord, don't let him wake up*, she silently prayed, approaching the sofa.

Lord Brerely snored lightly, lifting a shoulder to burrow more comfortably into the cushions.

Letitia gritted her teeth to keep from gasping. Blood pounding frantically through her veins, she rose to her knees and grasped the furry beast, drawing him toward her. Racky's claws snarled in the fabric of his lordship's unmentionables. Damn! Her gaze fearfully fixed on the earl's slumbering face, she gently tried to pry the animal free.

She had almost succeeded, when Lord Brerely's brown eyes opened to meet her horrified green ones. They stared at each other for one awful moment. Mesmerized, Letitia watched his face as realization begin to dawn.

"Jesus!" Lord Brerely sprang upward, nearly

knocking her down, but successfully loosening himself from Racky's clutches. "Goddam!"

"Lower your voice, my lord," she murmured urgently, leaping to her feet. "Someone might hear and . . ."

"Dammit!" he roared, fumbling to fasten his unmentionables.

Letitia backed toward the door. "Please, Lord Brerely, I can explain! Racky got loose again, you see, and . . ."

"I ought to throw you onto the sofa and have done with it!" he shouted ruthlessly.

"My lord!" she cried, incensed.

"I give up!" He stalked toward her. "Take off your clothes, Miss Grey, and let's have at it!"

"Lord Brerely! You're mad!"

He stopped in front of her. "It's what you want, isn't it?" he taunted. "You've attempted to undress me, so . . ."

Letitia dropped the raccoon to the floor. With a lightning reflex, she drew back her arm and slapped him across the face with all her might. Lord Brerely staggered back a step. He lifted a hand to his injured cheek.

"There!" she snapped. "That's what you deserve for your insults! I demand an apology!"

The blow had the effect of settling him somewhat, but he was still very angry. "You demand! What about me?"

"I would have apologized had you given me a chance! This whole, unfortunate matter was purely an accident! I certainly did not *plan* it!" She clenched her jaw, trying to fight back tears. "I was trying to remove Racky to save you from embarrassment!"

"I don't believe it," he growled, fastening his shirt.

"Then you are wrong! You know, by now, how mischievous Racky is!"

He haphazardly knotted his neckcloth. "You were attempting to compromise me!" he viciously accused her.

"Believe what you will!" Letitia whirled toward the door.

Lord Brerely reached it in one long stride. "Get out of my way! I'm leaving here. Now!" He flung himself out of the room and disappeared into the hall.

"Chit—chit?" Her pet tugged at her skirt.

"Oh, Racky!" Bursting into tears, she lifted him into her arms. "Everything is ruined now. He hates me."

She stepped out of the room. With blurry, wet eyes, she saw Lord Brerely snatch his portmanteau from his valet's hand and dart through the front door. Sobbing, Letitia ran up the stairs to her chamber, ignoring the stares of the curious servants.

Safely inside, she deposited Racky on the bed, wiped her eyes, and went to the window for one last gaze at the man she'd hoped to love. How could he have been so cruel? She sank to the window seat and pulled back the drapery.

The earl was careening down the drive at a very reckless pace. No doubt his rage had gotten the better of his common sense. She held her breath as the curricle's wheel dropped with a lurch onto the turf. Good heavens! If he didn't catch hold of his temper, he'd kill himself! Gasping with horror, she leaned out the window.

Lord Brerely seemed to regain his equilibrium. He settled the team and eased the vehicle back onto the lane, but suddenly the horses began to kick and buck. Letitia cried out as the curricle tilted up on its side and tipped over, flinging the earl to the grass. He staggered to his feet, swinging and batting his

arms. Then, half-running, half-stumbling, he hastened toward the ornamental pool at the center of
the lawn.

"Letitia?" Lady Grey asked, bursting into the
room. "What is going on? What happened in the
library?"

"Not now, Mama!" She fairly flew from the window seat. "Get help! There's been a terrible accident!"

"What . . ."

"It's Lord Brerely! His curricle has turned over!"
Rushing past her bewildered parent, Letitia sped
out of her chamber and dashed down the stairs.
Repeating her plea for assistance to Formby, she
ran, as fast as her legs would carry her, toward the
scene of disaster.

11

The pool was located some distance from the house. As she ran down the long green expanse of lawn, Letitia could see that Lord Brerely's fine bay team had kicked themselves free from the curricle. They were gyrating strangely in all directions, shying, bucking, rearing, and leaping. Their shod hooves flashed in the morning sunshine, and the remains of their leather harness whipped their sides. What had gotten into them? They were acting as though they'd completely lost their minds! She had never seen horses, or any other animal for that matter, behave so unusually. Neither the horrible accident nor the flapping equipment should have caused such a frenzied reaction. They were absolutely hysterical! But they were the least of her worries. She fixed her attention upon the man in the pond.

Lord Brerely was just as berserk as his team. He thrashed in the water like a veritable maniac. At times, she could scarcely see him for the violent splashing and turbulence. For one heart-stopping moment when he was submerged, she thought he was drowning, but he rose to the surface and dived purposefully under again. Obviously, he could swim, but dear God, what was happening to him? She lifted her skirts to her knees and sped faster.

"Lord Brerely!" she cried, reaching the water's edge.

He saw her, waved his arms as if he wished her to leave, and ducked under once more.

"What is wrong?" she called, and shrieked as something very sharp stabbed her leg. A second keen point pierced her neck. A third one speared her arm. Bees! They were viciously assaulting her! With a scream of anguish, Letitia plunged into the pool.

Taking a deep breath, she descended to the murky depths of the water. Now she knew what had caused the chaos. When Lord Brerely dropped his wheel off the drive, he must have run over a nest of bees concealed in the soft ground alongside the path. Though he'd set the vehicle to rights, the angry insects had stormed from their home to revenge themselves upon him and his horses. The team had responded wildly and painfully, wrecking the curricle and throwing Lord Brerely out. Stung and frantic, he'd dashed for the pool, the nearest safe haven.

Letitia's lungs cried out for air, forcing her to resurface. As soon as she did, she felt something ruffle her hair. The irate bees were plainly waiting above the water for their prey. Quickly, she dove under again.

How could they get out of this tangle? They? How could *she* get out of it? Didn't Lord Brerely despise her? Hadn't he insulted her beyond all bounds of decency? Let him find his own way out of this mayhem! He well deserved this stinging reprimand, and more!

She rose to the surface again, and gasped a ragged breath of air. Vaguely aware of a disturbance on the bank, she struck out, under water, for the opposite side. Perhaps the bees weren't so abundant there.

Dragging herself from the pool, she lay on her stomach, waiting for further onslaught. Nothing happened. She must have evaded the tiny attackers. With a long sigh of mingled pain and relief, she rolled to her side and gazed right into the darkly fringed eyes of Lord Brerely, lying beside her in the grass. She blinked in disbelief.

"You!" she cried.

He moaned. "We've escaped them."

Letitia hauled herself to a sitting position and stared at the sight across the pond. A horde of servants, Lady Grey, Julianne, and Lord William were savagely swatting bees. Lord Brerely's bay horses were galloping toward the stable. Her father and his bachelor guests were riding anxiously across the lawn. She fell back and lay still.

"Are you all right?" she asked guardedly.

"No," he whimpered. "I'm stung all over."

"We'd better get out of here, while the bees are occupied. It's everyone for themselves!"

"I can't," he grunted. "My ribs are killing me!"

"What?"

"My ribs! I must have injured them in the accident!"

"Oh, yes, the *accident*. We know all about *accidents*, don't we, my lord?" She tossed her head, wincing as the sting throbbed on her neck. "Suit yourself. I am getting out of here just as quickly as I can!"

"Letitia!" he implored. "Don't leave me! Please help me up."

"Hmm!" she grumbled, standing. "It suits you, indeed, to be humble when you are in need, and to use my first name, as if we were the best of friends. I haven't forgotten how you berated me and threatened to subject me to scandalous acts!"

"I am truly sorry for that," he said pitifully. "I'm sure I was in error."

"Yes, you were!" she snapped.

"Please?" he asked sheepishly. "If those bees return . . ."

"Very well, *Christopher*."

As she helped him to his feet, she saw his complexion pale beneath the redness of the bee stings. He gritted his teeth. Weakly, he lay his hand on her shoulder, attempting to balance himself.

"You really *are* injured, aren't you?" she asked, sudden fear clutching her stomach and eliminating all her anger toward him.

"I remember something striking me hard in the ribs. It must have been a part of the curricle." He grimaced. "It even hurts to breathe."

"Perhaps you'd best sit down."

"I'd rather not. If I did that, I'd have to get up again."

"Then lean on me," Letitia advised.

"I'm too heavy."

"Nonsense, my lord. I can manage. I'm a country girl, remember?" She peered across the pool and saw that the bee attack had diminished. The would-be rescuers had returned to normal, with only a few slaps here and there. Lady Grey was waving her hands and railing at her husband. Lord William and Julianne were gazing at each other. The servants were talking and gesturing, while the bachelors stared at each other with misgivings.

"I need some help!" Letitia called. "Lord Brerely has been injured!"

Lord Grey and his guests, Lady Grey, Julianne, and Lord William detached themselves from the milling servants and started around the bank.

"Do you think your ribs are broken, my lord?" Letitia queried.

"It feels like broken ribs should feel," he muttered pitifully. "How should I know? I've never had anything like this happen before."

"Don't be nasty," she chided.

"I'm not. I *hurt!*"

"All right. Just rest on my shoulder."

Goodness! He was being such a baby about all of this! Where was the arrogant, powerful Lord Brerely? He was acting like a little boy who'd fallen down and skinned his knees. Letitia could have laughed at the transformation, but she caught herself in time. After all, she didn't really know how badly he was injured. Perhaps he had good reason to be miserable.

That thought overset her more than she wished to admit. Broken ribs could be serious. A sharp piece of bone could puncture one's important internal organs. What if he was inwardly bleeding? What if he died?

Panic assailed her. Multiple bee stings could be dangerous, too. From the appearance of him, he had suffered a great many of them. Much more than she. They might make him terribly ill, even critically so.

Lord Brerely's hand seemed to grow heavier on her shoulder. He wavered against her. Staggering slightly under his weight, Letitia worriedly slipped her arm around his waist.

"Papa!" she shrilled. "Lord Brerely needs a doctor! Immediately!"

"Yes," said the earl, trying to smile, "I believe you're right." His long, dark eyelashes flickered. Slowly, he began to sink down.

"Lord Brerely!" she gasped, struggling to keep him upright.

Lord William dashed up, saving the earl from a fall. He grasped his brother under the arms and eased him to the ground. "Damme, Chris," was all he could say, but Lord Brerely couldn't hear him. He had fainted dead away.

Letitia burst into tears. "It's all my fault! If I had

been able to find out how Racky escapes, or if I'd put him in the stable, as Mama wished, this would never have happened! I am to blame!"

Julianne drew her away from the scene. "Everything will be all right."

"No, it won't! He will always hate me! If he lives!" she wept. "I should have handled things differently in the library. When I saw his dishabille, I should have sent for his valet. But no, I tried to repair matters on my own! I was afraid of what would happen to Racky! Oh, Julie, I am a bad person! Such a very bad person!"

"Shh," her sister soothed. "Later, you may tell me all. This sounds like a topic of conversation that should be kept private."

"It is." Letitia collapsed to the grass, burying her face in her hands. "But I deserve my just punishment! Racky was opening Lord Brerely's . . ."

"*Shut up!*" Julianne commanded. "You are becoming hysterical, and, in a moment, I shall have to slap you!"

"But if you had witnessed . . ."

Her sister gave her a hard shake. "Come to your senses, Tish! I have never seen you like this!"

"I love him," she whispered. "And now, he despises me!"

Julianne gathered her sister into her arms. "You are hurt, and overset, and you're failing to view matters in their proper perspective. You'll see. All will be well."

"No, it won't!" she screeched, her frenzy renewed. "If he dies, I shall kill myself! I might do so anyway!"

"I'm sorry to do this, Tish." Drawing back, Julianne smacked her smartly on the cheek.

Letitia's head snapped sideways. Her tears dried instantly. She stared in amazement at the younger girl.

"I'm sorry, Tish," Julianne repeated, "but you needed that."

"I cannot believe it!" she sputtered, sensible now. "You are not a violent person."

"One does what one must."

"I suppose so," she murmured. "I was awful, wasn't I?"

"There was a reason for it," her sister consoled her. "You're in love with him."

Letitia sighed. "For what good it will do me."

She gazed dry-eyed and clearheaded at the scene before her. Lord William was chafing his brother's wrists in an attempt to revive him. A group of servants was running across the lawn, carrying a gate upon which to transport Lord Brerely to the house. Lord Grey was barking orders. Lady Grey was wringing her hands.

"We must help." Letitia started to get up.

Julianne jerked her arm, causing her to sit back down. "You yourself need help. You are stung all over."

"I have only a few stings. I am all right. Really, Julie, I am fine now."

"No!" ordered her sister.

With a small scowl, Letitia obeyed. Julianne was being terribly bossy. Besides, she was suddenly feeling very drowsy. She saw Lord Brerely lift his head and felt a vast sense of relief. He had regained consciousness. Perhaps he would be all right. Her eyelids drooped.

Lady Grey approached, glaring. "My, that was quite a scene, Letitia! Such hysterics! Had I not been assisting Lord Brerely, I would have struck you myself! My goodness, I have never been as mortified as I have been this morning!"

"Please save your critique for later, Mama," Julianne said bravely. "Letitia is not well. We must take her to the house."

Letitia's eyes widened at her sister's effrontery. Being in love with William had certainly bolstered Julianne's confidence. What was more amazing was that the girl got away with it.

Lady Grey peered closely at her elder daughter. "My poor darling! There are welts on your face! Oh, my dear Letitia! We must take care of you!"

Her mother made as if to gather her to her bosom, but Letitia avoided her, shuffling to her feet. "I am all right, Mama. I am merely sleepy now, probably from the stings. But I shall stay awake until I am certain that Lord Brerely will recover."

"Bee stings! Cracked ribs! He is a man; he will come round. But you, my darling, need assistance."

"Mama . . ."

"I'll hear none of it! You will come with us!"

With her insistent mother on one arm and the dictatorial Julianne on the other, Letitia had no choice but to accompany them to the house.

"Ow!" Chris couldn't help but protest as the physician probed his ribs. "Dammit, is this necessary?"

"I am sorry, my lord, but I must ascertain the extent of the damage." Dr. Graham frowned and bent to his task.

"Ouch!" the earl objected, the pain nearly lifting him from the bed. "Isn't there a better way? Can't I just *tell* you where it hurts?"

"I made an oath to my profession to practice honest medicine, sir. I am a well-trained, ethical physician! I am not a charlatan!"

"I am sure you are not, but . . ."

"Lie still, and cease cringing away from me!" the doctor ordered.

"We could hold him down," Willie offered, eyes twinkling.

"I am not a child!" Chris yelped.

"That's a matter of opinion." His brother rolled his eyes heavenward. "He's scarcely been ill a day in his life, Dr. Graham. He isn't very patient."

" 'Tis understandable," the man agreed. "Healthy men like Lord Brerely are most surly when forced to accept medical treatment."

"My brother dislikes being forced, period," Willie remarked.

"Rather conceited, eh?"

"Terribly so, but he's still a good man. He . . ."

"Do you have to talk about me as if I weren't here?" Chris demanded.

"He does have a temper," his brother continued.

"I can see that." The physician nodded. "I have a country practice, so I see few lords, but most men behave rather obnoxiously when they are confined to bed."

"Confined? What do you . . ." Chris inhaled sharply as the doctor palpated a particularly sensitive spot.

"That's all, my lord. You can rest for a moment." He rummaged in his black bag. "Your ribs are cracked, but it isn't too serious. I'll wrap them tightly with a linen bandage, for support, you understand. Then I'll pick out all those bee stingers and put some salve on the welts. You'll be healed within a few weeks."

"A few weeks!" Chris cried.

"Oh, you won't have to stay in bed that long. You just won't be able to be active."

"Doctor!" he sputtered, panic in his voice. "I was leaving Greywood Manor! I was on my way elsewhere!"

"I'm sorry, my lord, but your plans have changed."

Willie grinned gleefully. "The Greys won't mind, Chris. They are the very best of hosts!"

"You don't understand . . ."

"Rise up now, Lord Brerely," Dr. Graham interrupted, "and sit on the side of the bed. Let's get on with it!"

The effort made him breathless with agony. Every time he moved, he felt as if a thousand needles were jabbing through his side. The stings didn't improve matters, either. The welts throbbed and burned, making him half sick to his stomach. Chris had never been so wretched.

The physician went about his work, tightly wrapping the long strip of cloth around Chris's middle. Every circle seemed tauter. When he was finished, the earl could scarcely draw a decent breath.

Then came the treatment of the bee stings. Dr. Graham scraped and scoured, making certain that all of the stingers were removed. At least the salve did ease the pain of the wounds, but Chris was grateful to lie back on the bed.

"Better now, my lord?" the doctor asked.

"Not really."

"Well, think on the fact that you were lucky. You could have come out of this in much more desperate straits."

"I suppose," he answered doubtfully.

The doctor pulled up Chris's head and poured a dose of medicine down his throat.

"What's that?" Chris asked.

"Laudanum, for the pain. It will put you to sleep, too, my lord. Rest is what you need." He clicked shut his bag. "I'll return tomorrow."

"Wonderful," said the earl, without enthusiasm.

"I'll go down with you," Willie told the physician. "You may instruct me in how to care for him."

Chris heard the door shut behind them and sighed. He was bound to Greywood Manor. Bedfast, no less! What would happen now? He'd have to make certain that either Willie or Nickerson

remained at his side at all times. What else could
he do? He couldn't get up and leave, and threaten
his recovery. But he couldn't endanger his future,
either.

His eyelids grew heavy. The laudanum was having its effect, easing the pain and making him
sleepy. Though he abhorred the feeling of being
helpless, the respite from pain was welcome.

"Chit—chit."

Chris stared up at the canopy overhead. A
grinning, masked face peered down. Chris's mouth
dropped open in disbelief.

"Oh, damn!" he lamented.

"Chit—chit?"

"I give up. I shall succumb to fate. I cannot survive this trap. And . . . and I cannot stay awake . . ."

Closing his eyes, the earl abruptly fell asleep.

Lying in her bed, Letitia watched her old nanny
remove the last of the bee stingers from her arm
with a dull table knife. The process didn't hurt,
not *too* much. What was difficult was trying to
stay awake, when she was so very drowsy. But
she didn't want to drift off until she found out
how Lord Brerely had fared. Surely he would be
all right, but she must know for certain.

"There now, my pet." Nanny dabbed on the salve
that Dr. Graham had given her. "Won't be long till
you'll be feeling fine!"

"My poor child!" Standing behind the elderly
nurse, Lady Grey fluttered her hands. "Are you
sure you don't need Dr. Graham?"

Letitia shook her head. "I'll be all right, Mama.
I've been stung before, haven't I, Nanny?"

The pensioned retainer sagely nodded. "That you
have! I surely remember! You were forever being
stung by bees or skinning your knees. Miss Julianne
was much easier to care for!" She chuckled, winking

at the younger girl, who was sitting at the foot of the bed, her chin in her hands.

"That may be," Lady Grey said shortly, "but Nanny . . . her face! It's so blotchy and swollen. I fear for the eventual outcome!"

"In a few days, there'll be nary a mark," the nurse assured her. "Now let's go away and let the poppet sleep. It's the best thing for her right now."

"Shouldn't someone stay with her?"

"Mama, it isn't necessary," Letitia declared. "None of you need miss your lunch. I shall be fine. But before I go to sleep, I want to know about Lord Brerely."

"Time enough for that later," Lady Grey ordered. "Nanny thinks you should sleep, and that is what you must do."

"Mama, really, I . . ."

"That will be all, Letitia. First and foremost, you will think of yourself. I shall have a tray sent up in a few hours." She motioned to Nanny and Julianne. "We'll leave you to your rest."

"Fiddlesticks!" she fumed as they left the room. "A few minutes more wouldn't have mattered."

She heard their footsteps echo down the hall. Shortly after, louder, booted feet strode by. Dr. Graham must have finished with Lord Brerely. What was the outcome? If the physician was leaving, he must be satisfied that the earl was not in serious danger.

She slipped from the bed. She would find out for herself how he was. Shrugging into her dressing robe, she left the room.

Happily, no one was about to view her state of undress. That would certainly be scandalous! Her mother would never forgive her. But wasn't this Lady Grey's fault? If the viscountess had taken the time to inquire about Lord Brerely's condition, she wouldn't have had to take matters into her own hands. Warily, she crept down the hall.

Pausing at Lord Brerely's door, she pressed her ear against it. There were no sounds from within. Cautiously, she turned the knob and peeked in.

Lord Brerely lay asleep in the center of the big bed. The sheets were drawn only to his waist, revealing a tightly drawn bandage that covered most of his beautiful chest. Though parts of him were bloated with bee stings, he seemed comfortable and peaceful. Satisfied, Letitia turned away. He would be all right.

As she started to close the door, she caught sight of a movement at the head of the bed. Racky shinnied down the bedpost to help himself to the earl's mints. Oh, no! How many horrors could happen in one single day?

Letitia silently entered the room as the raccoon, sweet in hand, hopped to the pillow beside Lord Brerely's face. Pray God she could remove the pesky creature before his lordship awoke! She tiptoed to the bed. Holding her breath, fixing her gaze on the earl's dark-fringed eyelids, she snatched up her pet. She was turning to leave, when she caught a glimpse of brown eyes flickering open.

"Oh, God," groaned Lord Brerely.

12

"My lord!" Letitia cried.

"Yes, Letitia," he muttered wearily, "it is I. Who did you expect to find lying here in my bed? And you may as well call me Chris, as my friends do. At least, I hope that we will manage to be friends during our long life together."

"What are you talking about?" She eyed him warily. "I don't know what you mean."

"We're to be married, aren't we? Just look at us! Compromise after compromise," he bitterly declared. "I'm stuck flat on my back. How can I escape?"

Letitia gasped. "You don't mean to tattle, do you?"

"You aren't trying to trap me?" he asked, astonished.

She bristled. "Certainly not! I would force no man to marry me against his will! My future husband will marry me because he *wants* to, and because he loves me."

"You are truly serious about that, aren't you?"

"Of course I am!"

He seemed to relax. His head sank more deeply into the pillow. His breathing returned to normal.

"Really, Chris," she went on, "isn't that what you would want from your future wife?"

"I suppose so," he answered slowly, "but it isn't likely."

"Why ever not?"

He shrugged, then winced at the pain of the motion. "My future wife would probably *want* me . . . my title and money, that is, but love? There is precious little of that in most marriages."

Letitia frowned. What a cynical attitude! No wonder he acted so suspicious of the opposite sex, always expecting traps.

"Don't your parents love each other?" she queried, curious as to why he had formed such a skeptical view of marriage. "My parents do."

"Yes." He nodded thoughtfully. "They love each other very much. They are quite fortunate."

"Are any of your friends married?" she prodded. "Do they love their wives? Do their wives love them?"

"Yes, they're lucky, too."

"So why shouldn't you have the same?"

"I don't know," he mused.

"You have a terrible opinion of women, Chris. Perhaps some have used unfair methods in an attempt to snare you, but not all members of my sex are like that. You may consider me to be a naive country girl, but I intend to have happiness in my life. Since I cannot imagine that a forced marriage would be very pleasurable, I have no desire to be partner to one."

Feeling awfully tired after that oration, she sat down on the edge of the bed. Racky squirmed from her arms and scurried across the mattress to curl up beside Chris. She reached for her pet, but the earl waved her away.

"Let him go. He must have a fixation on coming in here. The mints, I imagine."

Letitia smiled. "Perhaps he likes you."

"How very fortunate," he replied sardonically. "Well, if you are not bent on snaring me, and are so opposed to a forced marriage, I suppose that you must have come here in search of him."

"Actually, no," she admitted. "Truthfully, I didn't realize he was missing. I came to see how you had fared."

"I shall survive."

"You *look* miserable," she informed him.

"So do you." His gaze swept up and down her body, studying her thoroughly and lingering particularly on her thinly veiled curves. "I speak of your face, that is."

Letitia flushed under his scrutiny. She suddenly remembered her shocking dishabille. Goodness! Here she was, clad only in her nightclothes, sitting companionably on Lord Brerely's bed. If someone came in, it would be awful! How could she be so shameless? What could he possibly think of her?

Chris forced his swollen face into some semblance of a grin. "Truly, you look quite fetching . . . in other respects."

Her rosiness deepened to a brilliant shade of scarlet. "I had better leave," she said hurriedly. Standing, she reached for the slumbering raccoon.

"Leave him," the earl stated. "He looks so comfortable."

"You don't mind?" Letitia asked in surprise.

"He can keep me company. If I am going to be bedfast, I shall need plenty of that."

"I shall visit you," she murmured, "if you'd like that."

"I'll look forward to it. Do you play chess? Oh, never mind! We'll think of something for entertainment. But let us make sure we are appropriately attired for the occasion," he added wickedly.

His observation made her cheeks burn worse than any sting. Nervously, Letitia gathered her robe more closely around her. She backed toward the door, feeling as if his warm stare was devouring her body.

"Sleep well . . . Chris."

"Believe me, I shall rest much better now that I know I can depend on your honesty."

"I would never, *ever* set out to trap you," she assured him again, then peeped into the hall to make certain that it was vacant, and hastened out of his chamber.

Letitia let herself into her room and sought her bed. Thank heavens that all had gone well! They had mended their quarrel. He looked forward to seeing her again. He didn't even mind Racky being in his room. Everything was wonderful! With a sigh, she cuddled into the soft down pillow and dozed.

With the aid of the laudanum, Chris slept well throughout the day. In the early evening, he awakened to a loud crunching noise. Opening his eyes, he saw Racky sitting on the pillow beside his head, blissfully munching a mint.

"Is that all you get for dinner?" he asked mildly.

"Oh, my lord!" Nickerson rushed from the dressing room. "I am so sorry! I attempted to remove that beast from your bed, but it was impossible. He growled and tried to bite me!"

Chris watched the pointed, scissor-like jaws with their needle-sharp teeth and could well believe in his valet's intimidation.

"He seemed peaceful enough with you, sir, and I didn't wish to disturb you, so I didn't call for help. I hope that I made the proper decision."

"The raccoon doesn't annoy me anymore, Nickerson. I don't mind his presence."

Nickerson exhaled with deep relief.

Chris tried to sit up in the bed but the pain was too intense. He ceased his effort. "I feel as if I've been trampled by a hundred horses."

"Allow me to assist you, my lord." According the raccoon a wide berth, Nickerson propped up the rest of the pillows against the headboard of the bed and assisted his master to a sitting position.

Chris gritted his teeth against the agony. "My face and neck feel like a mass of pulp, and my ribs . . ." He tried and failed to take a deep breath.

"It was a most unfortunate accident," the valet agreed sympathetically. "Shall I fetch you something to eat, sir?"

"I'd like a glass of brandy. And maybe some soup would be good. I don't feel like chewing anything, Nickerson."

"I'll see to it at once. And now that you're awake, I shall obtain assistance in removing that bothersome beast from the chamber."

"Let the raccoon stay, Nickerson."

The valet stared at him as if he'd also suffered an injury to his brain. "My lord, you cannot allow an *animal* to share your bed! He will shed hair. Furthermore, if he got it into his head to bite you, you would be defenseless, in your condition."

"If he were apt to bite me, he'd have done so before now, and he is rather entertaining. Besides, if Lady Grey hears of any more of his exploits, she'll have him relegated to the stable. I don't want to overset Letitia."

"Letitia . . ."

"Miss Grey," Chris corrected.

Nickerson's eyes narrowed suspiciously. "I am aware of her given name, my lord." He waited for further clarification, but his master was not forthcoming. "Very well, sir," he finally said.

If his face hadn't hurt so badly, Chris would have laughed. He had let slip Miss Grey's Christian name, and now his valet was wildly speculating. Few times did a man use a lady's first name, unless they were very close friends or relations, or unless they were soon to approach the altar.

Nickerson left the room and returned shortly, followed by Miss Julianne. "The young lady says she will remove the nuisance, my lord."

"How are you, Lord Brerely?" the girl asked brightly, plucking Racky off the pillow.

"Frankly, I'm miserable." He managed a small smile.

"I'm sorry, but surely you'll feel better soon."

"I hope so. I'm not very patient with lying in bed. How is your sister?"

"Letitia will be up and about tomorrow. She seems to be sleeping now, but I believe she's faking it. Mama tried to feed her a dose of laudanum, but I saw Tish pour it into the bedclothes when Mama's back was turned." She giggled. "Tish has no patience with illness, either."

For the first time, Chris actually studied the girl whom Willie wished to bring into the family. Julianne was pert and pretty. She had the same dark hair as her sister, and identical sparkling green eyes, but Letitia's beauty was of the deeper, more classical sort, and her curves were more fully developed. Letitia was the type of woman to whom age would bring as much magnificence as youth.

"I must be going to dinner," Miss Julianne told him.

"Of course," he said hastily. "Don't allow me to make you late."

"Don't you wish some dinner, too?" she asked sweetly.

"Nickerson will be bringing me some soup. Come see me again, Miss Julianne. It's going to be lonely up here."

"I shall indeed. We will all endeavor to keep you entertained, Lord Brerely. It is our Christian duty to care for the sick." She waved jauntily over her shoulder as Nickerson bowed her out.

"A splendid young lady," the valet judged with approval, "and so, indeed, is her sister. Is she not, my lord?"

"Oh, indeed."

Nickerson waited for further comment. When none came, he nodded with slight disappointment. "I'll fetch you some nourishment, my lord," he mumbled, and went about his errand.

He returned promptly, bearing a huge tray, which he settled gently on Chris's lap. Delicious aromas rose from the vast selection of choice delicacies. There were two varieties of soup, one of beef and the other of turtle. Accompanying these were a side of trout, sliced roasted beef, an entire quail, boiled potatoes, cauliflower, and asparagus. The meal was rounded out by bread and butter, strawberries and cream, a fruit tart, a large bowl of custard, and a bottle of wine. Chris helplessly stared at the tray and picked up his glass of brandy.

"I can't eat all of this."

"Cook was most insistent, my lord. She said you might eat with something she calls 'a coming appetite.'"

Chris groaned. "I have an appetite all right. I just don't think I can chew, and this tray feels like hell on my ribs."

"I'm sorry, sir. Is there anything I can do to help?"

"No, Nickerson, thank you. Why don't you go and eat your own dinner? I'll be occupied for a while."

"Yes, sir." The valet departed.

The earl had almost finished the bowl of delectable beef soup when there came a scratch at the door. "Come in!"

The door opened, and Letitia peeked in. "Is your valet here?"

"No, he's dining."

She hesitated. "Maybe I should come back later, when he is here to chaperon."

"It never bothered you before," he remarked.

She blushed.

"It will be all right. Just leave the door open," Chris urged, suddenly in need of company, *her* company, but wishing he had his nightshirt on.

Letitia entered the room and securely closed the door behind her. "I'll take my chances with propriety," she said. "Mama thinks I'm asleep. I don't want her to know where I am. I'll stay only a few minutes."

"Did you want anything in particular?" Chris inquired.

She nodded, approaching the bed. "Oh, yes. I wanted to thank you, Chris, for not telling on Racky."

He shrugged. "He isn't so bad, I suppose."

"If you really don't wish him to come in here, I . . . I'll try to do something about it."

"I don't mind, Letitia. Nickerson is the one who objects. He doesn't believe in people and animals sleeping in the same bed."

"Racky is very clean. I bathe him frequently." She peered enviously at his tray. "That looks so delicious."

"I wish I could eat it," he said regretfully.

"You don't want it?"

"It hurts to eat. Would you like to have the rest?"

She nodded eagerly. "I am starved! Mama had a tray sent up in the mid-afternoon, and I suppose I'll have another one later."

Chris hurriedly finished his soup.

"Take it. That's all I want."

Letitia removed the tray from his lap and set it on the bedside table, drawing up a chair. Chris retained his glass of brandy and sipped it, watching her plunge into the hearty repast. As usual, she had an honest hunger. He wondered why Lady Grey hadn't schooled her in the feminine art of eating timidly when in the presence of a male. Perhaps she had, and Letitia had refused to comply.

Despite the welts on her face, the young lady looked very attractive tonight. Dressed in a simple yellow gown, she seemed fresh and cool. She hadn't put up her dark hair. Instead, she had contained it loosely with a band of ribbon over the crown of her head, allowing it to stream down her back. Chris was mesmerized.

She glanced sideways and caught him gazing at her. "Is something wrong?"

"No, nothing. I was admiring your appearance."

Her cheeks tinged with color. "Even with these great lumps on my face and arms?"

"Even so."

Letitia giggled. "My lord, I believe you have injured your brain as well as your ribs."

He tried to grin. "You're the second person to think so today."

"Indeed? Who was the other?"

"Nickerson. When I told him to leave the raccoon alone."

She laughed heartily. "Poor Nickerson! I feel so sorry for the servants, insofar as Racky is concerned. He truly is a pest to them. Of course, they have had a respite these past days, since he has centered his mischief on you. In the library . . ." She stopped, sobering and lowering her eyes. "I am sorry. I shouldn't have brought up that subject."

"I, too, prefer to forget it." He sighed. "I don't like remembering what a brute I was. In fact, a great deal of my conduct toward you has left much to be desired."

"Oh, no, Chris," she said rapidly. "It was all my fault. You were within your rights. In the library, I should have run away and called your valet. I should never have taken the chance of causing you embarrassment!"

"Let us put it behind us and start anew," he recommended.

"I . . . I would like that."

"Then that is what we'll do. Eat your dinner, Letitia. It's getting cold."

"I have had enough." She laid down the fork and took a sip of wine. "Now, my lord, let us discuss what we shall plan for your amusement."

He knew what he would prefer to do for diversion, but he certainly couldn't reveal it to her. He would like to pull her into his bed and to kiss her most thoroughly. In truth, he would like to do much more. His own thoughts shocked him. Letitia was a lady. He shouldn't think of her in such terms.

But he couldn't help it. She would be so soft and pliable in his arms. And she was woman enough to be responsive. She wouldn't lie there, unmoving. She would be an active participant in their lovemaking.

He felt himself flush with uncomfortable heat. It was lucky his ribs pained him so, or he might have done something stupid and sealed his own fate. He took as deep a breath as possible.

"Chris?" she asked worriedly.

"Yes?"

"Are you all right? You look as though you've become feverish."

"The stings are burning," he lied.

Letitia frowned. "Didn't the doctor leave some salve?"

"Over there on the chest."

She rose, crossing the room to fetch it. "Nickerson should have applied some of this when you awakened."

"He isn't accustomed to taking care of an indisposed master."

"Well, I shall instruct him," she said firmly.

Chris tensed in preparation for pain as she sat down on the bed and began to dab on the medication, but he needn't have bothered. Her hand was as light as a feather. When she spread salve on a sting over his mouth, he kissed her fingers.

Letitia faltered, blushing furiously.

"You are an angel," he whispered, slipping his arm around her waist.

"My lord, I . . ."

"Hush." He moved to draw her closer, but his ribs screamed with torment. "Ow!" he cried spontaneously.

"Chris," she chided tenderly, "you must take care of yourself."

"I was attempting to." He grinned self-consciously. "Frankly, I felt a great need to kiss you. To seal our pact of friendship?"

Letitia smiled. Leaning forward, she briefly touched her lips to his. Then, slightly flustered, she returned to dressing his wounds.

It wasn't enough, and it wasn't exactly the type of kiss that Chris had envisioned. But it would have to do. As long as he was in pain and flat on his back, he couldn't initiate more.

There was a scratch at the door and Nickerson entered, his mouth dropping open at the scene before him. "My lord! Miss Grey!"

Sitting back, Letitia, though rather embarrassed, took the offensive. "Shame on you, Nickerson! You should have tended his lordship's wounds!"

"I was going to, miss." He shuffled his feet. "After dinner, when he takes his laudanum."

"You should apply the salve more frequently than that."

"Yes, miss." An unholy glint shone in his eyes. "But I can see that he's in good hands!"

"Indeed." Letitia stood up, wiping her hands on her handkerchief. "Good night, Lord Brerely. I hope that you are much improved by morning."

"Good night, Miss Grey. I shall look forward to your next visit."

With a conspiratorial smile for him and a nod to Nickerson, she glided out of the room.

The valet shut the door behind her. "Well, my lord?"

Heart throbbing with happiness, Letitia entered her own chamber.

"Where have you been?" Julianne shrilled. "I've been waiting for you! I left Willie cooling his heels while I came up to see how you were."

"I've been visiting Lord Brerely," she answered smugly.

"Tish! His door was shut! Surely you weren't alone with him!"

"Not all of the time. Nickerson came in at the last. Oh, Julianne, he kissed me!"

Her sister's eyes widened. "He didn't!"

"Well . . . actually I kissed him, but he wanted me to."

"Tish, you're going to create a scandal! What if Nickerson tattles? What if Mama finds out?"

Pensively, Letitia sat down on the bed. "I'm sure that Chris will inform Nickerson not to tell." She took off her slippers and began to remove her hosiery.

"You call him by his first name?" Julianne gasped in awe.

"He asked me to. Julie, he is so wonderful!"

Her sister dashed over to hug her and to assist her with the tapes of her dress. "Wouldn't it be marvelous if I married Willie and you wed Lord Brerely? We would be double sisters!"

Letitia laughed joyfully.

"But now I must rush. I don't want to keep Willie waiting! I'll come back later and you may tell me *everything!*" She darted away. "And do hurry to bed, Letitia. It would be perfectly awful if Mama came along!"

Humming merrily to herself, Letitia went to her dressing room, slipped out of her gown, and donned her night rail. She climbed into bed, a smile still curving her lips, those lips that had sweetly touched his. Closing her eyes, she settled down to dream of him.

13

L etitia arose with the morning sun and dashed to her dressing-room mirror. During the night, she'd had a particularly disturbing dream in which the welts on her face had enlarged and turned a violent shade of purple. Seeing her, Dr. Graham had shaken his head and pronounced that the disfigurement would remain for the rest of her life. Chris had turned from her in disgust and proclaimed that he never wished to lay eyes on her again. The nightmare had been so vivid that it had awakened her. At the time, she'd recognized it for what it was, a nasty, but imaginary vision, and she hadn't scrambled from bed to light candles and peer at herself. Still, she was anxious for reassurance.

Sitting down at the dressing table, she gazed into the glass and sighed with relief. The stings were much improved. The swelling had gone down. Only rosy, splotchy marks were left to remind her of the assault. She smiled and went about her morning ablutions.

The rest of her nighttime fantasies had been wonderful ones. Over and over, she had dreamed of Chris's kisses and of him holding her close. It had been perfect.

Wrapped in the warmth of her memories, she strolled to the wardrobe and examined her choices of costume. Chris had complimented her appearance in the unembellished yellow gown. She pulled out a similar one of apple-green muslin and laid it across a chair. What would she do with her hair? She suspected that he had been entranced by her loose, flowing locks. He had certainly stared long enough! But Lady Grey would never countenance her wearing her tresses unfettered. Maudie would have to bind it into a bun.

Briefly, she closed her eyes. She hoped she would appear pretty to him. After all the ups and downs of their acquaintanceship, she must be absolutely flawless from now on.

"Good morning, miss." Her abigail entered the room, followed by Nanny. "Here is your tea."

"Thank you, Maudie." Letitia went into the chamber. "I was just choosing what I shall wear today."

The two servants exchanged knowing looks.

"I had it from Mr. Nickerson that Lord Brerely spent a peaceful night," the maid offered casually.

"I am glad to hear that," she remarked just as diffidently, but her eyes sparkled with excitement.

"Sit down and let me see your face," Nanny ordered.

Letitia obeyed.

"Much better." The nurse picked up the jar of salve.

"Oh, no, Nanny, please!" she protested. "It makes me look like a spotted dog!"

"Do you want to get better?"

"I *am* better. I refuse to use that medicine. I really do!"

"Lady Grey isn't going to like this," the old retainer muttered.

"When she sees how much I have improved, she won't mind."

"Humph!" Nanny set the salve aside. "We'll see about that."

Letitia sipped her cup of tea and nibbled a piece of toast and jam.

Maudie appeared in the doorway to the dressing room, carrying the green dress across her arm. "Is this what you wish to wear, miss?"

"Yes. That's it."

"You're not going riding?" the abigail asked incredulously.

"I don't believe I shall."

"Humph!" Nanny snorted again. "She's going to visit that earl."

Letitia arched a brow. "Yes, I shall look in on him on my way to breakfast. What is wrong with that?"

"It isn't proper. Going to a man's room!"

"He is ill, Nanny. I am paying a respectable sick call."

"It still isn't proper. Not in the morning," she grumbled. "He might be performing his private functions."

Letitia laughed. "I shall rap on the door to gain admission! Now, Nanny, doesn't that suit your notions of propriety?"

"Humph!"

Letitia wondered what her old nurse would say if she knew that she had twice visited Lord Brerely's chamber yesterday, and both had been very *improper* occasions. Probably, Nanny's mouth would drop open, and her teeth would fall out. Then the elderly woman would plunge over in a dead faint.

"I don't see nothin' wrong with it," Maudie stated, taking sides. She'd always been jealous of Nanny's infrequent presence in the house. Miss Letitia was *her* charge now, and the pensioned nurse should stay in her snug cottage where she belonged.

Seeing a joust for power in the offing, Letitia rose. "I'll dress now," she announced by way of distraction. "I am surely ready to leave this tiresome room."

"Humph," said Nanny as she departed, no doubt to find Lady Grey and report on Letitia's refusal of the medication.

"That mean-tempered nanny's old-fashioned," Maudie declared.

"She only wants what's best for me," Letitia gently chided.

"That may be, but she's behind the times!" The abigail helped her young mistress into her gown and becomingly did up her hair. "You look real pretty, miss, even with those blotches!"

"Thank you, Maudie. I hope so."

"Good luck with his lordship!" the maid called as she ushered her charge from the room.

Letitia paused in front of Lord Brerely's chamber, suddenly flooded with shyness. If he was much improved, he might not desire her company. But no, that couldn't be. Not after last night! Gathering her courage, she tapped lightly on the door.

Nickerson opened it. "Good morning, miss."

"Good morning, Nickerson." She peered past him toward the bed.

Chris was propped up in bed, a breakfast tray on his lap. In the chair beside him was Lord William. The two had broken off their conversation and were smiling at her.

"Come in," the earl invited.

She crossed the room. "You look greatly restored this morning, my lord." She smiled.

"I feel a bit better."

He looked better, too. His eyes were brighter, and, though his face retained some of the swelling, it seemed that much of it had gone down. Nickerson had applied the salve, so she couldn't tell a lot about it. His appetite had not resumed, however. He was eating some broth and ignoring the rest of the victuals.

William offered her his chair and pulled up another.

Letitia sat down. "You should at least attempt to eat some of the rest of the food, my lord."

"It hurts my ribs to chew," he said, somewhat querulously.

"The eggs look delicious," she encouraged. "They shouldn't require much effort to eat."

"I don't want any."

"You could try them." Leaning forward, she scooped up a forkful and held it out. "Here."

"You're awfully bossy today," he observed.

"If you expect to keep your strength up, you must eat." Letitia thrust the fork closer to his mouth.

"Oh, all right." Chris took the morsel and chewed cautiously.

"There. That wasn't bad, was it?" She swept up another.

William laughed. "What a homey, tranquil scene!"

"Give me that!" The earl took the fork from her hand. "I'm not so ill that I have to be hand-fed."

Letitia sat back, satisfied when he continued to eat the eggs.

"You should lie back and enjoy being babied, Chris," his brother advised teasingly. "A lady's ministrations can be quite comforting. I'm envious! I almost wish I'd received more than two bee stings."

Lord Brerely favored him with a glare. "You always were a capricious boy, Willie, and now you're a dim-witted man."

William chuckled.

Chris turned his attention to Letitia, eyeing her appreciatively. "You're looking better, too."

She flushed under his scrutiny. "I am much improved."

The earl's brother looked back and forth at each of them, his expression full of speculation. "I didn't realize that you two had seen each other after the accident."

"I slipped out of Mama's clutches and stopped by for a moment," Letitia admitted. "Please say nothing about it."

"That's right, Willie," Chris emphasized. "We mustn't cause Leti . . . Miss Grey to get in trouble."

Lord William nodded slowly, a grin spreading across his face. "I won't tattle."

Luckily they ended the topic, for just that moment, Lady Grey sailed through the open door. "Good morning, Lord Brerely, Lord William." She glowered at her daughter. "Letitia! Nanny informs me that you have refused to allow her to put salve on your face!"

"I see that Chris is not the only one to be babied," William intoned, snickering.

Lady Grey overheard. "Young man, I am not to be criticized!"

William blanched. "My lady, I apologize! I did not mean . . . I am so sorry! We were joking about . . . It was out of context! I am mortified beyond . . ."

"Have done!" cried the viscountess, exasperated. "I have forgotten it already!" She turned to her daughter. "Letitia, it is you with whom I am most displeased!"

"I am recovered, Mama," she objected. "I do not need that ugly salve."

"Do you wish to be disfigured for the rest of your life?"

Letitia giggled, remembering her dream.

"I fail to find the humor in this, young lady!"

"Perhaps the medication isn't all that necessary," Lord Brerely suggested, coming to her aid.

But Lady Grey was not to be mollified. "Are you skilled in the art of healing, young man?" she demanded.

"No, ma'am," he meekly murmured, "I am not."

"Then stay out of this! Letitia, you will go at once to your room, where Nanny is awaiting you."

"Yes, ma'am," she replied glumly, "but I don't see why."

"At once!"

"Fiddlesticks!" Letitia headed toward the door. "I am not a baby, Mama. I am . . ." She cast a twinkling smile over her shoulder at the two gentlemen. " A woman!" she finished.

"At the moment, that is a matter for debate, my girl!" Prodding her in the back, Lady Grey marched her out of the room.

Chris was glad when Letitia, Willie, and Julianne assembled in his chamber after they'd finished their breakfast. Already he was aching from lying flat on his back, but it wasn't very comfortable to turn on his side or his stomach. The three would certainly take his mind off his difficulties. Julianne was sunny, as usual. Letitia, her face thick with salve, was, nevertheless, cheerful. His brother, however, looked grim. He didn't have to wonder long about Willie's dismay, for the young man spilled it immediately.

"Chris knows about us, Julianne. I've already told him that I intend to ask your father for your hand this morning," he announced.

Letitia caught her breath. She hadn't heard the news yet. "That's wonderful, Lord William!"

"Please call me Willie," he told her. "I'm glad you approve."

"I am delighted!" She squeezed her sister's hand. Julianne glowed.

"But there is a problem now," Willie said morosely.

"What can it be?" his prospective fiancée wailed.

"I insulted your mother."

"Oh, no!" Tears formed in Julianne's green eyes. "How could you have done that?"

Willie informed her of his comment on babying. "She took great offense," he lamented.

"Nonsense!" Letitia flatly denied. "I'll wager she's forgotten it already."

"I am not so sure about that," he said broodingly. "She might have told your father. You didn't help matters either, Chris, when you confronted her about that salve."

"For which she gave me a rich set-down." He grinned. "She received immense satisfaction."

Willie shook his head. "I'm not so sure. Maybe I'd better wait."

Julianne's shoulders slumped. A tear slid down her cheek. "Perhaps you wish to change your mind," she whispered.

"Oh, no, my darling, never! Please, don't cry!" Dabbing her cheek with his handkerchief, he proceeded to comfort her. "I love you beyond all else! Forgive me, sweetheart!"

Chris rolled his eyes heavenward. Never would he make such a cake of himself over a woman! Willie was thoroughly, ridiculously besotted. In fact, he was finding it difficult not to laugh at the lovebirds. He winked at Letitia, who acknowledged in kind.

"I think you should ask him and get it over with, Willie," he suggested.

"Do you really?"

"Yes, I do. I don't think I can stand much more of your lovesickness."

His brother flared up. "This isn't amusing, Chris!

This is the most important thing I've ever done, and I'll thank you not to jest! If you weren't lying in bed, I'd call you out. I swear I would!"

"Willie, Chris was only trying to tease you out of your distress," Letitia soothed.

"I wish I could believe that!" He stared daggers at the earl, then seized on Letitia's use of his brother's Christian name. "So we are *all* on a first-name basis! I wonder what else is in the wind?"

"Go now and speak with my father," she returned. "I have reason to believe that he will look kindly on your match with Julianne."

"You do?" He gaped at her.

She nodded.

Chris saw her surreptitiously cross her fingers and wondered if she really had some private knowledge or if she was bluffing.

"I'll speak for you if necessary, Willie," he offered.

"I, too," Letitia seconded.

"And of course, I will!" Julianne cried, drying her eyes and tugging at his hand. "Come, Willie. Now is as good a time as any! If Mama has taken your joke as an insult and told Papa, you can explain that you didn't mean it as such. My father is a reasonable man. He'll understand."

"Well, I . . ."

"Besides, with the house party breaking up, someone else may ask for her first," Letitia prompted-ed.

A look of fear came over Willie's face. "I shall go now!"

"I'll go with you as far as the library!" Giddy with excitement, Julianne dragged him across the room.

"His fate is probably sealed," Chris remarked, watching them go.

"Fate?" Letitia sank down in the chair nearest the bed. "Is that how you think of it? As some dreadful fate? They are so happy. They belong together!"

"You're right, I suppose. It was a poor choice of words." He grinned sheepishly. "I don't envy Willie his task. I'd be shaking in my boots."

"You, my lord?" She smiled. "With your suave sophistication? You're bamming me."

"No, I'm not," he said with heartfelt fervor. "But tell me. I saw you cross your fingers. Are you truly sure that Willie will receive a favorable response?"

"I *think* he will. Papa told me that he was not averse to him. Your brother's youth is his only drawback."

"I know. I tried to discourage him, but he was adamant. I assure you that I and my family will look after them. Willie is upright and sincere. He'll make Julianne a good husband."

"She, in turn, will be an excellent wife to him. Unlike me, she is so very talented in the domestic arts."

"Unlike you?" He chuckled. "I cannot believe that Lady Grey has not schooled you proficiently in the management of a household."

She laughed. "Yes, I can manage, but Julianne far outshines me with all her frilly little touches."

"Some men do not care for fussiness. Some men like dogs in the house."

"Well, as you know, I like animals."

"Speaking of which," Chris mused, "I haven't seen Racky today."

She shrugged in amazement. "He seems strangely content to take apart an old shawl of mine. Shall I fetch him?"

"Yes, let's see what he's up to," he urged.

Letitia left, returning with the fuzzy raccoon. She set him on the bed. Racky promptly rushed up to Chris's face and pinched his nose.

"Ouch!" Chris exclaimed. "There's a bee sting there!"

She giggled. "You requested his presence."

"Yes, and I'm not sorry. He's quite entertaining." Reaching over, he grabbed a mint and offered it to the creature.

Racky snatched the sweet from Chris's palm, shinnied up the bedpost to sit on the canopy, and munched his treat.

"What's this about the house party ending?" Chris asked.

"The guests thought Mama would have her hands full caring for the sick." Letitia sighed. "Truly, I think that they have satisfied their curiosity and are ready to leave, anyway."

He wondered if any of them would ask for her hand. Probably not. They were confirmed bachelors. Most of them would marry eventually, but not just now. Furthermore, she hadn't spent much time with them. He hoped that his doubts were correct. Among that group, he couldn't think of a single man who would make Letitia happy. Except for himself, of course! But he wasn't ready to take that irreversible step either.

"Are you sorry?" he queried.

"That they are leaving? No," she answered quietly. "None of them overly impressed me."

"Good!" Chris exhaled, surprised to find that he had been holding his breath. "None of them are good enough for you."

She laughed. "Is that supposed to be a compliment?"

"Yes. Yes, it is!" He grinned. "You're very special."

"Thank you, my lord."

He took her hand and brought it to his mouth. "Don't ever forget it," he murmured, his lips caressing her trembling fingers.

A shout rose up from below. Running feet sounded on the stairs and in the hall. Julianne and Willie dashed in the door.

"He agreed!" Willie howled, whirling his fiancée high in the air.

"We're engaged!" shrilled Julianne. "We're going to be married!"

Letitia snatched her hand from Chris's grasp. Leaping up, she hurried to hug the ecstatic couple. The three of them danced around the room.

Forcing a smile, Chris watched the revelry. How could his brother accept, so easily and willingly, his coming nuptials? Was Willie too young to recognize the magnitude of the event?

He eyed Letitia twirling lithely, her swirling dress outlining her delectable curves. Letitia was just as elated about it as the two youthful lovers. It must be him. He must have escaped so many marriage traps that he'd become jaded at the very idea of matrimony. It couldn't be maturity. Letitia was rejoicing, and Letitia, by God, was no baby.

Letitia paused in her celebration to glance at Chris. He was a bit left out of it all, fixed as he was in his bed. Though he was smiling, the curve of his lips seemed rather constrained. She detached herself from the celebrating couple and went to him. Seating herself, she fleetingly pressed his hand.

"Isn't it wonderful?" she declared.

"Indeed." His voice seemed almost wistful.

"They are so very happy."

"Yes."

She studied his face. "You *are* pleased for them, aren't you?"

"Of course," he said amiably. "I am always glad to see people get what they want."

"You don't act like it," she couldn't help saying.

"What do you want me to do?" he demanded. "Jump out of bed and join in?"

"Certainly not! But you look . . . you look as if you don't quite approve."

"I told you I did! How many times must I say it?" he snapped.

Hurt, Letitia bit her lower lip. "You needn't be so short with me."

He covered her hand, which was still lying next to his. "I'm sorry, Letitia. Never fear, I shall offer my best wishes to my brother and your sister as soon as they cease their rotations."

Something was bothering him terribly. She wished he would confide in her. She wished she could hold him in her arms and comfort him.

"I'm just weary of being in bed," he said, as if he'd read her mind, "and my ribs hurt."

"Shall I fetch you a dose of laudanum?"

"All right."

Eager to help him, she hurried to bring the medicine. Mixing it with a small amount of water, she held it to his mouth. Once again, his hand covered hers as he swallowed.

"Thank you."

She felt warm all over. "I shall remove these two from your room, and that pesky Racky too, so that you may rest."

"Fine." He smiled at her. "And Letitia? I *am* happy for them, and I intend to make sure that they know it."

14

Time sped by much too quickly for Letitia. Each passing day brought Chris that much closer to complete recovery, and Letitia wondered what would happen when the doctor gave him a clean bill of health.

They had grown quite close in the hours they'd spent together. She was sure that he had come to trust her and to care for her. But was it enough? When Dr. Graham permitted him to travel, would he linger, just to be with her? Or would he simply say good-bye and depart?

The thought of him leaving disturbed her so much that she decided to take the reins into her own hands and broach the subject. If he didn't wish to discuss it, she would afford him the opportunity to avoid it. She waited until after a visit from Dr. Graham, who had probably given Chris a good report and put him in the best of moods.

Beaming broadly, Nickerson answered her rap on the door. "Good news, Miss Grey!"

"That's wonderful." She looked past the valet to the earl, who was sitting up in a chair, fully dressed and smiling at her. "Are you completely recovered, my lord?"

"I'm very close to it. The doctor is allowing me to go downstairs. Nothing more strenuous yet, but it's an improvement."

A small stab of regret nicked her heart. Confined to his room, he'd appreciated her presence. Would he continue to do so now?

Letitia crossed the room and sat down beside him. "I am so happy for you. You've probably been terribly bored."

"Thanks to you, I have not. You must be the one who's been most weary of it, trying to come up with ways to amuse me."

"Oh, no! Never!" she said, a bit too hastily, and flushed. "You may have beat me at piquet and trounced me at chess, but I have enjoyed our time together, especially our conversations."

He eyed her lingeringly. "So have I."

Letitia glanced away. "If you have recuperated to this extent, I suppose that it won't be long until you leave Greywood Manor. Have you other plans for the summer?"

"At this moment, I was to have been visiting friends in Kent." He grinned ruefully. "But no matter! The invitation will keep."

"I imagine that you are anxious to see your friends."

"A bit," he admitted.

"I remember your descriptions of them. They seem like very pleasant people."

"They are. I believe you would like them, Letitia. And they would like you," he added thoughtfully, rising and extending his hand. "Since I'm allowed more freedom, I'd like to go downstairs. Will you accompany me? We could sit for a while on the side veranda. The doctor has forbidden me to leave the house, but the porch is part of it, too, isn't it? I'd certainly like to be out in the fresh air."

Laughingly, she placed her hand in his and stood. "So would I, though I rode this morning. I don't know why Dr. Graham would object to our sitting out there."

"Good! That is what we'll do, and you can tell me how the horse went. Nickerson? You are excused for the afternoon. You deserve a holiday from the sickroom!"

"Thank you, my lord." Not taking a chance on Lord Brerely changing his mind, the valet smoothed his coat and hurried out the door.

Chris chuckled. "There's a girl in the kitchen who interests him. Poor Nickerson! He hasn't had much relief from me lately to pursue his own interests."

"He is admirably loyal." She smiled up at him. "It is no wonder. You are a very considerate employer."

He looked down at her, lacing his fingers through hers and drawing her closer. "Letitia, when I leave . . ."

"Yes, Chris?" she whispered.

"Letitia . . ." He dropped her hand and slipped his arms around her shoulders, bringing her nearer still, so close that her breasts lightly brushed his chest.

Her heart thumped wildly. Blood surged through her veins, rendering her almost breathless. Her knees seemed to dissolve. Momentarily frightened by her own shattering response, Letitia tried to draw away.

"Don't," he murmured, retaining his gentle control of her. "I wouldn't harm you. I want only the best for you. You see . . . well . . . The strangest thing has happened!" He grinned crookedly. "I . . . I find that I've fallen in love with you."

She softened, shyly slipping her arms around his waist. "And I with you," she breathed. "Oh, Chris!"

Happiness glowed in his dark eyes. Leisurely, as if to savor every second, he brought his lips to hers.

His kiss was all she'd ever dreamed that it would

be. He was skilled at the art, tumultuously setting her mouth afire with an unleashed hunger. She wished that he would never stop. Indeed, she longed for him to do much more. The incredible new feelings that surged through her body were almost overpowering. What could he think of her uninhibited reaction to his caress? Summoning all her willpower, she touched his cheek, her tender signal ending the magical moment.

He raised his head and smiled.

"I think we had best go downstairs," she said quietly. "I fear scandal."

He realized it, too. "Yes."

Chris took her hand and led her into the hall. "Where is your father? Is he in the house?"

Letitia felt that if her heart beat any faster, she would certainly have a seizure. He was going to ask for her hand! Oh, happy, beautiful day!

"He . . . he and Mama were in the salon when I came up."

"I would like to speak with him, if it meets with your approval?" He paused, studying her expression. "Letitia, will you marry me?"

"Yes. Oh, yes!" She threw her arms around him, and he drew her even closer than he had before. The now-familiar frisson of desire swept through her as she felt the hard-muscled planes of his body. He was magnificent, and he was hers.

Chris briefly kissed her lips and tucked a strand of her hair back behind her ear. "Then let us make our engagement official."

Silently, they descended the stairs. Letitia clung to his arm, hoping that the support he was giving her did not damage his ribs further. But she couldn't help it. Her legs almost seemed to have disappeared. Handsome, wonderful, *perfect* Christopher Brerely! He would be hers, forever and ever.

They turned at the newel post and glided, dream-like, down the hall toward the salon. How pleased her father would be! How excited, her mother! Julianne and Willie would be thrilled, too. And she, Letitia Grey, would be the happiest creature on the face of the earth!

Voices drifted from the half-opened door of the salon. Her father had not yet returned to the stable. He would be available for the glorious interview.

"You see?" Lord Grey was saying to his lady, with a chuckle. "My Marriage Mart has been a complete success! Ha! We didn't have to go to London after all! And you didn't think I could pull it off! You thought my eligible bachelors would be too wary!"

The viscountess snorted. "You caught a green boy . . ."

Letitia's heart leaped to her mouth. "They are occupied," she said, trembling, drowning out her mother's voice. "Let us come back later."

The pleasant expression on Chris's face faded. He stood his ground, listening.

"Besides," Lady Grey continued, "your so-called Marriage Mart is only fifty percent successful. I see no one suing for Letitia's hand."

"Just wait!" Her husband laughed gleefully. "Brerely will come up to scratch!"

"Fustian!" she replied caustically. "The earl is experienced. He can see right through your ridiculous scheme."

"Please, Chris," Letitia begged. "No good is served by eavesdropping. What you are hearing is taken from context!"

"Be still, Letitia."

He spoke softly, but she quailed at the determined note of command in his voice. Pleadingly, she looked up at him. There was no warmth now, in his dark eyes, only cold, hard anger.

"I cannot bear this nonsense, and that is just

what it is!" Almost frantic, Letitia turned away. "It is absolute nonsense!"

Chris grasped her wrist, squeezing it painfully and halting her flight. "No, you don't. You'll listen."

"Letitia will snare Brerely," her father relentlessly went on. "Right in the beginning, she told me that he'd do for her. Just wait! She has him where she wants him. We'll soon see her spring her trap! Letitia has always been successful in her endeavors. In fact, I'll make you a wager on it!"

The blood drained from Letitia's face. If she heard one more word, she thought she would surely faint. Dear heaven, how could she ever explain this to the earl? She had wanted him, yes. But she had not used unfair means to try to snag him. Hadn't she told him that she would never wed a man who didn't want to marry her? Pray God that Chris would remember her vow.

Evidently, he had heard enough, too. He dragged her back down the hall, a short distance away from the door, and whirled her around to stand before him. Rage blazed in his eyes.

"I trusted you, Letitia! Apparently, I was wrong!" he spat out. "You are just like all the others! You are lying and deceitful! God, but I was a fool! I thought you were different."

"Chris, I . . ."

"It's *Lord Brerely* to you!"

She drew a deep breath. "My lord, I can explain. Yes, I wanted you! And I love you!" She wavered on those last words, tears spilling down her cheeks. She tried, unsuccessfully, to speak around the lump that constricted her throat. Mutely, she shook her head.

"I am waiting!" he snapped.

She swallowed painfully. "If . . . if I had wished to trap you, why did I throw away the numerous chances I had to do just that? Didn't my actions prove that I had no such intention?"

He laughed, shortly and without humor. "That was part of your grand plan. You wanted *me* to want *you*. Your snare was extremely subtle, Miss Grey. I must give you credit for that! You should try it on some other unsuspecting man. I am sure that you will eventually capture your quarry."

Numbly, Letitia shook her head. "I want no other, and I had no plan," she murmured sadly. "Why can't you believe me, Chris? I *love* you."

"You'll get over it."

"You told me you loved me," she whispered, pain twisting her stomach.

"Betrayal and trickery have a way of destroying that illusive emotion," he sneered, striding toward the stairs.

"Oh, Chris." Her legs too weak to support her for another moment, she sank down onto one of the little gilded chairs that lined the passage. "If what we have between us is destroyed, then you have caused it yourself. You have done it with your stubborn arrogance and your poisonous distrust."

He turned on his heel. "If I mistrust, it is because of you, and others like you!"

His further comparison of her to others struck her like a heavy blow. Letitia clenched her jaw. Throbbing with anger, she leaped to her unsteady feet.

"You are afraid of women, my lord! You are afraid of what you feel for me! Very well!" she shouted. "If what you overhear others say abolishes your love for me, then I am best off without you!"

Her screech brought Lord Grey to the hall. "Brerely! Letitia! What . . ."

Chris favored him with an intense look of malice and proceeded upstairs.

"Letitia!" her father exclaimed. "What is going on here? Brerely downstairs and . . ."

Her temper flaming, she pushed him into the salon and slammed the door. "Yes! The doctor gave him permission for a bit more exercise! We came downstairs to sit on the veranda and . . . and he wanted to talk with you!"

"How nice, my dear." Lady Grey fluttered, holding her hands to her ears. "But why are you shrieking so?"

"Because we overheard a certain conversation!" she stormed.

Lord Grey blanched.

"Oh, dear," moaned his lady.

"How could you?" Letitia wrenched out. "You have ruined everything! He . . . he had just told me that he loved me, and that he wanted to speak with you!"

Her father started for the door. "I'll have a word with him."

She darted sideways, blocking his way. "You have said enough, Papa, and what you implied was untrue! I wanted him; I loved him! But I would never have set a trap for him! I wouldn't have had him, if he hadn't wanted me, too!"

"Then that is what we shall explain." He gently tried to edge around her.

"Don't you think I've already tried?" she shrilled with hurt and exasperation. "After what he heard, he refuses to believe me!"

"I will tell him I was jesting." Lord Grey nodded with satisfaction. "Yes, that is what I shall do. I'll tell him I was teasing my wife! He'll understand." He fondly touched her cheek. "Don't fret, Tish, I'll straighten out the situation."

"No!" she cried. "I wouldn't have him now! Not after this!"

"But Brerely would make the best of husbands," her mother protested feebly.

"No, he wouldn't! He would be a wretched spouse!"

"He is rich . . . titled. My goodness, he will be a marquess one day! My daughter . . . a marchioness," she marveled.

"You are not listening to me!" Letitia blared. "I will not marry him!"

"Lower your voice, my dear." Lord Grey took her arm and led her to the sofa, seating her beside her mother. "This matter bears discussion."

"There is no discussion to it! I will not have him for a husband!"

Her father moved to the sideboard. "I believe we could use a restorative. Then we will talk of this in a sane, sensible manner."

Letitia accepted the glass of sherry he pressed into her hand. "Nothing can be done, Papa. I have made up my mind."

He raised an eyebrow. "I thought you professed to love the man."

"I do, and that is why I won't marry him!"

"That doesn't make sense, Letitia," Lady Grey said, puzzled. "If you love him, why should you hesitate?"

"Because he would break my heart!"

"I just don't understand," her mother lamented. "If your papa makes an explanation, and if Lord Brerely loves you, everything will be all right."

Letitia merely shook her head, unhappily sipping her sherry. Why couldn't they comprehend? If Chris doubted her now, he would always do so.

"But he will be a marquess!" the viscountess wailed.

"I have told you, Mama. I wouldn't marry him if he were the King of England!"

Lady Grey pressed her lips together into a narrow, angry line. "Perhaps you can talk some wisdom into her head," she told her husband.

"Letitia." He dragged up a chair in front of her, sat down, and took her hand. "We love you and want what is best for you. Marriage to Brerely would provide you security for a lifetime."

"So would remaining here, as your unmarried daughter. I shall participate fully in your equine enterprise," she announced, "and I shall be just fine! You may depend on me to assist you at all times, for I shall *never* marry."

"You silly girl!" her mother fumed. "Alfred, go and speak at once to Lord Brerely. Let us remedy this unfortunate situation immediately!"

"You will be wasting your breath," Letitia declared. "He didn't trust me. I refuse to wed a man who doesn't believe in me. Can't you see? It would be the worst sort of marriage. He would be suspicious of me at all times."

There was a scratch at the door, and Formby entered. "Sir, madam, you have visitors. My Lord and Lady Trinarton."

"Dear God in heaven!" Lady Grey cried. "Now what shall we do? The entire house is at sixes and sevens, and now we must entertain the marquess and the marchioness!"

"Not I," swore Letitia, vehemently. "I shall not meet them."

"I have placed my lord and lady in the drawing room and sent for refreshments," the butler said with a curious glance at the young lady.

"Thank you, Formby," the viscount said, dismissing him. "We'll be along."

The servant bowed and made his departure.

"What are we going to do?" Lady Grey shrieked.

"We shall entertain our visitors," her husband said mildly.

"But what shall we do about Letitia?"

"I believe that our daughter will decide to exercise her good manners for the sake of Julianne, if for no other reason. Am I not correct, Tish?"

He was right. Julianne would be meeting her future in-laws for the very first time. All must be proper.

"Very well, Papa," she miserably informed him, "but I must have time to freshen my face and to . . . to gather my wits."

"Of course," he said sympathetically.

"And what of my wits?" Lady Grey blustered. "This is all your fault, Alfred! You and your damned Marriage Mart! I knew it would come to no good!"

"We'll rise above it." He extended his arm. "Come, my dear."

She grudgingly accepted his escort. "Dammit, dammit, *dammit!* I shall never forget the events of today. *Never!*" With a final disparaging glance at Letitia, she went forth to greet the guests.

"So you see, Willie?" Chris muttered, wrapping up his story. "I thought I loved her, but I was wrong. She's just like all the others."

"Don't be so hasty to leap to a conclusion," William advised. "Sit down and discuss it with her."

"We did *discuss* it." He lifted the glass of brandy to his lips, drained it, and poured himself another.

"You're going to get foxed."

"I don't give a damn," he growled. "I hope I do. And then I'm going to leave this place."

"Chris, you can't!"

"For once, you'll have to get along without my support, Willie. If you're man enough to get married, you're man enough to stay here by yourself!"

"I'm not talking about that," his brother replied. "What about your ribs? The doctor will never permit you to travel!"

The earl uttered an obscenity.

"Chris, you can't take a chance on hurting yourself."

"Damn my ribs! I don't care! Don't you see? I have to get away from her!"

He polished off his drink. Willie tried to remove the bottle, but his brother beat him to it. He replenished his glass again.

"I thought I loved her," he repeated morosely. "The worst part of it is . . . I still do. I *do* love her, I've never felt this way about a woman, and I doubt that I ever will again."

"Then stay! You can work it out!"

"No." He resolutely shook his head. "It's over."

Willie scowled. "The trouble with you is that you have too much pride."

"I am the heir to the Marquess of Trinarton. I'm supposed to have pride." He forced a grin. "Breed pride into your sons, Willie. They'll be my heirs, for I shall never wed."

"Don't be ridiculous, Chris, you—" Willie halted, hearing a faint rap on the door.

"Come in!" the earl shouted.

A footman appeared. "My lords, Lord and Lady Trinarton are awaiting you in the drawing room."

"Oh, God." Chris swayed to his feet. "That's all I need."

"Dammit, you're half-seas over!" Willie complained. "Shall I say that you're feeling ill?"

"Hell, no. Mother'd be up here in a flash."

"They won't approve of your drinking to excess."

"Well, I have good reason!" he said querulously.

His brother narrowed his eyes. "Do you intend to explain it to them?"

"Good Lord, no! They'd hop right into the midst of this tangle!"

"They'll realize that something is wrong," Willie surmised. "They always do."

"Not this time." Chris gritted his teeth. "I've

fooled them before. I can do it again. Above all else, I don't want them to know *anything* about Letitia and me. I mean that, Willie. You'll keep your mouth shut!"

"Of course, Chris." The younger man grinned mischievously. "Of course!"

15

"Please forgive us our unannounced arrival," Lady Trinarton implored after the four parents had greeted each other. "When we received William's letter, containing the news of Christopher's accident and William's betrothal, I could not bear to wait another minute before paying a visit!"

"You are always welcome in our home," Lady Grey replied graciously. "Set your mind at ease; your elder son is much improved. The physician allowed him to come downstairs today."

"That is a relief!" the marquess responded. "Of course, we were very worried about him, but that is not the only reason for our visit. We are terribly anxious to see William, and to meet your Julianne."

"I hope you approve of the match?" Lord Grey asked enthusiastically.

"Well, certainly we were concerned about William's age," the young man's father said, "but he is a good, steady boy, and he is so enamored, how could we do anything but give them our blessing?"

"Your Julianne sounds absolutely delightful!" Lady Trinarton exclaimed. "I do look forward to having a daughter. You won't mind me spoiling her a bit, will you? I'd like to take her shopping with me in London. Having only had sons, I've missed the enjoyment of buying dresses and pretties for a young lady."

"With that venture, my wife will probably drive me to the poorhouse," the marquess complained, but laughed good-naturedly.

"Julianne will be delighted to shop with you," Lady Grey assured her. "Our daughter loves fashion and is very stylish, as you will soon see. We have sent word upstairs that you are here. Julianne and both of your sons should arrive at any moment."

"I believe you have another daughter?" Lord Trinarton pleasantly queried.

Batting her eyelashes, Lady Grey hesitated, unable to speak. Her husband was forced to respond.

"Yes, we do. Our elder daughter, Letitia, should be along later. She has been rather indisposed today." The viscount glanced nervously at his wife.

Catching his gaze, she burst into tears. "Oh, dear, I must apologize!" she wept. "I thought I could put it out of my mind, but I just cannot bear it!"

"Goodness! You poor lady!" The marchioness hastened to the sofa to comfort her. "Is your daughter seriously ill?"

"I fear it is terribly serious!" she sobbed. "Your son, Lord Brerely . . . and Letitia . . . Alfred, you must explain! I simply cannot find the words!"

"Must you carry on so, my dear?" he replied in aggravation, then addressed his guests. "It seems that Brerely and Letitia have developed a *tendre* for each other, but recently they've had a grave quarrel."

"Christopher?" the marquess inquired incredulously, leaning forward. "A *tendre?*"

"Apparently so."

"Gracious!" exclaimed the marchioness. "That is wonderful news!"

"Oh, no, it is not! I fear it shall all come to naught!" Lady Grey wailed. "And Letitia loves him so!"

"There, there." Lady Trinarton patted her hand. "We shall intercede in the tangle and straighten it out. Christopher? Interested in a lady? What a welcome miracle! We were giving up hope . . ."

"My dear," Lord Trinarton pointedly interrupted, rising.

Chris stood stiffly in the doorway, his face a stony mask. Behind him, Willie frantically motioned for silence.

Lady Trinarton quickly gathered her wits. Lightly hopping up, she hurried to embrace her sons. "My darlings, what a joyous day this is! William, we are so happy with your betrothal! And Christopher . . ." Her nose twitched. "We know that your situation will improve."

"Mother!" Willie quickly drew her away. "Just wait till you meet Julianne!"

"Oh, yes, I am most anxious to meet her, and Letitia, too!"

Lord Trinarton patted his younger son on the back and shook hands with Chris. "Well, son, I see that you are recovering from your injury." He sniffed knowingly. "Good medicine, no doubt."

"Of excellent quality, Father," his heir answered tightly.

"Yes, I'm sure that Lord Grey keeps a very fine cellar," he said in an undertone. "We'll discuss this later. You know that brandy will not solve your problems, Christopher."

"I haven't any problems, so there's nothing to discuss."

"We'll see about that." The marquess turned to

face the Greys. "I must thank you for assisting my son. I'm sure he will be completely recovered in no time at all!"

At that moment, Julianne appeared. "Mama! Papa! Letitia is sorely distressed! She refused to allow me to enter her chamber, and her eyes . . ."

"Your sister will be all right, my dear," Lady Grey rapidly stated, drying her eyes.

"But she's . . ." Julianne gasped. "Mama! You have been crying, too! What is going on?"

"Julianne!" Lord Grey said sternly. "Lord and Lady Trinarton are here."

"Oh, yes. I do apologize. My lord. My lady." Swiftly recalling her manners, she dropped into an elegant curtsy. As she rose, a look of horror assailed her face. "Is that what is wrong? Is that why everyone is weeping? They disapprove of William's and my engagement, and they have come to put period to it!"

Before a reply could be made, Julianne slipped to the floor in a graceful swoon.

When Letitia despondently dragged herself to the drawing room, she was shocked to see Julianne collapsed in a faint on the carpet, Lady Grey waving a vinaigrette under her nose, and a very attractive woman, who must be Chris's mother, chafing her sister's wrists. A stricken William hovered helplessly nearby. Lord Grey and Lord Trinarton had retreated to the sideboard to pour themselves a drink of brandy. Chris stood, alone and rigid, by the mantel.

Though she tried to keep from it, Letitia couldn't refrain from meeting his gaze. She almost shuddered. Even from across the room, she could discern the cold anger and loathing in his eyes. She looked away, fearful that she would cry again. Kneeling, she pulled Julianne's mussed skirt down over her ankles.

"What happened, Mama?"

Chris's mother answered. "Poor child! Somehow she took it into her head that we did not approve of the engagement." She sat back on her heels. "You must be Letitia."

"Yes, ma'am."

Lady Trinarton smiled with elation. "You are quite lovely, my dear, even with those reddened eyes. But never fear. We shall straighten matters out."

"W-what?" Letitia stammered.

"Lovers' quarrels can be very painful." Before the marchioness could go on, Julianne began to revive, and she turned her attention to the girl.

Lady Trinarton knew, Letitia realized with a flood of hot embarrassment. The marchioness knew about her and Chris! Who could have told her? Certainly not her elder son. Chris would never have done that. Willie? Maybe, if he'd been made aware of what had happened. Lady Grey glanced at her with tear-streaked cheeks, and Letitia suddenly knew the answer. Her mother had told! Dear heavens! How could she ever hold up her head again in the Trinartons' presence?

She rose to her feet and went to the window, standing with her back to the company and staring at the green expanse of lawn. How could Lady Grey have mortified her so? It was bad enough to remain in the same room with Chris. Now it was almost impossible. Letitia wished she could flee down the road and never stop running until she reached the next county. How could she ever endure this pain? Losing Chris was heartbreaking, but having everyone know it was even worse.

"Tish?" Lord Grey appeared by her side. "Won't you come with me? I wish to introduce you to Lord Trinarton."

"If I must." Numbly, she took his arm and walked across the room to make her curtsy to Chris's father.

The marquess bowed over her hand, openly studying her appearance. "My dear, you are quite lovely."

I will never be your dear, she wanted to shout. *We shall never be so informal. I'll not be a close member of your family. Your son hates me.*

Instead, she smiled lifelessly. "Thank you, my lord."

Lord Grey poured her a glass of sherry. "Here is refreshment, Letitia."

She shook her head, eyeing Julianne, who was being assisted to her feet by her distraught fiancé. "I should aid my sister."

"Balderdash!" Her father pressed the drink into her hand. "There are hens aplenty clucking over the gel!"

"Plus my moonstruck boy!" Lord Trinarton chortled and turned to his elder son. "Christopher, come and converse with us!"

Letitia paled.

"There are roosters aplenty crowing over her," Chris cynically observed in blatant mockery of Lord Grey's previous statement.

His father frowned at his son's lapse of etiquette. "I beg your pardon?"

Letitia flinched, noting the autocratic undercurrent in the marquess's voice. The question contained a command. There was no doubt about it. She couldn't help feeling sorry for Chris. He, no more than she, wanted any part of this, and yet, being a gentleman and a loyal son, he could scarcely refuse.

Chris woodenly moved forward and filled a glass with brandy.

Lord Trinarton's scowl deepened.

Butterflies fluttered in Letitia's stomach as she sensed the awkward tides flowing around them. She wished she could go to Julianne, or better still, escape from the room, but she knew that her father would not permit it. He and Lord Trinarton, in their maladroit way, were trying to promote a reconciliation between their daughter and son. Their efforts were doomed. It wouldn't work. In fact, their interference made it much more final. Chris was too stubborn to give in to them, and she had made up her mind.

The earl leaned, abruptly and slightly unsteadily, against the sideboard. With his strangely ungainly motion, she realized the reason for the marquess's deeper frown. Along with his obvious irritability, his son was becoming quite foxed.

Despite her embarrassment and her heartache, Letitia desperately wanted to giggle. She had never seen Chris like this! He enjoyed a glass of brandy, but he had never drunk to excess. Their altercation had overset him more than he would care to admit. It was rather satisfying.

Lord Grey caught the earl's ungraceful movement. "Brerely?" he questioned.

Chris winced. "My injury is annoying me."

"Of course. Seeing you dressed and downstairs, one tends to forget your affliction," the viscount said with compassion, but he grinned perceptively.

Letitia swiftly sipped her wine to conceal her smirk, but Chris saw it. He favored her with a searing glare. Setting his glass firmly on the sideboard, he straightened.

"I believe that I should lie down for a while. Dr. Graham told me to rest whenever necessary."

"Yes, my lord," she mockingly observed, lifting

her chin. "You appear to be in need of it now."

He started to respond directly to her, then, apparently, thought better of it. He addressed his father and Lord Grey. "You will excuse me?"

"Certainly," Letitia's father answered. "We shall see you at dinner?"

"I hope I shall feel up to it," Chris replied politely.

Lord Trinarton also set his drink aside. "I shall accompany you, son."

Chris's brows knitted, but he didn't attempt to deter the marquess. Together, the two left the room.

"Ha-ha!" Lord Grey chuckled. "Trinarton will talk some sense into his head!"

It was Letitia's turn to stiffen. "That makes little difference, Papa."

"Why, it makes a great deal of difference! After his papa gets through with him, Brerely will renew his suit!"

"In which case," she murmured succinctly, "I shall turn him down!" Turning on her heel, she sought the company of the ladies and a well-deserved seat.

"Christopher," Lord Trinarton began as his son slipped between the sheets, "it is time we had a serious talk."

"I thought you assumed that I was too foxed for that sort of thing." Chris feigned a yawn.

"No, I don't believe you are that far and away."

"Father, I am rather weary. Remember, this is my first day to escape my chamber."

"This will only take a few minutes." Lord Trinarton drew up a chair. "I am not aware of the whole that went on between you and Miss Grey, but your feelings for her must have been vital enough to have driven you to the brandy bottle. It isn't like you, son. Not since your salad days have I known you to over-imbibe. You must care a great deal for the lady."

Chris sighed. Sooner or later, he was going to have to discuss this. It was best to get it over with now.

"Yes, Father, I did. But I discovered her to be dishonest and deceitful."

"She did not strike me as that sort."

"You were only momentarily in her company. She fooled me for a very long time. Trust me, I don't want a woman like her for a wife."

Lord Trinarton shook his head in disbelief. "Will you tell me what happened?"

Chris did. He told him the entire story, including the compromising incidents. If he hadn't, his father would have found out most of it, anyway. With the matter already known, Willie would feel no compunction about telling everything he knew.

The marquess listened, nodding. "You eavesdropped, Christopher. What you heard came out of context."

"That's what *she* said."

"Don't you think that she could be right?"

"I heard what I heard," he resolutely insisted.

"Lord Grey could have merely been boasting to his wife," Lord Trinarton suggested.

Chris shook his head. "I won't be pressured, Father. I won't be caught in some woman's damned trap!"

"Didn't you *really* love her?"

"I thought I did," he quietly acknowledged.

"Then why can't you believe her?"

"I told you. I won't be caught in a snare like some dumb animal!"

Lord Trinarton rested his hands on his knees and leaned forward. "Christopher! The young lady had you snagged in several compromising situations!

Yet she didn't drop her net. Doesn't that prove her honesty?"

"Not necessarily."

"Dammit, you are too prideful for your own good! You finally found a lady with whom you wished to spend the rest of your life. Why are you throwing it away for a trivial reason?"

Chris seethed. "It isn't insignificant to me!"

His father stood. "I can see that I am getting nowhere here. You will not listen to reason."

"I'm sorry that you are disappointed."

Lord Trinarton looked at him long and hard. "Promise me that you will think about this, Christopher. If you do not consider it wisely, *you* will be the one who is disappointed. And that dissatisfaction will last for a lifetime."

Chris closed his eyes. Presently, he heard his father leave the room. No doubt the man would speak with Willie. The two of them would probably approach him again. It would do them no good. He had made up his mind.

Even if, by a long stretch of the imagination, they might change his attitude, the whole matter was hopeless. Letitia would never have him now. She was a vastly stubborn chit.

"Go away!" Letitia begged, lifting her head from her pillow. "You will not have the least influence on me!"

Lady Grey and Julianne ignored her appeal, entering her chamber and closing the door.

"Letitia," her mother began, "you must listen to us."

"Please," entreated Julianne. "Do you never wish to know happiness?"

"I have known it!" she snapped. "And I know the hurt it can bring!"

"But love can be mended," the viscountess told her.

"Yes!" agreed her sister. "Lovers' quarrels can be so sweetly concluded."

Letitia pulled the covers over her head.

Julianne tried unsuccessfully to pull the sheet away from her sister's face. "You love him. Why are you letting him go so easily?"

Grimly, she gripped the edge of her shroud. "I am not. *He* let go of *me!*"

"He will come round! Willie will . . ."

Furiously, Letitia threw back the bedclothes and sat up. "How many times must I say it? He distrusts me! I could never be happy with such a man! It is over! *Over*, I say, and nothing any of you do will change it! Gad, I cannot believe that you are harassing me so. It wasn't *my* fault!"

"Maybe not," Lady Grey said in a huff, "but it will be your fault if you refuse Lord Brerely when he asks you to marry him!"

She shook her head. "He will not ask. He has too much pride, and he is too arrogant."

"If he did solicit your hand, would you accept?" her mother inquired.

Letitia caught her breath. "If . . . if he apologized, I would consider it. But it will not happen!"

"You do love him, don't you?" Julianne beseeched.

"I . . ." She sank down in the bed. "I thought I did," she whispered, "but he was not the man I saw him to be. I do know this about him. He will never seek me out, never again! You are wasting your time and your hopes. Chris is just too proud and too wary."

"He will be my brother-in-law," her sister said mournfully.

"That he will, and he will be an excellent one.

You must not allow what has happened to color your relationship with him. You may depend upon him," she advised.

"Indeed? You couldn't."

"The situation is different."

"That is true," Lady Grey seconded. "You must not permit this upset to disturb your place in William's family."

"Yes, Julie," Letitia agreed. "Cannot we be happy for you, and forget all about me?"

"I cannot do that, Tish. You are my sister, and I love you. If you are sad, so am I."

"You must not be! If you are, you will make Willie wretched. You don't want that, do you?"

"No, but the matter does deal with his brother."

"The matter, Julianne, rests between Chris and myself," Letitia said firmly. "It has nothing to do with anyone else."

"That is true," Lady Grey proclaimed urgently. "Julianne, you must not jeopardize your relationship with William! Come, let us go now, and leave your sister in peace. Further discussion of this will do no one good!"

"But . . ." Julianne stuttered.

"Come, come!" The viscountess speedily escorted her to the door. "We shall see you at dinner, Letitia."

Letitia smiled wryly. Her mother had been frightened enough that Julianne would inadvertently bungle her liaison with Willie to give no further attention to her elder daughter's broken heart. But what did it matter? She didn't wish sympathy. She only wanted to be alone, and now she had been granted that one desire. She closed her eyes and tried to nap.

Julianne took William's hand as they strolled through the garden. The flowers were blooming riotously. A gentle breeze chased away the afternoon heat. She was with the man she loved. But she couldn't be entirely cheerful, not with her sister lying miserably in bed. Wasn't there any way that Letitia and Chris could be brought to reason?

"Willie," she said, "I wish there was something we could do about my sister and your brother. I believe that all could be resolved if they were not so stubborn."

He squeezed her hand and winked at her. "I've already done it, my love."

She stopped in her tracks, peering up at him. "You have?"

"If you can help bring Letitia around, I've taken care of Chris."

"What did you do?" she gasped.

"Mother and Father will have little influence on him. His friends, however, will. With our fathers' permission, I've sent for them."

"You have?" she cried. "Oh, but, Willie, will they get here in time?"

"I hope so. We've sent a groom to ride posthaste to their house party in Kent. They all should be there, and, knowing them, they'll hurry to our assistance."

Julianne danced on her toes. "I pray it will work!"

"Chris values his friends' opinion. It's our only chance."

"Thank you, thank you! I do so wish Letitia to be happy!"

"And I wish Chris to be the same. They're perfect for each other. Just like we are!" Bending his head, he sought her lips.

16

Despite pleas from his parents and brother, Chris remained in his chamber as much as possible, appearing only for meals. Nor would he listen to his family's appeals regarding a reconciliation with Letitia.

In fact, he wasn't at all sure how he'd come so close to leg-shackling himself in the first place. Somehow, he'd been taken in by an innocent country girl who pretended to share a great deal in common with him, who amused him more than any female he'd met, and who claimed to love him. His inattentiveness worried him. More than that, however, he was disturbed by his innermost feelings. He'd thought himself in love with her. Indeed, he loved her still.

But all of that was finished. No matter what his parents desired, he hadn't been interested in marriage when he came to Greywood Manor, and he certainly wasn't drawn to it now.

Letitia, resisting familial pressure in much the same manner as Chris, remained closeted in her bedroom, she took her breakfast there, and emerged only for luncheon and dinner. She did not even go to the stables. She, too, had turned against marriage. In her heart, she knew that there was only one man she would ever love. If she couldn't have him as her husband, she wanted no other. But that hope had dissipated. All she could do was to muddle through the final days of his unsettling presence at Greywood Manor, and plan ahead for a life without him.

Lord and Lady Grey, Lord and Lady Trinarton, William, and Julianne were forced to give up attempts to effect a compromise between Chris and Letitia. It was useless to try to talk logic with a pair as stubborn and prideful as those two were, and the tension created by the chilly couple was almost unbearable. Furthermore, it was infuriating to see the pair throwing away this chance for happiness. Their only hope was that the earl's friends would arrive with a solution to the dilemma, before Dr. Graham gave Chris permission to travel. Everyone knew that the earl would flee at the earliest possible opportunity.

Even Racky was affected by the swirling conflict. He was no longer welcome in Chris's chamber. He did succeed, though, in maintaining contact with Lord Brerely, and usually managed to pilfer a mint before his lordship saw him and rang a peal over his head.

Letitia had still not discovered her pet's means of escape. One moment, Racky would be contentedly playing in her room. The next, she would hear a lordly bellow, announcing his presence in Chris's chamber. Then Julianne or William would remove the offender and return him to her. Lady Grey debated his eviction to the stable, but decided to allow him to stay in the house. He seemed to be the only thing that provided Letitia with a diversion.

Even the servants were involved in the dispute. Gaining the entire story through their vastly accurate grapevine, they argued the matter, took sides, and made wagers on the outcome. With all of this distraction, Greywood Manor was not running very smoothly when three large, luxurious traveling coaches drew up in front one day.

Hearing the commotion on the drive, Chris strolled to his window and looked out, scarcely believing his eyes. He immediately recognized the noble crests on the doors of the vehicles. What in the hell were his friends doing here?

Spellbound, he watched as Allesandra and Brandon Rackthall, Ellen and Harry Singleton, Clarissa and Brougham Abingdon, and Aubrey Standish emerged. Good God, what had caused Aubrey, that firmly dedicated bachelor, to come here? He, of all people, had shunned Lord Grey's Marriage Mart. And why had the others brought their wives, as if the Greys were holding a house party? No one had told him of any plans for entertainment. It just didn't make sense.

Of course, he had written to his friends, telling them about his accident, but he'd assured them that he wasn't seriously injured. They couldn't have been so worried about his condition that they'd made a special trip to see him. Perhaps they were simply using the event as an excuse to see Lord Grey's horses and stables. But that didn't seem right. If that was the motive, the gentlemen would have come alone.

Chris groaned. No matter what the reason, they couldn't have arrived at a worse time. Now he would be unable to keep to his chamber, as he preferred. He'd have to socialize with his friends, or they would know that something was terribly wrong. In truth, they'd probably find out anyway. Someone, Willie in particular, would be sure to enlighten them about him and Letitia. Then what would he do? He would especially have to watch out for machinations from Allesandra, that beautiful little matchmaker.

He started as he heard a door slam, running foot-steps, and a loud rapping in the hall.

"Julianne!" his brother cried. "Get up from your nap! They're here!"

They're here? Seething, Chris clenched his jaw. Suddenly, awfully, he knew why his friends had traveled to Greywood Manor. It was nothing to do with his letter, his mishap, or Lord Grey's horses. That scheming Willie had sent for them! Rot his meddlesome hide!

Visions of fratricide danced temptingly through his mind, but he knew he couldn't kill his brother. Wasn't that brat the one destined to carry on the family lineage? Besides, Chris didn't relish spending the rest of his life in exile on the Continent. No, he couldn't murder Willie, but he could show him what he thought of his fiendish scheme. He would capture that knave in the hall, dash him against the fine paneling, and bloody his nose.

Furious, Chris whirled on his heel to rush to the ambush, and received for his troubles a breath-taking stab of pain in his ribs. Hell! He wasn't in the condition to engage in a bruising-match with his brother, or he'd come out the loser. In self-defense, Willie would punch him back. He'd end up spending a month in bed at Greywood Manor, thus giving Letitia a grand new chance to design and spring a foolproof trap.

There was one thing, however, he could do. He could give Willie a dressing-down that he would never forget! Gingerly holding his side, Chris hurriedly exited his room and saw his brother and Julianne trotting toward the stairs.

"William!" he roared.

The young man halted and turned around, grinning sheepishly. "Oh, Chris! You'll never guess what has happened. We have surprise visitors!"

He ground his teeth, wishing he could plant

Willie a facer right then and there. "I don't have to guess, dammit! I looked out the window! Furthermore, I know *why* they're here!"

"But aren't you glad to see your friends?" Julianne asked sweetly.

"No!" he exploded. "You did this, Willie! You interfering, prying thatch-gallows!"

"You shouldn't speak to your brother like that," scolded the young lady.

"Shut up, Julianne!" the earl shouted. "This is between Willie and me!"

"Now, see here, Chris," his brother began as Letitia's door burst open and a very incensed young lady rushed out.

"Don't you dare talk to my sister in that ugly manner, you odious brute!" Letitia shrilled.

Angrily, he turned to her. "Stay out of this, Letitia! It is none of your affair!"

"It most certainly is! If you think I am going to stand by and listen to you speak to my sister as if she were worse than a cur, you are sadly mistaken!"

"She's going to be *my* sister-in-law, and I'll speak to her any way I want!" he barked.

"No, you won't!" Willie broke in and took a step toward him, but Julianne grasped her fiancé's arm and dragged him down the stairs to the front hall, where servants, Greys, Trinartons, and guests were peering curiously upward.

"Besides," Chris thundered, "you weren't *standing by!* You were in your room! Why don't you go back in there and mind your own business, you impudent hoyden!"

"Arrogant coxcomb! Why don't you?"

"Because . . ." He glanced around to find that Willie and Julianne had vanished. "Now see what you've caused!"

Her answer was a slamming of the door, so clamorous that Chris thought his eardrums would rupture.

The devil take her! He spun around sharply, and winced. Clutching his protesting ribs, he returned to his chamber and ran straight into Nickerson.

"What in the hell are you doing? Eavesdropping?" he cried.

"No, sir." A faint smile flitted across the valet's face. "Actually, my lord, it wasn't necessary."

"That vexatious chit!"

"Yes, yes," he soothed.

"Help me undress, Nickerson," Chris instructed shortly.

"You aren't going down to greet your friends?"

"No, I'm in pain! I'm going to bed! I want some laudanum! That vixen caused my ribs to hurt!"

The valet assisted him out of his coat. "Did she strike you, my lord?" he asked sympathetically, eyes twinkling.

"No! But she caused it just the same!"

"Yes, yes." Biting back a smirk, Nickerson undressed his gentleman and tucked him into bed, administering a large, tranquilizing dose of medicine.

"Don't permit anyone to wake me," Chris warned. "I want to sleep and sleep. I don't care if I never wake up!"

"But then you would be dead, sir."

"I feel like I already am. Dead and in hell."

"Yes, my lord." Nickerson withdrew. He quietly worked in the dressing room until he was certain his master was sound asleep. Then he darted from the room and down the servants' stairway to the kitchen, where he could share in the unbridled gossip.

When the din in the upstairs hall had ceased, the mortified Lady Grey led her guests to the draw-

ing room, directing Formby to bring refreshments
and to notify Lord Brerely and her daughter that
their presence was desired. The skillful butler and
his footmen brought trays of refreshments in short
order, served the company drinks from the sideboard, and reluctantly left the fascinating scene.
When Letitia and Chris did not appear so quickly, the conversation naturally drifted to them.

"Are you certain that they even *like*, let alone
love, each other?" asked the Duchess of Rackthall,
sipping her glass of ratafia.

"Of course, Allesandra." Her husband chuckled.
"I've never known Chris to be in such a state."

"They do," Willie assured her. "Chris told her he
loved her."

"Letitia told him the same," Julianne offered timidly, holding her fiancé's hand. "Do you really think
you'll be able to salvage the situation?"

The Greys and the Trinartons interrupted their
partaking of food and drink to hear the answer.

Chris's four male friends solemnly eyed each other. They were much more aware than the women
of how stubborn Lord Brerely could be. They also
knew of his almost obsessive apprehension of being
trapped in a marriage he didn't want.

"Brandon?" the duchess prompted.

"It won't be easy," he admitted.

"Chris shies away from marriage as much as I
do," Lord Standish remarked.

"Gad, surely not that much, Aubrey," the Marquess of Singleton said dryly.

"He's also too obstinate for his own good," added
Lord Abingdon. "He won't be pushed."

"If that is true, perhaps our being here will make
matters worse," murmured Ellen Singleton, "especially if he realizes why we have come."

Willie looked miserable. "He already does. That's
what that fuss in the hall was about."

"Well, we're here now," the duke stated. "We won't leave without trying to talk some sense into him."

"The four of you should speak with him first," his wife suggested. "If that doesn't work, we ladies will try."

"Is there anything else we can do?" inquired Lady Singleton.

"Maybe . . ." Julianne began haltingly, clearly intimidated by the fashionable young matrons. "Maybe you could tell Letitia what you know of Lord Brerely, ma'am. If she understood more about him, she might come round."

"Tell us a bit about her," Lady Abingdon requested.

"Oh, poor Letitia!" Lady Grey put in mournfully. "She is so in love. If she cannot have Lord Brerely, she will have no one!"

"She is stubborn, too, Mama," her younger daughter reminded her, "and she has enormous pride. She will be difficult."

"It sounds as if the two of them are so much alike that they are at cross purposes," the duchess remarked. "Can you influence Chris to apologize for his part in this, Brandon?"

He flinched. "Can you persuade the lady to do the same?"

"I don't know. Which should go first?" she mused in a tone indicating that she expected no answer.

The duke took a long sip of brandy. "Yes, that's one of our major problems, isn't it?"

Formby quietly entered the room, bent to whisper in Lord Grey's ear, then departed.

The viscount cleared his throat. "I am informed that Lord Brerely will not be joining us. His injured ribs are distressing him. He has taken a dose of laudanum and gone to bed."

Chris's friends exchanged glances of anxiety.

"The coward," growled his father. "Those ribs are his means of escape."

"My daughter, however, is freshening up and will soon be down," the viscount announced. "She begs your forgiveness for her tardiness."

"Well," said Lady Trinarton, "as you must know, Letitia is a most admirable gel!"

Lady Grey glowed with pride. Letitia, unlike Chris, did not know the meaning of the visit from the earl's friends, but she was just as overset by this awful tangle as he. Yet, no matter what her inward turmoil, she was steadfastly preparing to perform the duty expected of the daughter of the house. It couldn't be easy for her, and each one of their noble guests was well aware of it! They were impressed by her, sight unseen.

His drink finished, Lord Grey, catching her eye, winked and rose. "Gentlemen, will you join me in a second glass of brandy?"

The Duke of Rackthall nodded, his blue eyes twinkling. "I think we should toast your daughter's aplomb."

"And my son's thick skull," grumbled Lord Trinarton.

Nervously lifting her hand to delay Formby's opening of the drawing-room door, Letitia paused to catch her breath. What a bumble-broth! First, she had been awakened from her nap by loud voices in the hall. When she'd heard Chris berating sweet Julianne, she'd sprung to her sister's defense. Moments later, it seemed, she'd been alerted to the arrival of the earl's friends. Pray God they hadn't heard the upstairs altercation. If she received any inkling that they had, she would be mortified for the rest of her life. She was tempted to ask Formby, but she decided she'd best keep her silence. She, and not Julianne, should have been the one told to shut up today. But drat it, Chris deserved every snapping word! Still simmering from his effrontery, she nodded rather curtly to the butler.

She was unprepared for the sight within. The room seemed filled with people. Immediately, she noted that Chris was not present, but four other wondrously handsome, absolutely elegant gentlemen stood by the sideboard with Willie, Lord Trinarton, and her father. Three of the most beautiful, stylish ladies that she had ever seen were chatting pleasantly with Lady Trinarton, Julianne, and her mother. So these dazzling men and women were Chris's friends! But that shouldn't be surprising. Wasn't he just as enchanting and polished?

Her heart sank. No doubt, it was just as well that she and Chris had ended all hope of a future together. With her definite lack of town bronze, she couldn't fit in with these people. In no time at all, he would probably have become weary of his horse-loving country wife. They would have been wretched.

All at once, everyone seemed to be looking at her. Quaking inwardly, Letitia lifted her chin. She glided into the room, hoping that her quivering knees would hold her up.

As introductions were made, she recognized the names from her long conversations with Chris. It only remained to fit them to faces. And to summon the nerve to converse with them!

"Come and sit here, my dear." Lady Grey patted the place on the sofa between herself and Lady Trinarton.

Letitia was thankful that her parent had come to her rescue. If she'd had to sit next to one of the others, she would surely have swooned. Even so, she was struck speechless and sat quietly, allowing the discourse to flow around her. She noticed that her sister did the same. Even though Julianne was much more outgoing than she, the girl was equally unnerved by the magnificent ladies, too.

"I understand that you are an excellent horse-woman."

Letitia started. "Forgive me, Your Grace. I fear I was woolgathering," she confessed.

The duchess repeated her statement, adding, "Perhaps you could take us riding."

"Of . . . of course," Letitia stammered.

"The three of us are country girls at heart. We enjoy nothing more than a good, long ride."

Letitia stared at her in disbelief.

The duchess smiled. "You are surprised?"

"Yes," she admitted, flushing.

"Well, it is true. We prefer a rural setting. At certain times, the three of us have even managed estates."

"You *have*?" Letitia blurted.

Her Grace nodded. "All of our parents died early. Clarissa oversaw the property while rearing her younger brother and sister. Ellen inherited hers and directed its affairs for several years before she married Harry. I administered my brother's domain while he was in the army."

"Goodness! You are all to be congratulated!" Lady Grey said enthusiastically. "I am sure I could never do such a thing!"

Letitia was amazed. Life, it seemed, hadn't always been perfect for the three young matrons. She herself had probably had an easier upbringing. These ladies had experienced difficult times. If they were mired in the country, how had they gained their social polish?

It was as if the duchess read her mind. "I never even set foot in London before my marriage."

"I had a Season." The Marchioness of Singleton laughed. "It was a complete disaster! Only recently have I managed to avoid tripping on carpets and spilling champagne, and I still cannot be depended upon not to cause some awful calamity! But Clarissa had a successful Season."

Lady Abingdon rolled her eyes. "Really, Ellen, it was my sister's Season, not mine."

"True enough, but *you* were the one who came away with a husband!"

Letitia smiled, listening to the casual camaraderie displayed by the ladies. They did not seem so fearsome now. Indeed, she felt she could become friends with them. But that would never happen. After this visit, she doubted she'd ever see them again.

Julianne would. Julianne's marriage would take her right into the heart of Society. Smile fading, she tried not to be jealous of her sister's good fortune. She didn't wish to spend Seasons in London, anyway. She much preferred her provincial life.

She concentrated on being happy for Julianne. It was a wonderful stroke of luck that the girl had been introduced to these ladies, who were surely the cream of tonnish Society. Her sister would love the city and its social events. She'd be run ragged by all the parties. Knowing these women, and having Lady Trinarton as a mother-in-law, would grant her social prestige. Julianne would be pampered, just like the duchess, the countess, and the marchioness. Those women might have known hard times in the past, but it was perfectly clear by nothing more than their fashionable travel ensembles that they were indulged by their husbands.

She would never be coddled by a gentleman. Nor would she ever be cuddled by one. Her father would remain the only man in her life. When her parents passed on, she would be left here alone. She blinked back tears.

Oh, Chris, she thought, remembering the warmth

of his arms and the sweet ecstasy of his kiss, why couldn't it have worked out?

"Letitia!" her mother said sharply, reminding her of the presence of their guests. "Gracious! You are a thousand miles away today!"

"I'm sorry," she whispered.

"We were discussing the horses once more," Lady Grey explained. "I was wondering if you would agree to ride with the ladies in the morning?"

"Yes," she answered numbly. "I would be delighted."

"I am sure we will have a splendid gallop," the duchess predicted, eyeing her searchingly. "And a comfortable chat," she added with relish.

17

Under the influence of the laudanum, Chris slept through the afternoon, evening, and the entire night. Awakening in the early morning, he glanced out the window at the pale promise of the day to come and was pleased to see that he had whiled away at least a portion of his friends' visit. He swung out of bed, grimly ready to be up and about.

His previous day's retreat had been cowardly. For that, he was slightly ashamed of himself. He did not consider himself to be a man who ran away from trouble. Of late, however, he seemed to be doing so frequently. It was the easiest thing to do. He wondered what Bran, Harry, Brough, and Aubrey thought of his behavior.

Just now, his closest male friends probably had a very low opinion of him. They were smart. His use of his injured ribs as an excuse would not fool them. They would know why he had avoided them. By now, if not before, they would have been made aware of every minute detail of what had happened between him and Letitia.

Stretching, Chris rang for Nickerson and went into the dressing room to perform his morning ablutions. He would have to face his friends today. He couldn't elude them forever. However, he was up rather early. He could have his meal, as usual, in the dining room. With any luck, he would be alone at this hour, thus postponing the inevitable meeting until later.

Yes, that was entirely logical. His friends had traveled the day before. They would have spent the evening in the drawing room, doubtlessly staying up late to talk about him. Then, he thought with a knowing chuckle, they'd probably made love to their wives. All that activity had surely made them weary. Hopefully, they would sleep late.

"*Chit—chit!*"

"Oh, damn!" He looked into the bedroom and saw Racky perched on the canopy of the bed, munching a mint.

The raccoon fixed his bright, beady eyes on Chris and cocked his head from side to side. "*Chit—chit.*"

"You just don't give up, do you?" the earl asked.

The animal trilled joyfully.

"Good morning, my lord," Nickerson greeted him, arriving with a tray of tea and toast. He followed Chris's gaze, an expression of horror twisting his face. "There's that damnable beast!"

Racky shinnied down the bedpost, snatched another treat, and hopped to the pillow.

"Yesterday he was here while you were sleeping, sir. I was having dinner, so I was unaware of his invasion. He got into a stack of your cravats and scattered them all over the floor, rendering them filthy and wrinkled! I had to launder and press them at midnight!"

"I'm sorry, Nickerson." Chris crossed the room and picked up the soft, furry creature.

"What are you going to do, my lord? Throw him out the window?"

He absently stroked the animal's back and scratched its ears. "I'm going to set him out in the hall. I don't wish to wake up the household."

Racky nuzzled the earl's neck and dispensed a sticky kiss on his cheek.

Idly, Chris wondered if the raccoon had kissed Letitia this morning. His spirits sank. He didn't like to visualize such intimacies concerning the lady, even if they were only comprised of the playful capers of an animal. The painful memory of her silky skin and her soft lips was still much too sharp. Glumly, he returned the creature to the bed.

"Let the animal remain for a while," he said.

"But my lord!"

"He won't bother anything, now that you've put my clothes away."

"He shows his teeth to me!"

Chris ignored him. "Come, Nickerson, and help me dress. I want to go down immediately. There isn't anyone breakfasting yet, is there?"

"I don't know, sir. I could go and see."

"No, it doesn't matter. I'll go anyway."

Hurriedly, Chris dressed in breeches, boots, and bottle-green coat. With Nickerson's continued complaints about Racky ringing in his ears, he descended the stairs. A footman bowed and opened the dining-room door.

"Good morning, Chris." A chorus of deep male voices hailed him.

He stared at all four of his gentlemen friends.

"Feeling better today?" Bran asked casually.

"I suppose."

Waving aside Formby's offer to serve him, he filled his own plate at the buffet. The butler poured him a cup of tea and withdrew to his pantry. Chris sat down beside Aubrey and began to eat.

The duke got right to the point. "You know why we're here. There is no sense in any of us denying it."

"Yes." Chris snorted. "You're here because of my meddlesome family."

"Not really," Harry Singleton returned. "We've come because you're our friend, and because we heard you were having a problem."

"Then you've come in vain. I've already solved it."

The marquess raised an eyebrow. "It doesn't seem that way."

"See here, Harry, everyone." He laid down his knife and fork. "I'll admit to acquiring a *tendre* for Miss Letitia Grey, but it is finished now. I found the lady to be dishonest and untrustworthy. There is nothing more to say about the situation, and nothing more to do. So won't you let me eat my meal in peace?"

"We just don't want you to make a mistake you'll regret, all because of some trivial incident," Brandon told him.

"Trivial? It was hardly that!" Picking up his utensils, Chris savagely stabbed a slice of ham. "She lied to me! She tried to trick me! Would you wish me to wed a woman like that?"

"Strange," his friend mused. "She didn't strike me as being deceitful."

"*All* women are treacherous, Bran."

The duke's blue eyes narrowed dangerously. "I beg your pardon?"

"I wasn't referring to Allesandra, Ellen, or Clarissa," Chris swiftly apologized. "Let's admit to it! You, and Harry, and Brough have gotten the best. There aren't any more women like them."

Brandon relaxed. "I agree that the three of us are fortunate in our choice of wives, but I do *not* believe the rest of your assumption."

"Well, it's true, isn't it, Aubrey?" Chris questioned, certain of finding an ally in that elusive bachelor.

Lord Standish leisurely swallowed a mouthful

of tea and set down his cup. "No, Chris. You're wrong," he slowly declared.

"What? *You, too?*" He angrily shook his head. "You're one hell of a Judas! You're the very man who was so fixed against coming to Grey's party! In fact, all of you laughed about Lord Grey's Marriage Mart and 'grey mares'!"

The four had the grace to look ashamed.

"It's a wonder you aren't laughing now, about me almost getting caught, dammit!" Chris railed. "I'm surprised you aren't riding about the countryside, spreading the news of my folly!"

"Chris . . ." Aubrey began.

But he had them, and he wasn't about to let them go. "You, Aubrey! Think of all the jokes you constantly crack about Lady Christina chasing you, and you running like hell from her snares! I don't see any of us trying to help her catch you! Not even Harry, and Christina is Ellen's best friend!"

"That isn't the same," Lord Standish muttered.

"It sure as hell is! And all the rest of you! We've escaped more marriage traps than any one of us can remember!"

"Why must you refer to marriage as a trap?" Brough Abingdon asked quietly. "I don't feel trapped."

"Your circumstance is not the same!" Chris snapped.

"Indeed? How so?"

"I told you! Your wives are far superior to other members of their sex!"

Lord Abingdon nodded. "Yes, they are top-drawer, but they are not the only females of their caliber. Miss Grey is pretty, sweet, and charming, and I believe her to be honest."

"If you had been her victim, you'd be reciting a different verse," he growled. "Leave off, gentle-

men! The matter is ended! Even if I wished to
renew my suit, Letitia would turn me down. She
hates me. You should hear the names she's called
me!"

The duke shrugged. "She is merely hurt and
angry. If you would apologize . . ."

"Apologize!" Chris exploded. "Are you mad? I've
nothing to apologize *for!* She is the one who should
seek penance from me! If you think I'd beg forgiveness from that sharp-tongued wench, you're
far wide of the mark!"

"Well." Aubrey leaned back in his chair, tenting
his hands and thoughtfully eyeing the earl. "It
seems as if Chris's *tendre* is truly concluded."

"I'm glad that someone has finally gotten that
through his head. Now we can enjoy the rest of
your visit. Lord Grey has a most impressive stable." With a sigh, he began to eat in earnest.

"You know," Lord Standish said reflectively, "I
was somewhat wrong in my conclusions about Lord
Grey's Marriage Mart. I assumed that the man was
attempting to pawn off a couple of antidotes. That
wasn't the case. Both ladies are extremely attractive.
Miss Julianne has already been claimed, but . . .
Chris, since you have come to care nothing for
Miss Grey, I'm sure you wouldn't mind if I . . .
uh . . . developed an interest in her."

Chris nearly choked on his eggs as a wrench of
jealousy twisted his stomach. Coughing, he grasped
his cup of tea and took a hasty gulp. He stared with
disbelief into his friend's sultry blue eyes.

"You're a damned fool, Aubrey."

"Why? A man has to wed sometime, and my
father's been pressuring me a great deal lately,"
he drawled.

"Since when have you ever paid heed to your
father?" Chris scoffed.

Lord Standish grinned. "Perhaps this time, the old curmudgeon's right. Miss Grey should suit his expectations."

"What about Lady Christina?" Chris demanded.

"Too volatile."

"If you think Lady Christina is too capricious, you should see Letitia in action!"

"Can't be as disturbing as Lady Christina. I like a woman of spirit! Besides," he chuckled, "she'd come to my bed with a dowry of the finest horses in the land."

His bed? Chris felt sick all over. Letitia couldn't marry Aubrey! It was all wrong! They'd never get along together!

"Yes," his friend went on contemplatively, "I believe I'll press my suit. The lady is mending a broken heart. She should fall easily for me."

"No," Chris said flatly.

"But why not? You aren't interested."

"That's right, but . . ."

Chris glanced around the table. The men had ceased eating and were smilingly attentive to the exchange. He flushed. He had demonstrated that he was not indifferent to Letitia, and they knew it. He set his jaw.

"Go ahead, Aubrey. Court her," he muttered, rising to leave. "You have my best wishes."

As the ladies, attired in their riding costumes, descended the stairs, the duke caught his lady's arm and drew her aside.

"Allesandra, it's up to you. He's still in love with her, but he's too damned stubborn to make the first move toward reconciliation. She will have to do it."

The duchess shuddered. "Then I don't hold much hope. Not only is she said to be as immovable as he, but any well-reared lady is taught that the gentleman must make the first move. For her to do so would be considered fast."

"There's nothing else. Aubrey is trying to make him jealous, but it seems to cause him to be that much more unyielding. You ladies are our only hope. If you fail, so does the match, and it will be the gravest mistake the two of them could ever make." He shook his head. "When we talk about it, he just becomes angry."

Allesandra nibbled her lip. "Brandon, are you certain we are doing the right thing?"

"I'm positive," he vowed. "They love each other."

"But they fight like cats and dogs!"

"I believe that if they settle this, there will never be another quarrel between them." The duke kissed her pert nose. "Good luck, darling."

She moaned. "We'll need it!"

The morning was perfect for horseback riding. The air was fresh and clear, and not so hot yet as to be oppressive. After warming their horses, the four ladies enjoyed an exhilarating gallop, then took a walk in the woods to cool their mounts. At a clearing by a stream, they dismounted to collect themselves as well. Handing their reins to their attending grooms, they strolled a short distance along the bank.

"This is such a pleasant spot," the Duchess of Rackthall observed. "May we sit for a while?"

"If you wish, Your Grace," Letitia agreed.

"Oh, please do not be so formal. I'd be far more comfortable if you would address me by my first name, and I'm certain that Ellen and Clarissa feel the same."

The other ladies nodded.

"I feel as if we are already the best of friends,"

Allesandra said, seating herself on a large rock. "We are so much alike."

No, thought Letitia, you are wrong. How could they be the best of friends when they would probably never see each other again? And how could they be alike? They were beautiful, stylish ladies, married to handsome, wealthy peers. She was destined to be a dried-up old maid.

Conversation was desultory until the duchess suddenly giggled. "Brandon and I had the silliest quarrel the other day."

"I cannot picture the two of you arguing over anything!" Ellen laughed. "Harry and I, yes. He can be so stubborn!"

"Well, so can Brandon. The whole matter was his fault entirely, and he knew it! But I was the one who was forced to apologize. Men! They can be so hardheaded. I believe that they consider it a blow to their masculine pride if they are compelled to admit they were wrong."

"How very true," chorused the other matrons.

"But it isn't fair!" Letitia blurted.

All eyes turned curiously in her direction. She flushed. She had no business advancing her opinion to these women.

"You are correct, of course," said Allesandra, "but in loving and understanding Brandon, I am willing to give him that much."

Ellen's blue eyes sparkled. "Furthermore, mending matters can be quite enjoyable."

"Sometimes I needn't say a word to Brough," Clarissa revealed. "I simply put my arms around him and kiss him."

Letitia's heart thumped painfully. She thought of Chris's arms, warm and tender, as he held her so lovingly. She remembered the searing touch of his lips. Her throat ached. Without warning, she burst into tears.

"Oh, my dear!" Allesandra hurried to her side, slipping her arm around her waist.

"I know you don't understand," Letitia choked out. "It's Lord Brerely. He and I . . ."

"We know," the duchess said softly. "That is why we are here. Chris is our friend, and now you are, too. We want both of you to be happy."

"He hates me!" she cried.

"No, dear, we believe that he loves you very much. And don't you love him, too?"

"With all my heart, but . . ."

"Yes?" the duchess prompted.

"He distrusts me. He considers me deceitful. He did love me once. I am sure of it. But he doesn't love me now."

"That is not true," the duchess declared. "He's heartbroken."

"I have no doubt that it will quickly mend itself." Letitia dried her tears, mortified by her outburst. How could she have been so emotional in front of the ladies? They might call her friend, but, in all actuality, they scarcely knew her.

"Don't you wish to marry him?"

She shook her head. "I cannot wed a man who doubts my integrity."

"If you talked with him, Letitia . . ." Ellen Singleton began.

"No," she said adamantly.

"We've told you how stubborn and prideful our husbands are. Men can be so vain when it comes to admitting their guilt. In his heart, Chris knows that he was wrong, but he is too proud to acknowledge it. If you took the first step . . ."

"No," repeated Letitia.

"Don't throw away your chance at happiness," Clarissa implored. "You'll be sorry for the rest of your life."

"He accused me wrongly!"

"Yes, he did, but he isn't going to back down! Letitia, it is such a small price to pay."

She had difficulty in controlling her soaring anger. They didn't truly understand! They hadn't been there. Their own quarrels with their husbands were petty in comparison. None of these ladies knew what it was like to have the man she loved turn on her in a ghastly fury of loathing and blame.

"I cannot go to him," she declared, struggling to keep her temper within bounds. "I, too, have my pride!"

"Perhaps you have too much of it," said Allesandra, dryly.

"Well, at least I have something left from this snarl."

"Yes, for you won't have Chris." She seemed to brighten. "You might be interested in Aubrey. He's very charming, and his dimples are simply devastating!"

"I don't wish to wed Lord Standish," Letitia avowed. "I will not marry anyone."

"No one but Chris?"

"That is finished." She stood. "We should start back to the house. It is almost time for luncheon."

"Very well," Allesandra murmured with disappointment. "Letitia, will you do me a favor?"

"Of course."

"Will you think on what we have said and give it your serious consideration? A simple move on your part could salvage this calamity."

She had given her word, and she couldn't take it back. "I will ponder it. But why must it be me? Why can't you speak with Chris?"

The duchess gazed pityingly at her. "Our husbands already have."

*   *   *

Chris did not appear for luncheon; nor did he attend dinner. After the evening meal, when the gentlemen finished their port and joined the ladies in the drawing room, Julianne consented to play the piano. While Willie turned the pages of her music, the four older members of the company gathered around a table for a game of piquet, while Chris's friends surrounded Letitia.

"I tried to see Chris this afternoon," the duke remarked, "but he's gone to ground in his chamber. The door is locked."

"We put too much pressure on him," Lord Singleton stated.

"We had no choice," said Lord Abingdon.

Letitia tried to pretend that she was not listening to their overt discussion of the matter that should have been hers and Chris's alone. She knew that they meant well, and that they truly cared about the dreadful situation, but they should keep their noses to themselves. There was little she could do about it, however. She could only maintain her aplomb. She certainly couldn't give these lofty peers the setdown they deserved.

"Letitia, have you given a thought to what we discussed this morning?" Allesandra asked.

"Yes," she replied, "and the answer is no."

"Then there is nothing more that I can do to sway you."

"No, ma'am, there is not!"

"Too stubborn," the duke intoned. "Both of them are too stubborn for their own good. All would be solved if you weren't so afraid to make the first step, you silly chit!"

"Brandon!" gasped his wife.

"I'm sorry," he said in a voice that held no remorse. "A man has his pride. Why can't this witless little girl comprehend what we're telling her?"

"How dare you!" Letitia cried, belligerently lifting her chin. Exalted duke or no, she certainly would not permit him to talk of her in such a manner. "Why can't *you* understand that I have my pride as well?"

"I do, and it's damned overblown."

Letitia rose. "Your Grace, you are domineering and opinionated! Obviously, you have a low regard for women!"

"On the contrary, Miss Grey, I hold a very high esteem for your sex, especially for my wife. She is loving enough to smooth over our few quarrels, even when she and I know damned well when I am at fault! You, Miss Grey, know nothing of men, and you refuse to learn!"

"You will not speak to me like this!" Letitia sharply told him. "Obviously, you do not understand women!"

Lord Singleton began to laugh. "Miss Grey, Bran has had women groveling at his feet for the better portion of his life. Insofar as I know, you and Allesandra have been the only females to stand up to his insolence. Congratulations!"

"Shh, Harry," Ellen whispered.

"Bran's usually quite charming, but right now he's frustrated," he went on, ignoring her. "May I explain, please?"

He had such a sweet and beguiling expression in his gray eyes that Letitia found it difficult to deny him. She nodded abruptly. "Very well."

"We men are raised to be dominant. From the moment we're born, we're led to believe that women were put on this earth to pamper us. We're taught that we're always right. We're the masters! So you see? Our wives have grown to understand this." He smiled fondly at Ellen. "She always seems to give me the upper hand, but I constantly find that I end up doing that which she wishes. Do you understand?"

"A little," she said slowly.

"One more thing. Chris has always been terrified of being trapped into marriage. When he heard your parents' discussion, he was overwhelmed. It was unfortunate that the two of you were together when that occurred. If he'd had the chance to digest it, things might have been different."

Letitia sighed. "He was so angry. And then I behaved that way, too."

"You simply reacted in kind, just as you did to Bran's irritation."

She blushed and glanced at the duke. "I apologize, Your Grace. We are all experiencing a great deal of tension."

He smiled and kissed her hand. "Goodness, Miss Grey, can this truly be you? Apologizing to a man?"

She smiled.

"Especially when I was the one at fault?"

"I scarcely stopped to think who should go first," she conceded. "I owed you an apology, too."

"Then would it be so hard to do the same with Chris?" Lord Abingdon urged. "After all, you love him."

She took a deep breath and made her decision. "I shall attempt it."

"Excellent!" shouted the marquess. "This is cause for celebration!"

"It certainly is," said the duke, "but we still have one minor problem. How will we get Chris out of his room so that she can work her magic? She must see him face-to-face, for remember, Letitia, a touch can often say more than words."

Together, they all sat down to unravel that knotty dilemma.

18

His substantial breakfast untouched, Chris sat at the small table by his chamber window and pondered his situation. At least his room was comfortable, and the view of the well-tended front lawn of Greywood Manor was salubrious, even though the brick-bordered pool reminded him of his catastrophe. Those were the only positive things he could conceive about his present state.

His friends were probably disgusted with him for hiding in his room. By now, they'd be convinced that he was a spineless dolt, without the courage to stand up to his problems, and not worthy of their friendship. They wouldn't want anything to do with him, ever again. He'd have to find new companions, maybe Morley or Rotham, or some of the few others who had attended the infamous Marriage Mart house party. Those gentlemen would understand and be sympathetic to his plight.

Chris was saddened by the certain loss of his closest friends. Though of varying ages and from different geographical backgrounds, they had suffered through their early years of school together and proceeded to university. When they'd gone up to London, they had naturally gravitated toward each other. Like other young, high-spirited blades, they had survived enough misadventures, mistakes, and misbehavior to boggle the mind. But they'd come through their salad days and gained the fine gloss of town bronze and sophistication that they evidenced today. After all those years, it would be strange to be without their company.

He would also miss their wives. Allesandra, Ellen, and Clarissa were lovely, kind, fun-loving ladies, the best that any man could hope to find. He felt, and they treated him, just like a brother.

The group had been shocked when Bran had been the first to wed. He had simply gone out and married the beautiful Allesandra without their knowledge. Most likely he had planned it that way, for the purpose of avoiding discussions such as plagued Chris now.

Harry's courtship had astounded them. They certainly hadn't been aware that he was considering parson's mousetrap. And they were amazed at his choice of brides, but guileless, artless Ellen had been the perfect match for the suave marquess.

Brough was a different story. He'd always been more settled than the rest. When he selected the attractive widow, Clarissa, no one was surprised.

He and Aubrey were the only bachelors remaining in the original group of men-about-town. Though Aubrey was overtly pursued by the Lady Christina, she would never catch him. Neither would Letitia. Aubrey couldn't mean what he said about her. He was bluffing and trying to make Chris jealous.

And himself? Well, that didn't matter. None of them would care what happened to him.

He wondered if the lot of them would give him the cut direct. Most likely, they would not. They held too many good memories which would prevent them from reacting in such a vindictive manner. His friends would be coolly polite. But they would not invite him to their homes, and they wouldn't converge at the club. The friendship was over. He'd best grow accustomed to it.

But in a large measure, wasn't it their fault, too? The men should have known better than to attempt to put pressure on him. No honorable male did such a thing to another. The ladies had possibly urged them to it, but they hadn't had to comply with their wives' wishes. Everyone knew that women's heads were stuffed with romantic nonsense.

Dammit! Why had it turned out like this? His friends were annoyed; his family was aggravated; and he was wretched over it. Why couldn't everyone mind their own business?

Chas looked down at his meal, sniffed the odor and felt like casting up his accounts. In his upsetting predicament, the very sight of food made him nauseous. Letitia undoubtedly wouldn't respond like that. He had never seen a female with such an honest, healthy appetite. She could do admirable justice to a full-scale banquet even if the sky was falling.

Letitia. She haunted him. No matter what she had or hadn't done, he hadn't really stopped loving her. She would have been the perfect wife for him.

She attracted him. Good God, he'd had a difficult time keeping his hands off her! He'd never known a respectable female to fill him with such rampant desire.

She fascinated him. Her mercurial swings of temperament were mesmerizing. With a lady like Letitia, a man's life would never be dull.

Her riding ability was another boon. His friends enjoyed riding with their wives and were proud of their talents, but Letitia was much more skillful. Yes, she could ride better than some men he had observed. She could have joined him safely in any equine activity he chose to undertake. And she sincerely cared about the well-being of animals, an attribute too frequently lacking in Society.

But it was too late. Even if he were able to set aside his pride and apologize, she would never forgive him. He wanted to hear, and think, no more about his terrible loss. It was over, finished. In all honor, he could do nothing about it.

He picked up a piece of toast and chewed it with disinterest. He'd have to eat something or he'd make himself sick. He definitely didn't need any more bed rest! He crammed another slice into his mouth and forced it down with a swallow of tepid tea. He hoped the trays were removed before Dr. Graham arrived. If the physician saw the incriminating evidence of uneaten food, he'd believe that Chris was ill and make a colossal issue of it.

"*Chit—chit—chit!*"

Chris glanced toward the direction of the chatter and saw Racky profiled in the window beside him. He couldn't keep from laughing out loud. So that was how the raccoon gained his secretive entry! Why hadn't they thought of that? They'd just been too busy assuming that the servants were careless.

"Good morning, Racky," he said, and then an inspired idea came to mind. Scooping up the animal, he set him in the middle of the table. "Eat your fill!"

Racky wonderingly cocked his head.

"Go ahead," Chris encouraged, picking up a rasher of bacon and extending it toward the pointed little jaws. "It's yours."

A smile seemed to form on the creature's face. He grasped the bacon and poked it into his mouth, crunching with pleasure. He licked his lips.

"Here." The earl held out the plate.

That was all it took. Uninhibitedly, Racky plunged into Chris's breakfast. Chris wondered how such a small stomach could hold all the food that was entering it.

There was a rap on the door, a pause, then a louder tap. "Chris! It's me, Brandon."

Dammit! They hadn't given up! Chris clenched his jaw. Forfeited friendship or no, he refused to listen to one more word about Letitia. Enough was enough!

"I'd like to speak with you," the duke entreated.

"Go away!" he bitterly returned.

Brandon jiggled the locked doorknob. "Really, Chris, this is childish. We need to talk!"

Chris bit back an obscene reply.

"You can't stay holed up in your room!" the duke persisted.

"Why not?" he snapped.

"It's ridiculous! Come out! I promise I won't say one word about you and Letitia!" the duke vowed.

The earl hesitated. Brandon would keep his word, but he couldn't make commitments for the other men. And certainly not for the ladies! The fair females would guarantee no such thing. This approach was just another ruse to draw him out and make him fair game for everyone's nagging tongues. He made up his mind. He would remain in his room until he left. Whether or not the doctor allowed it, and even if he had to hook up his own team, he would depart that night, when everyone was asleep. No one would see him leave and try to prevent it.

"No!" he said firmly. "Never!"

Other voices resounded in the hall. Chris heard the rumbling tones of Dr. Graham. Wildly, he shooed the raccoon from the table and went to the door.

"Out of my way," ordered the doctor. "I will see my patient alone, and I will not have him disturbed! Lord Brerely, you may open the door."

"You're unaccompanied?" Chris asked.

"Your valet is with me."

He cracked open the door, peeking out.

"Your would-be intruder is gone," the graying physician assured him.

Chris let them in.

"Such disruption at the entrance to a sickroom!" The doctor shook his head. "Are you feeling poorly, my lord? Is that why you did not wish to appear?"

"I'm feeling fine. I simply wasn't dressed properly," Chris lied, indicating his dressing robe.

"There's that damned beast!" Nickerson suddenly cried.

The earl turned to see Racky sitting on the windowsill, smacking his lips.

"He'll eat your breakfast!" shrilled the valet.

"It's all right. I've finished with it."

"But . . ."

Dr. Graham laughed. "I see it's Letitia's quaint little creature. He won't hurt you, Nickerson."

"He's a menace," muttered the valet.

The physician inspected the trays. "Very good, very good. A robust appetite is a excellent sign of recovery."

Chris smiled innocently.

"Now, my lord, let us examine you."

Chris sat down on the side of the bed and Nickerson removed his dressing robe.

The physician unwound the tight strips of binding. "See if you can take a deep breath, my lord."

Chris inhaled, careful not to display the slight discomfort he felt.

"No pain?"

"It feels wonderful." He tried not to wince as the doctor probed his ribs.

"Slightly tender still?" Dr. Graham guessed. "No matter. You're well on the mend! I want you to be careful for a few more days, then I see no reason why you can't go about as usual, so long as you take care to undertake no task that would require any strain. I wouldn't lift anything, or drive, or ride for a while, my lord."

"Yes, sir." It was marvelous to be rid of the bandage.

"Do practice breathing deeply, Lord Brerely."

"I shall."

Nickerson ushered the doctor out and returned. "Shall I assist your toilette, my lord, or shall I remove the trays before that little nuisance assaults them?" he asked, returning.

"Take away the trays and order a bath. I'd like to have a soak before dressing."

"As you wish." The valet moved to collect the breakfast remains. "Aaugh!" he screeched.

Chris started. "What is it?"

"My lord . . . oh, my lord . . . oh, my God . . ."

"What is it, Nickerson?" he exclaimed.

"Oh, sir, there is a hair on your plate! I have never been so shocked in all my life!" Nickerson's eyes filled with fury. "Just wait until I tell that kitchen staff what I think of this!"

"The Greys' kitchen is unexcelled," Chris soothed. "If there had been a hair in my food, I would have seen it. Perhaps it's one of mine."

The valet's rage turned to outright horror. He dashed to Chris's side. None too gently, he began to ruffle the earl's dark hair.

"Stop that!" He ducked away. "What are you doing?"

Nickerson stood back, mournfully hanging his head. "I regret to inform you, my lord, of a very serious event."

"What's happening?" Chris chuckled. "Are you afraid that my hair is falling out?"

"Oh, no, sir, it isn't quite *that* bad, but it is critical just the same. But never fear! I possess a special receipt for a dye."

"What in the hell are you talking about?" he demanded.

Nickerson twisted his face, as if he were in great pain. "The hair I found, my lord. It's gray!"

"Chit—chit!"

Chris looked toward the window to catch the glimpse of a departing ringed tail. "Don't worry, Nickerson. I'm sure it will be a long time before we need resort to such remedies." Despite all his previous depressing meditations, he burst out laughing.

"I'm sorry." With an unhappy glance at Chris's locked door, the Duke of Rackthall shook his head sympathetically. "I couldn't reason with him. He won't come out."

"Thank you, Your Grace, for trying." Letitia opened the door to her bedchamber. "It was probably a fruitless idea in the first place."

"He'll have to come out sometime," Brandon said hopefully.

"Yes, but when he does, he'll run so fast that no one will be able to catch him."

The duke slipped a frustrated hand through his golden-blond hair. "If you think of anything else, I, or any of us, will be glad to assist."

"Thank you," she repeated forlornly. "Please tell the others that I wish to be alone for a while."

"Very well." He bowed over her hand.

Letitia entered her room, fighting back the tears. Last night, after she had considered the discussion and agreed to try once more, she had felt confidence and elation. Now it was gone. She had lost Chris. There was nothing that she, or anyone else, could do to bring him back.

As she walked to the window, Racky came darting in. "What?" she exclaimed.

"*Chit—chit.*" With inflated stomach, he perched on the sill and licked his greasy lips. There was a distinct aroma of bacon about him. Bits of egg clung to his whiskers and chin.

"You've been eating . . . Chris's breakfast!"

The earl had been the only resident who'd dined in his room that morning. Her pet must have intruded and plundered his meal. Yet she'd heard no lordly bellow.

As Racky dropped to the floor and ran to her washstand to cleanse his face, Letitia quickly peered outside. There was a narrow ledge that extended along the front of the house, just below the chamber windows. That was how Racky escaped! She leaned out, considering. If she could creep along that shelf to Chris's bedroom . . .

No, it was too dangerous. One slip and she could crash to the hard ground below. To contemplate doing such a foolish thing was outside of absurd. She could be killed! But to think of losing her love, when she had even the smallest chance of changing his mind, was inconceivable.

Letitia hopped onto the sill and sat, looking down with a flutter of nerves. Even as a child, she hadn't cared for heights and had climbed trees only to prove that she could. Heavens! It seemed such a long way down! Could she do it? Was he worth the risk?

Pulling up her skirt, she tentatively eased a leg onto the ledge. It was too small to allow her to crawl on hands and knees. She would have to walk upright, placing one foot in front of the other very, very carefully. Using the width of the windowsill to facilitate her, she grasped the frame and ducked out. She wavered fearfully, then, biting her lip, she began her unnerving progress.

It was such a long way to his room. It hadn't seemed far in the hall, but out here, it constituted a terrifying, drawn-out journey. Would she never reach her destination?

She heard loud conversation from down below. Dear heavens, had she been discovered? She timidly looked down to see the head gardener arriving with his staff, just below her in a flower bed. If they chanced to look up and glimpse her, they would report her immediately to her father. Worse still, they would feast their eyes on the vision she made, her skirt held high above her knees. Furthermore, if tragedy struck, she would fall right down on top of them. It was appalling.

Giddy with anxiety, Letitia began to giggle and was forced to lean against the brick wall to maintain her stability while she gained control of her wits. Holding her skirts in one hand and covering her mouth with the other, she desperately sought for restraint. How could she laugh at a time like this? Had she lost her mind? She looked up at the sky and forced herself to remember the perilousness of her mission.

Thinking of losing Chris effectively sobered her. She proceeded onward, treading softly and painstakingly. She reached the earl's window and thankfully clutched the frame. She'd succeeded! Cautiously, she bent and peered inside.

Clad only in his dressing robe, Chris was lying on his back in the bed. He held an open book, which concealed his face. From the way his attire gaped open at the chest, she noted that Dr. Graham had removed all the bandaging. Letitia blushed. This was going to be a rather informal and scandalous interview.

She debated calling to him and decided against it. If he roared at her, she might startle and fall. No, she would enter silently, so that her feet would be firmly planted on the floor when he began to berate her.

Kneeling as best she could, she took a deep breath. It was now or never. As she began to advance a leg, a sharp object enmeshed her dress at her hip and pulled her up short. The abrupt and startling halt jerked her down. Letitia fell hard on the ledge, her legs swinging over the side. Desperately clinging to the sill, she screamed.

"My God!" The earl leaped from the bed.

"Chris!" she wrenched out. "I'm falling!"

"I'm here!" He caught her around the waist.

Letitia kicked violently. "I'm going to die! I'm falling!" she shrieked hysterically.

"No, you're not. I have you!" he assured her, pulling her torso securely across the windowsill.

"Oh, Chris!" Realizing that she was safe, she wrapped her arms around him. "Take me inside! Oh, please hurry!"

His fingers explored her hip. "You're caught on a nail."

Her face burned. "This is so mortifying."

"Mortifying, hell! You scared me to death!" he exclaimed.

"Don't be angry with me!" she wailed.

"Letitia, it's difficult for a man to be angry with you when he's feeling your luscious . . ."

She shuddered with a combination of embarrassment and something oddly akin to pleasure. "Just hurry."

"What the hell is going on here?" Lord Grey shouted from the lawn as several females squealed.

"Oh, please, Chris, just rip it free. They can probably see my . . . uh . . . derriere!"

"What a scandal." He laughed and tore her loose with a great rending of fabric, pulling her fully inside.

"It is not amusing!" Letitia regained her feet and tried to straighten her clothing, but he was holding her much too tightly.

"I think it is. It's the most elaborate and dangerous snare ever laid for me."

She bristled, pulling herself free. "It was not a trap, Lord Brerely."

"A moment ago it was *Chris*," he reminded her.

"Very well . . . Chris." She proudly drew herself up, unmindful of the split in her skirt, which revealed her entire shapely leg. "I have come here to talk with you, so I shall begin. I am a forthright person."

"Letitia!" bellowed Lord Grey.

She whirled to the window and leaned out. "Go along, Papa! I am conducting business here!" She turned back to Chris. "As I said, I am a forthright person."

"Letitia!" blared Lady Grey. "The scandal! The shame!"

She slammed the glass shut. "I am . . ."

"A forthright person." He grinned. "Continue."

Letitia tossed her head. "As such, I shall get right to the point! I am not certain that I am completely at fault, but I am terribly sorry that I disturbed you and . . ." She faltered, helplessly overcome by the soft look in his eyes. "I love you, Chris," she whispered.

"Come here, Letitia."

She took one step forward, eyeing him beseechingly.

Chris closed the distance and wrapped her in his arms. "I don't give a damn whose fault it was. Actually, everyone probably had a hand in it. But it doesn't matter now. Let us put it behind us and begin anew. I'd just as soon hear no mention of it ever again."

"You . . . you wouldn't? You don't care?"

"No."

His lips moved across the top of her head, his

breath ruffling her hair. Letitia leaned her cheek against his shockingly bare chest and listened to the swift throbbing of his heart. Oh, my, there was so much to learn about men!

"Will you forgive me?" she entreated. "For everything?"

"If you will forgive me."

Letitia nodded, pressing closer against him. "I have been so miserable."

"I, too, and all because of my self-defeating, stubborn pride," Chris conceded.

"I, too, am guilty of such," she admitted. "I suppose that pride has its place, so long as one does not become puffed up with it."

He smiled, lowering his lips to her forehead and cheeks. "Do you know what?" he inquired between caresses.

She gazed up at him, waiting for his answer.

"We are well and truly compromised."

"I will not hold you to it, my lord, no matter what others have witnessed, nor what gossip they spill," she pledged.

"You won't?" He raised a dark eyebrow.

"Certainly not! Haven't I told you in the past? I shall marry no man who doesn't want *me*."

"Well, then." Chris took her hand and dropped to one knee. "Miss Letitia Grey, may I persuade you to marry me? I love you, and I *do want you*. I want you in ways that you've never dreamed of," he added enigmatically.

Letitia slipped to her knees before him. "Oh, Chris, I shall try to be the very best of wives, and to make you the happiest man in the world!"

"I already am." He lowered his mouth to hers.

"Letitia!" Lord Grey banged on the door.

"Oh, my sweet, innocent daughter!" wailed her mother.

"Christopher!" Lord Trinarton added his poundings to the din.

Chris sighed, lifting her to her feet. "We'd best let them in before they have an apoplexy." Holding her hand, he walked with her to the door. Before he opened it, he turned to her. "No long engagements? I do not wish to wait a minute longer than I must."

"Whatever you want! We shall forestall our mamas and all their grand bridal plans!" She smiled bravely.

"Then we are ready for the onslaught." He jerked the door open and stepped back, slipping his arm securely around her waist.

The onlookers stood momentarily paralyzed. Their parents' faces were white with concern. But William and Julianne and Chris's friends and their wives were grinning broadly. Nickerson was leaning limply against the far wall. Suddenly, they surged forward.

Chris extended his hand to Lord Grey. "Sir, before anyone says another word, I would assure you that your daughter and I have reconciled our differences. May I present my suit for her hand at your very earliest convenience?"

"There is no need for formality!" Lord Grey exclaimed. "You're accepted!"

"Letitia!" wept Lady Grey. "You've done it!"

"I've done *nothing*, Mama!" she demurred, gazing up at her fiancé. "Nothing but fall in love."

The Trinartons cheered and hugged the couple. Julianne kissed her sister, and William shook his brother's hand. "See?" Willie taunted. "I was right, wasn't I?"

"Shut up, little brother," Chris jovially warned him. "From this moment forth, you will see to your own lady, and stay out of my affairs!"

Chris's gentlemen friends shook his hand and kissed the future bride. The ladies wiped moisture from their eyes and embraced them both.

"*Chit—chit—chit!*"

Chris went to the window, opened it, and picked up the raccoon. "This animal had a great deal to do with solving our troubles."

"Indeed?" several people exclaimed at once. "How?"

As Letitia and Chris related the tale, Racky scrambled from the earl's arms and scurried to the bedside table to savor a mint or two.

"That menace!" cried Nickerson, regaining his outraged dignity.

"That meddlesome nuisance!" echoed Lady Grey. "I shall have him evicted! Get a broom, Nickerson! Dash him to the floor!"

"With relish, my lady!"

She hesitated, considering. "On second thought, I believe we owe him his pleasure. Allow him to enjoy himself. After all, I haven't much longer to stand his mischief. After the wedding, he shall depart with Letitia."

"Oh, no!" The valet put a trembling hand to his chest. "My lord, you must reconsider this august decision!"

"Why, Nickerson," Chris said mildly, "if you are kind to Racky, I'm sure he will grow to like you."

His loyal servant groaned. "We should never have come here."

"On the contrary, I couldn't be happier that we did." He squeezed Letitia's waist. "I've had great success at Lord Grey's Marriage Mart!"

The viscount took a merry bow. "Glad to be of service!" He laughed and hugged Lady Grey. "You see, my dear? I was right!"

"Fustian!" she muttered.

Letitia flushed, leaning her head on Chris's shoulder and eyeing him lovingly.

"Have you any more daughters tucked away?" Chris wickedly asked Lord Grey. "My friend Aubrey is needful of a mate."

Lord Standish blanched. "Now that matters are settled, I must be leaving!"

Hurriedly, the last bachelor fled from the room as the crowd applauded.

Avon Romantic Treasures

Unforgettable, enthralling love stories,
sparkling with passion and adventure
from Romance's bestselling authors

COMANCHE WIND *by Genell Dellin*
76717-1/$4.50 US/$5.50 Can

THEN CAME YOU *by Lisa Kleypas*
77013-X/$4.50 US/$5.50 Can

VIRGIN STAR *by Jennifer Horsman*
76702-3/$4.50 US/$5.50 Can

MASTER OF MOONSPELL *by Deborah Camp*
76736-8/$4.50 US/$5.50 Can

SHADOW DANCE *by Anne Stuart*
76741-4/$4.50 US/$5.50 Can

FORTUNE'S FLAME *by Judith E. French*
76865-8/$4.50 US/$5.50 Can

FASCINATION *by Stella Cameron*
77074-1/$4.50 US/$5.50 Can

ANGEL EYES *by Suzannah Davis*
76822-4/$4.50 US/$5.50 Can

Avon Romances—
the best in exceptional authors and unforgettable novels!

FOREVER HIS Shelly Thacker
77035-0/$4.50 US/$5.50 Can

TOUCH ME WITH FIRE Nicole Jordan
77279-5/$4.50 US/$5.50 Can

OUTLAW HEART Samantha James
76936-0/$4.50 US/$5.50 Can

FLAME OF FURY Sharon Green
76827-5/$4.50 US/$5.50 Can

DARK CHAMPION Jo Beverley
76786-4/$4.50 US/$5.50 Can

BELOVED PRETENDER Joan Van Nuys
77207-8/$4.50 US/$5.50 Can

PASSIONATE SURRENDER Sheryl Sage
76684-1/$4.50 US/$5.50 Can

MASTER OF MY DREAMS Danelle Harmon
77227-2/$4.50 US/$5.50 Can

LORD OF THE NIGHT Cara Miles
76453-9/$4.50 US/$5.50 Can

WIND ACROSS TEXAS Donna Stephens
77273-6/$4.50 US/$5.50 Can

America Loves Lindsey!

The Timeless Romances
of #1 Bestselling Author
Johanna Lindsey